The world was a stage, then life went dark

THE

LIFE
FANTASTIC

A Novel in Three Acts

LIZA KETCHUM

MeritPress

Published by
Merit Press
an imprint of F+W Media, Inc.
10151 Carver Road, Suite 200
Blue Ash, OH 45242. U.S.A.
www.meritpressbooks.com

ISBN 10: 1-4405-9876-2
ISBN 13: 978-1-4405-9876-0
eISBN 10: 1-4405-9877-0
eISBN 13: 978-1-4405-9877-7

Printed in the United States of America.

10   9   8   7   6   5   4   3   2   1

Library of Congress Cataloging-in-Publication Data

Ketchum, Liza, author.
The life fantastic / Liza Ketchum.
Blue Ash, OH: Merit Press, 2017.
Includes bibliographical references.
LCCN 2016026860 (print) | LCCN 2016038608 (ebook) | ISBN 9781440598760 (hc)
| ISBN 1440598762 (hc) | ISBN 9781440598777 (ebook) | ISBN 1440598770 (ebook)
CYAC: Singers--Fiction. | Vaudeville--Fiction. | Race relations--Fiction. | Performing arts--Fiction. | United States--History--1913-1921--Fiction.
LCC PZ7.K488 Li 2017 (print) | LCC PZ7.K488 (ebook) | DDC [Fic]--dc23
LC record available at https://lccn.loc.gov/2016026860

Cover design by Sylvia McArdle.
Cover images © Mod Paperie; iStockphoto.com/aleksandarvelasevic; GoodGnom.

This book is available at quantity discounts for bulk purchases.
For information, please call 1-800-289-0963.

For my grandchildren:
Rushil and Kinari, Willa and Camille—
May your lives be filled with music, love, and laughter.

And in memory of:
My great-grandparents, who eloped
and ran away to the vaudeville stage;
My grandparents, who taught us the songs;
And my parents and my aunt Janet,
who kept the music alive.

A Note on Language

In 1913, the year that *The Life Fantastic* takes place, African Americans were called "colored" or "Negro," and they also referred to themselves that way. Although those terms may be offensive today, they were in common use at that time. Theater terms are listed in the Glossary at the end of this book.

ACKNOWLEDGMENTS

This novel has been blessed with a wide cast of characters who have provided invaluable help, information, and support over many years of creation and revision. For assistance with Vermont history, thanks to Jeff and Peg Barry, at the Brattleboro (Vermont) Historical Society, and Kevin O'Connor from the *Rutland Herald*. Librarians at the Boston Public Library, the Brooks Memorial Library (Brattleboro), the John F. Reed Library at Fort Lewis College (Durango, Colorado), and the New York Public Library for the Performing Arts at Lincoln Center (New York City) provided invaluable assistance. I wish that my dear, departed friend and librarian Deanna Held had lived to see this book in print. She was an indefatigable researcher.

Thanks to my cousin, singer and songwriter Coleman Harwell, for help with song lyrics and information about vaudeville in southern states; and to Fern Chasse and Sally Macquart-Moulin for assistance with French translation. Katherine Leiner, Makenna Goodman, Will and Jean Hobbs, and the Klema family provided meals, friendship, and moral support during my stay in Colorado.

Many smart and savvy readers offered excellent suggestions and advice as the book was revised. Those readers include Heather Arhenholz, Eileen Christelow, Pat Lowery Collins, Karen Hesse, Ellen Levine, Bob MacLean, Lisa Papademetriou, Phyllis Root, Hollis Shore, Eleanora E. Tate, Tinky Turner, Wendy Watson, Nancy Werlin, and Ellen Wittlinger.

I am lucky to have worked with talented and supportive students during my years as a teacher of writing. In several programs—the

Boyds Mills Whole Novel Workshops in Honesdale, Pennsylvania; Rhode Island College's Alliance for the Study and Teaching of Adolescent Literature (ASTAL); and Hamline University's MFA in Writing for Children and Young Adults program—students listened as I read from the novel, offered suggestions, and asked insightful questions. Some sent me books about the period or offered links to resources. To all the students I have taught over the years: I can't express how much I learned from you, as well as from my brilliant and loyal fellow faculty members.

Finally, my deepest gratitude to my agent, Ginger Knowlton, and to my husband, John Straus. Teresa sings because you never gave up on her story.

ENTR'ACTE 1

Setting: A shabby vaudeville theater in the upper Midwest, January 1906.

CHARACTERS:

TERESA (RESA) LECLAIR: age seven, a lively child with carrot-colored curls and a strong singing voice.

ALICE LECLAIR: Teresa's mother, a singer and dancer. Alice hides her pregnancy beneath the skirt and shawl of her gypsy costume.

FRANÇOIS LECLAIR: Teresa's father, a burly man with auburn hair and beard. He plays the fiddle.

CONROY: a small-time magician.

THE STAGE MANAGER: a nervous man in his late forties.

As the curtain goes up, we see into the wings, where CONROY tries to distract Teresa.

CONROY: (*Whispers.*) Hsst! Look, Resa. There's a rabbit in my top hat! (*Holds up a live rabbit by the ears.*)

TERESA: Go away. I want to hear Mama.

ALICE: (*Sings.*) Everybody works but Father . . . he sits around all day. (*Points at François and winks at the audience.*) Feet in front of the fire—smoking his pipe of clay. Mother takes in washing . . . so does sister Anne . . . (*Pantomimes scrubbing.*) Everybody works at our house . . . but my old man.

ALICE cocks her head at FRANÇOIS. She dances as he plays. The audience is restless. ALICE twirls and nearly falls.

ALICE: (*Sotto voce.*) I'm out of breath. Play something slow.

FRANÇOIS finishes the tune with a flourish.

FRANÇOIS: (*To the audience.*) We do a slow number now. This is for all those families who have troubles in their lives.

(*The audience falls silent. François plays the opening bars of the Stephen Foster tune "Hard Times."*)

TERESA: (*From the wings.*) Mama! That's our song!

CONROY: Hush, child.

TERESA: Let me go!

ALICE (*Sings.*) Let us pause in life's pleasures, and count its many tears, while we all sup sorrow with the poor . . .

TERESA: Mama, wait for me! (*She dashes onstage, grabs Mama's hand, sings.*) There's a song that will linger, forever in our ears . . .

FRANÇOIS: (*Still playing.*) Resa, stay with Conroy.

ALICE AND TERESA: (*Singing in unison.*) Oh! Hard times, come again no more.

CONROY: (*From the wings.*) Teresa! I'll let you hold the rabbit.

ALICE AND TERESA sway from side to side. Teresa's voice is clear and pure. She sings melody, her mother harmonizes. François shrugs and keeps playing.

STAGE MANAGER: (*In the wings.*) What's going on! No children on stage. The Gerry Society will close me down! Where's my hook?

ALICE AND TERESA: (*Singing.*) Tis the song, the sigh of the weary: Hard times, hard times, come again no more: Many days you have lingered, around my cabin door. Oh! Hard times come again no more.

THE STAGE MANAGER stalks toward Teresa, brandishing a long hook.

TERESA: Papa! The bad man is coming! He wants to hook me!

Hisses from the audience.

FRANÇOIS: (*Drops his bow and yells in French.*) *Ne touchez pas ma fille!*

STAGE MANAGER: Very well! I won't touch your daughter— I'll hook you instead! Get out of my theater. Right . . . now!

He hooks François around the waist and drags him into the wings. The audience boos and throws coins onto the stage apron. TERESA darts from one side of the stage to the other, scooping up pennies and nickels.

STAGE MANAGER: (*Enters again.*) Get this child off the stage!

ALICE: Teresa, come with Mama now. (*Her gypsy shawl comes untied.*)

TERESA: Wait! I want the money.

STAGE MANAGER: (*To Alice.*) How dare you perform in your condition!

FRANÇOIS: (*From the wings.*) Resa! *Viens ici.*

TERESA: Mama! Why can't we sing?

MAN IN FRONT ROW: Yes! Let the child sing!

Shouts from the audience. ALICE grips TERESA'S hand and yanks her offstage.

MAN IN FRONT ROW: Keep the little girl! Keep the little girl!

MORE MEMBERS OF THE AUDIENCE: (*Chanting.*) Keep the little girl! Keep the little girl!

TERESA: (*From the wings.*) Mama! Papa! They want me to sing!

THE AUDIENCE: (*Chants in unison, stomping and clapping.*) Keep the little girl! Keep the little girl!

Fade to black.

ACT ONE

A VOICE LIKE A NIGHTINGALE

BRATTLEBORO, VERMONT
MAY 1913

1.

"There's a song that will linger, forever in our ears . . ." Teresa picked out the tune on the upright piano with her right hand and filled in the chords with her left. "Ouch." That low E-flat was out of tune. "'Tis the song, the sigh of the weary . . ." She sang louder to send the chorus to Nonnie at the end of the hall. Her great-grandmother's cloudy eyesight kept her in her room, but she loved this song and had taught Teresa the chords.

"Hard times, hard times, come again no more . . ." Teresa's left hand fumbled for the chord in the bass. If only she could find the music for this piece.

"Try a B-flat chord."

Teresa spun around on the piano bench. Mama stood in the doorway, her market basket over her arm. She set it on the hall table and came into the music room. "Your voice sounds lovely. That was our song, wasn't it?"

"You surprised me." Teresa pulled her mother onto the bench and played the B-flat chord. Mama hummed as Teresa sang to the end. She hit the final chord with a flourish, and they both laughed.

"Remember when I performed onstage for the first time?" Teresa asked. "Where were we?"

"The Silver Circuit. It seems like another lifetime." Mama combed her fingers through Teresa's tangled curls. "Your voice was already strong. You were the star of our show for a few nights."

"A few nights? I thought I only performed once."

Mama shook her head. "Audiences loved you. They shouted for you to come on every day that we performed in that town. The stage manager had to let you sing, until the night we died."

"We *died*?"

"Our act failed; Papa broke a fiddle string and I tripped and fell. I was too far along with Pascal to keep dancing."

"Don't you miss it?" Teresa asked.

"Sometimes." Mama's brown eyes were dreamy as she gazed out the window. "I miss the feeling of family," she said. "The way we took care of each other. But I don't miss the work. Four shows a day in one-night stands. Fleabag hotels, unheated trains, stale sandwiches for supper—it's no life for children. And we'd never be headliners—"

"You could have been," Teresa said. "Besides, you work hard here at the boardinghouse—"

The front door slammed. "Where are my girls?" Papa's voice sounded from the hall.

Teresa glanced at Mama. "I haven't washed the dishes," she whispered.

Mama squeezed her knee. "We'll do them together."

Papa strode into the room and took off his hat. Flecks of sawdust drifted onto the carpet. Teresa cringed, waiting for his scolding, but Papa's eyes shone like copper pennies and he set his elbows on the back of the piano. "Resa, *ma chérie*. How would you like to use your musical talents to earn some money?"

Teresa jumped to her feet. "Are we going back on the road?"

Papa raised his eyebrows. "Don't be silly. Vaude is no life for a young girl. Besides, they are strict about child performers now. Those days are behind us."

"But Papa—"

"Don't start." Papa cleared his throat and hummed a note. "*Qu'est-que c'est?*" he asked. "What is this note?"

"A," Teresa said.

"And this?" Papa hummed another note.

"D-sharp." Teresa tried to push past him. "I'm too old for that game."

"*Attends un moment*—wait." Papa set a hand on her shoulder. "You're lucky you have this talent: perfect pitch. One good thing you inherited from your poor father, the cat scraper. What if you could use this skill to make money—good money?"

Mama hissed like an angry cat. "François. Don't you dare . . ."

The hair prickled on the back of Teresa's neck. "What are you talking about?"

Papa rubbed his hands. "When I was installing the stops on a parlor organ, I overheard the manager talking to my boss. He said they might hire someone in the tuning rooms."

"I won't have it." Mama stood up so fast she knocked the piano bench over. Teresa jumped out of the way and stared at her parents. Had they gone mad?

"Alice," Papa said. "Please." He reached for Mama, but she backed away, as if Papa were an angry dog about to attack. "It's only a possibility," Papa said. "You and Resa both complain there is too much work here. We could stop looking for more boarders if she brought in real money. You wouldn't need to cook, clean, and wash all day."

Teresa's mouth went dry. Did Papa expect her to support them? "I don't understand. You think I should work at Estey?"

"If they'd have you. It's only an idea," Papa said.

"A terrible idea." Mama's mouth was drawn into a straight line. "You want her to lose her voice, as I did?"

"Of course not," Papa said. "The tuning rooms are the cleanest part of the factory. No sawdust there."

Teresa clapped her hands over her ears as if she could already hear the pounding of the giant engine that powered the organ works, the whine of the saws, the clang of hammers in the room where Papa assembled the organs. "I'm still in school."

"Not for long," Papa said. "Summer will be here soon. Besides, you hate school."

"I hate YOU!" Teresa ran down the hall and slammed the front door. The rippled glass shivered and cracked, like the fissure that opened in her heart.

2.

Teresa stopped at the end of the walk to catch her breath, and squinted. One, two, then three lumpy orbs rose and fell above the bandstand across the street. Was Pascal juggling? She lifted her skirt and hurried over the trolley tracks. Two little boys sat in front of her brother, their eyes big as they watched him juggle fist-sized potatoes. Pascal kept his eyes fixed on the spuds as they spun up and down. He lifted one knee, tossed a small potato under his leg, and caught it on the other side without missing a beat. The boys clapped.

When Teresa joined in, one of the boys spun around and scowled. "Your *sister's* here!" He scrambled to his feet and hurried away. The other boy followed.

Pascal lost his rhythm. One potato split on the bandstand floor and the others rolled away in the grass. "Look what you made me do."

"Sorry." Teresa helped him clean up. "You're good. I like that trick where you send it under your leg."

"I need real juggling balls." Pascal stowed the potatoes in his pockets, giving his skinny legs a lumpy look. "I asked Papa, but he said no."

"Too expensive?"

Pascal put his hands on his hips, imitating Papa's stance. "*No child of mine will ever be in a dumb act.* I told Papa I'm not *dumb*, but he laughed at me." Pascal's blue eyes filled.

Teresa ruffled his yellow hair. "A 'dumb act' is where the performer doesn't speak. Acrobats, jugglers, people with animals—those are all dumb acts. They come on first in the lineup."

"How do you know so much?" Pascal asked.

"I remember. I was born on the road. Mama called me a 'trunk baby' because I slept in the drawer of her steamer trunk. It was my life for six years."

"I wish I'd been there." Pascal flicked his loose front tooth back and forth with his tongue. "Papa can't stop me from going onstage when I'm grown up."

Teresa raised her eyebrows. "You want that, too?"

"'Course. Don't you?"

"More than anything." Teresa glanced across the street. No sign of Papa.

"Remember the jugglers at the Pageant last year?" Pascal asked. "Juggling swords? And fire?" He whirled and danced, as if he were handling flaming torches. "I'm going to do *that* someday."

Teresa laughed. "You must have caught the vaudeville bug when you were in Mama's tummy."

Pascal's face twisted as if she'd fed him a worm. "What do you mean?"

"Never mind." The front door of the boardinghouse swung open. Mama beckoned to them from the porch. "Time to go," Teresa said.

Pascal dashed for the house, but Teresa lingered on the bandstand. She'd have to face Papa now. A poster tacked to one of the posts caught her eye. She stepped closer and read the sign.

AMATEUR NIGHT! SINGING CONTEST!
ARE YOU A CHILD WITH UNUSUAL MUSICAL
TALENT? COME SING YOUR FAVORITE TUNE,
WIN A SILVER DOLLAR AND A SECRET, SPECIAL
OPPORTUNITY! PRINCESS THEATER, TUESDAY
AT 8 P.M. CHILDREN 15 AND UNDER.

Tuesday: tonight. Mama would insist that Teresa go to choir practice as usual, knowing she needed to rehearse her solo for Sunday. Teresa always rode the trolley to church. If she got off at the Princess Theater instead—who would know the difference?

3.

Mr. Jensen was waiting for his supper when Teresa came in. Papa wouldn't scold her in front of their boarder; instead he chopped kindling on the back porch, Pascal loaded it into an old sap bucket, and Teresa helped Mama slice the vegetables—as if nothing had happened.

As she served the stew at the table, Teresa spilled on her old blouse—accidentally on purpose. "I can't go to choir with grease on my blouse," she told Mama.

"Put on your new shirtwaist," Mama said, "but keep it clean for church on Sunday. And fetch Nonnie's tray before you go, will you?"

"Nonnie should eat with us," Papa said. "It makes more work for your mother."

Teresa knew that her great-grandmother couldn't stand old Mr. Jensen and his quavery voice. Plus, Nonnie's failing eyesight embarrassed her. Sometimes Teresa helped Nonnie find the food on her plate—but Teresa wouldn't contradict Papa now.

Upstairs in her attic room, Teresa buttoned her shirtwaist, smoothed the ruffles at the sleeves, and crouched under the eaves to peer in the mirror. She tried to work a comb through her tight curls. Impossible. Hopefully, the judges would only pay attention to her voice.

Teresa slipped past the dining room, avoiding Papa, and stepped into Nonnie's room without knocking. The air smelled sickly sweet. A single lamp lit the chair where Nonnie sat wrapped in a flowered shawl, her face turned toward the window, as if she could see the spring shadows gathering outside. "Nonnie?"

"Resa!" Nonnie's voice was bright. "Come closer."

Teresa kissed Nonnie's forehead. Her skin was as thin as tissue paper.

"I missed you earlier," Nonnie said. "I'm having a little spell."

Teresa smiled. They played this secret game every night. She took the bottle of sherry, a gift from Nonnie's friend Miss Wilkins, out of the cupboard and poured the amber liquid into a glass waiting on the side table. Nonnie claimed that these spirits were her "medicine." Teresa waited while Nonnie took a small sip, then another. "Feel better?" she asked.

Nonnie smiled. "Much." She set the glass down. "Where are you, my dear?"

"Right next to you." Teresa touched Nonnie's shoulder. Her great-grandmother's eyes were milky. "I'm going downstreet soon."

Nonnie reached out a hand and smoothed Teresa's skirt. "Is that your new shirtwaist? I'm glad your mama listened to me. I told her you were bursting out of all your clothes. If only I could still sew for you."

"You made such beautiful things." Teresa felt fidgety. In the past year, her body had betrayed her, pushing out and up in every direction until she had more bust than Mama and was nearly as tall as Papa. Even her voice had changed. The choirmaster had chosen a contralto part for her solo this week. What would Mr. Tish say when she didn't show up tonight?

The piano sounded from the front parlor: *plunk plunk plunk ker-plunk*. "Listen to that," Nonnie said. "Someone should teach that child a more interesting tune. Thank goodness he's not strong enough to pump the Estey pedals. He'd drive us out of the house."

Pascal was picking out a melody one slow note at a time. "Sounds like 'Shoo Fly,'" Teresa said. "Somebody should shoo *him* away." She cringed as he missed the B-flat and covered her ears when he hit the C in the seventh measure. "Ouch! The piano's out of tune."

Nonnie smiled. "You could tune pianos someday with that skill of yours."

Teresa shivered. She wouldn't tell Nonnie about Papa's plan. It would only make her angry. "I want to sing," Teresa said.

"You will," Nonnie said. "Don't you have choir practice tonight?"

"I'm *supposed* to." Teresa dropped her voice to a whisper, although no one else could hear them. "Can I tell you a secret?"

"Of course, child." Nonnie winked and held up her glass. "You keep my secrets; I keep yours. Not running after a boy, are you?"

"Never. The ones in my class call me 'carrot top' and stare at my chest. No—I'm entering a singing contest."

"Good for you." Nonnie reached for Teresa's hand. "I love hearing you sing. You have the gift. Don't waste it, as your mama did, working at Estey. She had a pretty voice when she ran away with your father. Not as strong as yours, but lovely."

Teresa squatted on Nonnie's footstool. She was too big for it now, but she had always perched there to listen to Nonnie's stories. "Tell me again, how they eloped."

Nonnie laughed. "It was a scandal. Your papa stole Alice away in the dead of night, carrying nothing but a small valise. And vaudeville was called improper back then."

"Papa still says vaude is 'no place for a young girl.'"

Nonnie laughed. "Just what your grandpa said. Broke his heart when your mama eloped—and of course, your Grandma June never forgave your papa." Nonnie squeezed Teresa's hand. "And you know about the strange omen."

"Omen? What do you mean?"

"Your mama had a pet canary named Lebo." Nonnie spoke so softly that Teresa leaned closer to hear her. "Of course, she couldn't take the bird on the road. After they found your mama's bed empty, your grandpa pulled the cover off Lebo's cage. The canary was lying dead in the sawdust."

Teresa shivered. "I'd forgotten that story. No one ever talks about it."

"Why do you think, child? Your parents don't want *you* to run away with some Gypsy Davey."

Teresa laughed. "I know that song. A princess elopes with a handsome gypsy. 'And he won the heart of a la-dy . . .'" Teresa sang. "No gypsy in my life." She stood up and kissed Nonnie's withered cheek. She paused at the dresser to finger Nonnie's treasures, collecting dust: a chiffon scarf; a box of crumbling rose petals that had lost their scent; pieces of unfinished embroidery; and a glass vial of rouge. She glanced at her great-grandmother. The old woman's eyes were closed. Teresa tucked the rouge into her dress pocket and picked up Nonnie's tray.

"'Night Nonnie."

"Good night, Resa dear. Sing like an angel."

"I'll try."

4.

By the time the trolley clanked toward her, Teresa's palms were damp with fear. She gave the conductor her nickel and sat in the back, watching the familiar houses slide past. Maybe she should go to choir practice after all. What if she got stage fright? Last summer, when the town had its 150th birthday, she sang a solo in the Pageant, out on Island Park. She had stood in front of thousands of people, her heart pumping faster than the engines on the new automobiles draped with bunting, and her voice came out in a tortured squeak for the first few notes. Could that happen tonight?

Teresa jumped off the trolley at her stop and ran down the hill to the Princess. A poster nailed up beside the door advertised the upcoming show, with a picture of a woman called "The Rose of Abilene: The Girl with the Golden Voice." This singer wore a skimpy dress with a neckline cut deep at the bodice, and a feathered hat. Papa would never let her dress that way. She felt dingy and immature in her plain shirtwaist. If she had to compete against this "Rose," she'd better put on some rouge.

Teresa went through the dark lobby into the washroom and studied her face in the mirror. She rubbed some rouge onto both cheeks with her fingertip, but the makeup couldn't hide her freckles—in fact, the rouge made them bleed into an angry red tapestry, and the color clashed with her orange curls. She pursed her lips, ran another streak over her mouth, and took two deep breaths. She sang up and down an A scale, as they did in choir practice, then a B and a C, to warm her voice.

The Princess had a low tin ceiling and hard wooden chairs. The house lights were on and a single spotlight fell on the stage, where a small boy, about Pascal's age, sang, *"I dream of Jeanie with the light brown hair."*

Ouch. He was slightly off-key. And what a silly song for a little boy! Teresa went to the woman sitting at a desk near the stage.

"Name, please," the woman said, without looking up.

"Teresa LeClair."

The woman spelled it wrong, but Teresa didn't dare correct her. "You'll be tenth," the woman said and raked her eyes over Teresa's face and figure. "Didn't you read the rules? Contestants must be fifteen and under."

"I *am* fifteen."

"Date of birth," the woman said, her pencil poised.

"April first, 1898."

The woman sniffed. "You're seventeen if you're a day. You'll forfeit the prize if we find you're lying." She waved her away.

Teresa's cheeks felt warm. Could she help it that she had burst out in every direction? She sat in the third row. The next singer was a tiny girl who wore a velvet bow as big as her head. She croaked like a broody hen when she sang. Teresa knew she could do better, but her dress felt damp under her arms as she waited.

"Teresa La Clark," the woman finally called, mangling her name.

Teresa went to the piano. The pianist was a pudgy man whose rear end overflowed the piano stool. "Where's your music?"

"I—I don't have any." She felt stupid. "I'm going to sing 'Hard Times.' Do you know the tune?" She hummed a few bars.

He shook his head. "Bad luck. Next!"

"Wait. I'll sing it a cappella. I don't need the music." Teresa climbed the steps to the stage before anyone could shoo her away. Her heart bounced in her chest. She glanced at the front row where the judges sat: two men in dark suits and a woman in a brown dress. She was about to bolt when the lady judge nodded, as if to say: *You can do it.*

Teresa imagined she was back on the Silver Circuit, performing with Mama and Papa. She heard the E-flat note in her head, took a deep breath, and brought the melody into the theater. Her voice felt tentative on the first notes but strengthened as she reached the chorus. As she sang, the door from the lobby opened and two men slid into seats near the back. She raised her voice and pitched the song to them.

According to Papa, Mama was singing this song when they first met. Stephen Foster, who wrote it, told about the sorrows of being poor and hungry, but to Teresa, the song was about everything she and Mama and Papa left behind when they gave up touring. It was about the sorrow of Mama's voice going bad at the organ works, and Papa coming home tired and grumpy while his fiddle sat silent in its case.

"*Many days you have lingered, around my cabin door,*" Teresa sang, and she gave her voice the full power of her breath on the last line of the chorus: "*OH! Hard times come again no more.*"

She held the final note until her breath was gone, as the choirmaster had taught her. The theater was completely silent.

Did she sound terrible? Had she been off-key? Suddenly, clapping sounded and one of the men in the back stood up in front of his seat. "Very nice!" he called.

Teresa gave him a small bow. She wasn't sure what to do until the woman at the table called out another name. Teresa hurried off the stage. The piano player surprised her by giving her a thumbs-up. Her cheeks felt hot. She dropped into a seat a few rows back, too rattled to pay attention to the final contestants, and closed her eyes. She went so far away that the lady judge called her name twice before Teresa realized she had won.

5.

Teresa stood in front of the stage, fingering the silver dollar that was her prize, while one of the judges, a short man with a wide belly, introduced himself. "I'm Mr. Quincy, manager of the Princess." He pointed to the second judge, who had come up behind him. "This is Mr. Fenton, owner of Fenton's music shop."

Teresa nodded, still too shocked to speak, though she and Nonnie used to buy sheet music at Fenton's.

"We need a song plugger for Saturday's show," Mr. Quincy said. "You're just right for the job."

Teresa found her voice. "You want me to plug songs here—in Brattleboro?"

"That's right," Mr. Quincy said. "Saturday morning, when the shoppers are out, you'll sing a few songs for the upcoming show, in Fenton's, at Miss Wilkins's Café, J.E. Mann's—wherever we find a crowd. Hopefully, your singing will pull folks into the theater to see Rose Stanton, the star attraction."

"I'm plugging songs for Miss *Stanton?*" Teresa asked, feeling like a dumb echo.

"For Miss Stanton and for me," Mr. Fenton said. "If you sing as well as you did tonight, I'll sell more sheet music." He looked her over as if she were a horse for sale at the livery. "Could you wear something a bit more—sophisticated?"

"Of course." Teresa wouldn't tell him this was her very best dress. "What songs will I sing?" she asked.

Mr. Fenton reached into a bag and pulled out two sets of sheet music. "'Cousin of Mine' and 'Heaven Will Protect the Working Girl.' You know them?"

"Just 'Cousin of Mine.' But I can read music."

"Perfect." Mr. Fenton rubbed his hands together. "First band call is Saturday, nine o'clock sharp. You'll practice with the orchestra."

A real orchestra! Teresa shivered with pleasure. "May I come to the show?"

Mr. Quincy flipped open his gold watch, as if he might find the answer there. "I suppose. We'll leave a ticket in the lobby for the first house." He hurried up the aisle without saying goodbye.

The matinee was never as good as the last show, but Teresa didn't care. How could she turn down a free ticket? Unless Papa found out—but she wouldn't think about that now. She rubbed the silver dollar and slipped it into her pocket. It was her first real money from singing.

"Excuse me."

Teresa looked down at the woman judge, a short lady with eyes bright as shoe buttons. "Congratulations." The woman took Teresa's hand and gave it a warm squeeze. "I'm Lucy Connover from New York. I'm visiting friends in Brattleboro and heard they needed a judge. Where did you learn to sing?"

Teresa shrugged. In her house, singing was like walking or breathing: You just knew how to do it. "From my parents, and my great-grandmother."

"That melody you selected was lovely; one of Foster's best. I'm surprised the pianist didn't know it. You even picked the right key."

Should she tell this stranger that she had perfect pitch? It seemed like a strange thing to boast about, like being double-jointed, or knowing how to say the alphabet backward, the way Pascal could. "Thank you," she said.

Miss Connover stepped closer, speaking softly although the theater was nearly empty. "You have a powerful voice for a young girl. You're not really fifteen, are you?"

"I was fifteen on April first." Teresa tried to sound polite, since Miss Connover had awarded her the prize. "Everyone says I look old for my age." She glanced at the clock at the back of the theater. "Excuse me. I need to catch the last trolley home."

"I'm sorry," Miss Connover said. "I didn't mean to question your honesty. I'll walk you out." As they started up the aisle, she pulled a calling card from her beaded bag. "You're wasting your talent, singing in amateur contests. With proper musical training, you could sing opera."

Opera? Teresa stifled a laugh. Opera was for fancy people who traveled first class on the train, or for women like Miss Connover, whose stylish brown skirt skimmed her ankles. "I plan to sing in Hammerstein's Victoria Theatre," she said, though that was only a dream.

"I'm sure variety sounds glamorous from here," Miss Connover said. "But the life of a vaudeville performer is hard work and little money. Only the best make it to the big cities. If you'll pardon my saying so, nice girls don't end up in variety."

So Mama wasn't a *nice girl*? Teresa drew herself up tall. "My parents were vaudeville performers. And we loved being on the road." She pushed open the door to the lobby. "Excuse me. I have to catch the trolley."

Miss Connover looked flustered. "I didn't mean to insult your family. I do apologize." She pressed her calling card into Teresa's hand. "You sing beautifully. Come spend the summer with me. I'll give you voice lessons."

Before Teresa could tell her that her family could never afford such a thing, Miss Connover added, "Don't worry about the expense. I always need help around the house—if you wouldn't mind that sort of work."

"We run a boardinghouse, so I'm used to it." She'd had enough of those chores to last a lifetime. Still, scrubbing dishes and dirty clothes in New York City would be better than being locked up at Estey. She gave Miss Connover a quick smile. "Thank you for the offer. I'll think about it." Teresa hurried outside.

Miss Connover joined her under the streetlight and pinned on her broad-brimmed hat. "Good luck, Teresa LeClair. Whatever you decide, I won't forget you." She hurried away up the hill.

What an unusual woman! Teresa studied the embossed card in the lamplight. *Lucy Connover, #3 Gramercy Park, New York, New York. Instruction in piano, voice, and composition.* A musical note decorated the top corner.

Teresa sighed. She couldn't leave Brattleboro alone. Besides, when Papa heard what she'd done tonight, he'd never let her out of the house again. Her shoulders drooped. Whatever happened to the old Papa, the one who played fiddle tunes after work or showed off his Québécois clogging, his heavy boots rapping their wooden floors?

A trolley rattled past, headed for the final stop on Prospect Hill. In a few minutes, it would turn around and come back for its final run to West Brattleboro. Teresa had stepped out to the curb to cross the street when the theater door opened behind her. The man who had clapped for her performance tipped his cap. He was tall and dark-skinned, his short-cropped hair rooted with gray. "My compliments, Miss," he said, in a soft southern drawl. "Marvin Jones, here. You're gifted with a fine set of pipes."

Pipes? Teresa was flustered. "Excuse me?"

"Daddy means you can sing." A younger man emerged from the shadows, carrying a book under his arm. He was a taller, younger version of Mr. Jones, wearing a similar suit of dark wool.

"My son, Pietro Jones," Mr. Jones said.

Pietro touched the brim of his cap. His gold-flecked brown eyes met her gaze so steadily that Teresa had to look away. "Good to hear the competition," he said.

Teresa looked from one man to the other, confused.

"Pietro's teasing," Mr. Jones said. "We're on the program here Saturday—and we needed to take a look at the stage."

"Oh!" Teresa said. "So I'll see you perform. Do you sing?"

"I do, now and then. Mainly, we dance." Pietro took his father's walking stick and tapped out a syncopated rhythm with his feet, using the stick to punctuate the beat. The distant clang of the trolley drowned out Teresa's applause. "That's my ride to West Brattleboro," she said. "Nice to meet you."

"You, too, Miss LeClair," Mr. Jones said. "By the way—I heard you tell that lady judge your family takes in boarders. Any chance you have a room for tonight? We're headed to New Hampshire tomorrow to do another show."

Teresa bit her lip. "I'm not sure . . ."

"Daddy." Pietro's voice was hard. "Don't cause trouble. You know we got to find our own place in this all-white burg—"

"It's not you." Teresa's face felt hot, although the air was cool. "Papa won't rent rooms to anyone in vaudeville, even though we used to be on the road ourselves."

"So that's where you learned to sing," Mr. Jones said. "What will your daddy think about your winning the contest?"

Teresa shifted from one foot to another. The trolley bell clanged, growing closer.

"Where *do* entertainers stay, then?" Pietro asked.

"Try Miss Wilkins's Café." Teresa pointed up the hill. "She doesn't mind performers—at least, I don't think so. She's always been a friend to my mama and papa."

"You mean it depends on their skin color?" Pietro asked.

Teresa met his gaze. "Miss Wilkins looks like you." She hadn't thought about it much, but Pietro was right: Brattleboro was a very white town. "Miss Wilkins has rooms over her shop. And her bread is delicious."

"Sounds good." Mr. Jones touched his hat brim. "Thank you for the tip, Miss LeClair. And take care of that voice. If luck will have it, we'll see you Saturday."

The church clock struck the half hour. Teresa gave them a quick wave and dashed across the street to catch the trolley. She sank onto the wooden seat. She'd won a silver dollar, received an offer to learn opera, *and* been told she had a "fine set of pipes." Best of all, she'd been offered a job as a song plugger. The trolley wheels clanged and squealed. Somehow she needed to keep all this from Papa.

6.

The next morning, Teresa carried Nonnie's breakfast tray into her room and set it on the table. Nonnie was still asleep, but Teresa waited until she heard the *clump clump* of Papa's boots and the slam of the front door before she left for school. She'd been lucky last night; the house had been dark and quiet when she'd come home—as it often was after choir practice. Maybe her luck would hold all day.

After school, Teresa washed the stack of dishes in the sink, snapped the sheets off the line to fold them, and slipped her hand under the broody hens, setting their warm eggs into Mama's egg basket on the kitchen table. The boardinghouse was blissfully quiet: Pascal and a friend were skipping stones in the brook, and Mama wasn't home.

Now or never. Teresa shut the glass doors of the music room behind her and set the new sheet music on the piano. She ran through "Cousin of Mine," singing the verses softly without the piano—she knew the tune. But she nearly choked when she picked up the second song. The cover of the sheet music, under the title "Tillie's Nightmare," showed a woman in an enormous, ugly hat, her mouth wide open as if she'd just seen a hairy spider. Inside, the lyrics for "Heaven Will Protect the Working Girl" were as silly as the title, and the tune was harder to grasp. If only she could read music as easily as she could pick things up by ear.

She pulled Miss Connover's calling card from her skirt pocket. *Instruction in piano, voice, and composition.* She'd never thought about voice lessons. What did she need to learn? Mr. Tish, the choirmaster, only complained that she sang too loud.

She squinted at the sheet music, slowly matching the notes with the lyrics. "You are going far away, but remember what I say, When you are in the city's giddy whirl . . ." Teresa sang. Her hands went still on the keys. Was this song trying to tell her something?

She heard voices through the open window. Mama and Papa? Teresa stood up, lifted the cover on the piano bench, and stuffed her music under a stack of popular songs. She wedged herself into the spot between the piano and the parlor organ. She used to hide there when she was small. Now she wiggled her hips and crossed her arms to fit into the narrow space. She remembered how Nonnie and Mama used to sing together, until Mama's voice gave out. While Nonnie pumped the Estey organ, Teresa felt the vibration of the bass notes inside her body. Lately, the organ was as silent as Papa's fiddle.

The front door opened. Mama and Papa's voices were raised. Teresa ducked her head and held still.

"Did you know Teresa skipped choir practice last night?" Papa said.

"But I saw her go out," Mama said.

"I ran into Mr. Tish," Papa said. "He told me Resa never showed up, so he gave her solo to someone else."

Teresa itched all over. She was in for it now.

"That's strange," Mama said. "I wonder where she was?"

"Out with some boy, I'd guess," Papa said. "And if I find out who—"

How ridiculous. Teresa unfolded herself and opened the glass doors, catching a glimpse of her flushed face and snarled hair in the mirror. "It wasn't a boy," she said.

"*Bon soir*, Teresa." Papa's voice was ice. "How nice of you to join us this evening." When Teresa said nothing, he asked, "Who is he?"

"François, calm down." Mama turned to Teresa, her dark eyes worried. "Where *did* you go last night?"

"I competed in a singing contest. And I won!"

Mama's smile was quick as the flash of a lightning bug, but Papa frowned.

"One of the judges gave me her card." Teresa held it up. "She says—that I have real talent." Teresa felt her cheeks burn. Mama had warned her not to brag, but still, that *was* what Miss Connover had said. "She wants me to come to New York City. She says she'll teach me to be an opera singer."

"*Très intéressant.*" Papa ignored the card. "And may I ask what you told her?"

"I said—that I didn't want to sing opera."

"*Eh bien.* So. You're not as foolish as I thought."

Papa's words smarted like a slap. "I told her—" Teresa gulped. "That I plan to sing with a vaudeville troop someday."

Mama's shoulders slumped. "Resa—"

Teresa grabbed Papa's sleeve before he could protest. "Think of it, Papa. You always wanted to play Hammerstein's Victoria. And you hate working for Estey. You could play the fiddle again, if you'd practice. You were *good*. Remember?"

Papa shook his head, then turned away. Was that regret she saw in his eyes? Teresa pressed on. "If we were on the road, Mama wouldn't have to cook and clean all day. And Pascal's a great juggler. He could be our dumb act."

"I'm not dumb!" Pascal's high voice came from the landing. "And I can juggle four balls now—want to see?" He clattered down the stairs, braced his feet on the hall carpet, and pulled four wizened apples from his pockets. He began to juggle, tossing first two, then three, then four apples into the air, his head bobbing as his eyes followed them up and down. One apple went up and over the chandelier. The glass wands tinkled but didn't break, and Pascal caught the apple, then lifted one leg and tossed the apples from side to side, up and around and under his leg. The red orbs bobbled and spun.

Teresa couldn't help laughing. Mama covered her mouth, but her eyes twinkled and her laughter came out in a snort.

"*Mon Dieu!*" Papa roared. He scrubbed his hair and beard with both hands, as if he'd just wakened from a hundred-year sleep. "Have you all gone mad?"

Pascal missed a catch and the bruised apples rolled across the floor. "You *said*: No swearing about God," he whimpered.

"Pick. Those. Up." Papa's words came out like fisticuffs.

Teresa cringed as tears started in Pascal's eyes. She pulled her brother close. "Papa," she whispered. "Pascal is only playing."

"Excuse me." A reedy voice sounded from the upstairs hall. "Is everything all right?"

7.

No one moved for a long moment. Then Mama called out, "Excuse *us*, Mr. Jensen. We've had a little upset. Dinner will be ready in an hour." She shooed them all into the music room and shut the doors. Pascal plunked himself down on the upholstered stool by the organ and swung his legs from side to side. "It's not fair. Resa got to perform on the road when she was young, but I never had the chance. *Can* we go again, Papa?"

"*Non*," Papa said. "Besides—aren't you forgetting someone?" He jerked his thumb toward Nonnie's room.

Teresa and Pascal exchanged a guilty look. How could they forget Nonnie?

Mama smoothed Pascal's collar. "Go wash up. And Teresa, pour your brother a glass of lemonade. Then we'll fix the supper."

"*Un moment*," Papa said. "They need to hear what I have to say."

"François . . ." Mama began, but Papa shot her a warning look.

Papa rubbed his beard, as he did when he was excited. "You're a lucky girl, Teresa," he said. "You have an appointment with Estey's floor manager tomorrow."

"I won't go."

"Resa, you are testing my patience . . ."

"Stop, you two." Mama drew herself up. Though she was short, she seemed rooted like an oak when she was cross. "I won't have it. Teresa is too young."

"Not necessarily," Papa said. "If she can lie about choir practice, perhaps she can lie about her age. She certainly *looks* sixteen, or older."

"Would you teach our children to lie?" Mama asked.

Papa ignored Mama and turned to Teresa. His eyes seemed to glisten. "The manager is eager to meet you and witness your talent." He cleared his throat and hummed a B-flat. "What is that note?"

Teresa shook her head. "I'm not playing that game."

Papa's neck reddened. "Resa—I won't have this rudeness."

"What's wrong?" Pascal cried. He buried his face in Mama's skirts.

"Papa wants to shut me up in the tuning rooms," Teresa said.

Pascal's blue eyes swam. "Is that like jail?"

"Exactly," Teresa said.

"François—look how you've upset everyone," Mama said, stroking Pascal's hair. "Teresa is *not* going to work in that factory. And that's final."

"Now Alice. Surely you don't want me in trouble with my floor manager? I promised to bring Resa in tomorrow. We'll see what he says—and then, we decide. Together. How does that sound?"

"Horrible," Teresa said. Papa had become a stranger. A stranger who would lock her away and told her to lie. "It's not fair," she said.

"*La vie n'est pas juste,*" Papa said.

"If life isn't fair, what about you, Papa? You have perfect pitch, too. Why don't *you* work in the tuning rooms?"

"Tell her, François." Mama's voice was hard.

Papa's shoulders slumped. "My hearing is not so good after all those years with the big saws. But Estey has been good to me—work is quieter where I work now, assembling the organs. I'm finally a craftsman." Papa cupped Teresa's elbow. "Estey could give you a job for life. Many girls in this town would die for this chance."

"I don't want to die, Papa! I want to *live*—and sing."

Teresa raced upstairs to her attic bedroom, threw open the tiny window under the eaves, and breathed deep until her heart stopped racing. The dappled light was fading and a cardinal sang his mating song in the oak tree. "You're lucky," she told the bird. "You can sing wherever you want. No one will put you in a cage."

She perched on the edge of her bed and made a bargain with herself. She would go to Estey with Papa tomorrow. But on Saturdays, Papa worked the morning shift, and he always came straight home when the noon whistle blew. Hopefully, he wouldn't know she'd been plugging songs until she was done. He couldn't stop her from doing that—could he?

8.

Teresa rode the trolley to the end of the line on Thursday afternoon and trudged up the hill to Birge Street. Dark clouds scudded across the sky, their color matching the slate tiles that covered the roofs and sides of the factory. The identical buildings were lined up like soldiers in uniform. Smoke poured from the building housing the giant Corliss steam engine that powered the factory. It pounded in syncopation with the whine of saws in the lumberyard and the clang of metal in a distant building. How did Papa stand it? She could never work here.

A quick wind whipped the branches overhead. Teresa thought of all the happy times when she had come downstreet after school to do an errand for Mama, then waited for Papa so they could ride the trolley home together. Now she felt nothing but dread. She checked the clock on Building Number Five: 3:45. She was a few minutes early.

"Well, well; look who's here. Miss Hard Times herself."

Teresa whirled around and almost knocked into the young man she'd met at the contest. He looked younger, dressed in street clothes, but he still carried a book tucked into his open jacket. She'd forgotten his name. "Oh—hello . . ."

"Pietro. Pietro Jones." He tapped out a quick-step rhythm with his heavy boots.

"I thought you were performing in New Hampshire," Teresa said.

"We did, last night. I'm just walking through town, passin' time." He pointed to the Estey buildings. "I wanted to see this factory everyone brags about. It's quite the place. My grandmamma in Tennessee has one of their parlor organs. It has a pretty sound."

"We have one, too," Teresa said.

The streetcar clanged in the distance. Pietro glanced over his shoulder, as if looking for someone, but the street was empty. "I heard Estey employs half the town."

"Not half—but a lot of people. My papa works here."

Pietro raised his eyebrows. "Maybe he made Grandmamma's organ."

"Maybe part of it—but Papa was only a sawyer until last year. Now he puts the organs together." She frowned. "He wants me to talk to someone about a job."

Pietro whistled. "My, my. 'The girl with the golden pipes,' as my daddy called you. You'd work in a factory that makes *organ* pipes?"

Teresa's collar felt too tight around her neck. "I hope not," she said.

"Mm-mm. I know how that is," Pietro said. "My daddy's got his ideas and I've got mine."

"You don't want to dance with your father?"

Pietro frowned. "It's complicated. Marvin Jones and *Son*— that's our name. Like I don't rate my own name up there on the marquee. Besides—there are other things I might want to do."

"Like what?" Teresa couldn't believe she was having this conversation. Most boys treated her like an idiot.

Pietro tapped the spine of the book he carried but didn't reveal its cover. "I'm studying on it here in this book."

"What's the title? Is it your homework?"

"Wouldn't you like to know."

"Well of course! That's why I asked." The door of Building Number Five opened and two men in suits stepped out, pulling on their hats. Teresa glanced at the clock. Time to go.

When she turned around, Pietro was striding away toward Canal Street. "Well, excuse *me*," Teresa said to herself. "You can't even say goodbye?"

Daddy's got his ideas and I've got mine. She understood Pietro's words all too well.

∞∞∞

Teresa knocked on the door of Papa's building and a short man opened the door. He held a screwdriver in his hand and scowled at her as if she were an annoying insect. "What is it, Miss? Do you have a pass?"

"I'm here—to—to see my father," Teresa stammered. "François LeClair."

"Wait here." The man pointed to a small square of empty floor near the door and disappeared into a maze of organs—some finished, others in pieces—that stretched as far as she could see. The organs near the front of the room gleamed, their dark wood polished and shiny. Men in aprons worked on the instruments, some hammering, others drilling or sanding. The room smelled of sawdust and resin, and the din made her ears ring.

"Amazing, no?"

Teresa startled. Papa stood in front of her. He looked like a chef with his starched apron pulled tight over his chest and belly. "*Viens,*" he said, beckoning. "Mr. O'Malley waits for us."

They hurried through the rain into the next building and climbed a set of steep stairs. A tall man with a greased mustache waited at the top. "Mr. O'Malley: my daughter, Teresa," Papa said.

"Pleased to meet you." Mr. O'Malley shook Teresa's hand. "Your father tells me that you're sixteen—and that you have perfect pitch," he said.

Sixteen? Papa had lied! Teresa couldn't look at him.

Mr. O'Malley rubbed his hands together. "We don't employ too many gentlewomen at Estey," he said, "although they can be skilled at filing reeds. For tuning, however, the ear matters most."

He led them down a hall. Soft, reedy noises sounded from behind closed doors. Mr. O'Malley stopped in front of the last door and gave Teresa a severe look. "We don't want other companies to know how we make our reeds, so each tuner keeps his technique to himself. They say, when a tuner dies, the secret of his reeds dies with him." He paused, as if to let the words sink in. "Can you keep a secret?"

Before she could answer, Papa said, "Don't worry, Mr. O'Malley. You can trust our Resa." He turned to her. "*C'est vrai?*"

She heard the threat in his voice. "Yes, Papa. It's true."

"If you don't mind, Mr. LeClair, I'd like to test your daughter myself," Mr. O'Malley said. "It won't take long."

"Of course." Papa sent Teresa a warning look. She followed Mr. O'Malley into a small room lit by a tall window. He closed the door behind them, opened the drawer on a small table, and pulled out a handful of tuning forks. He tapped one against the windowsill. "Recognize that note?" Mr. O'Malley asked.

She hesitated. If she lied, Papa would never forgive her. "I'm sorry," she said, and tried to laugh. "I'm nervous. Could you hit it again?" When the note rang out against the table, Teresa said, "Middle C."

Mr. O'Malley tapped another fork. The rich sound reverberated in the quiet room. "F, below middle C," Teresa said.

The test went on. Mr. O'Malley played some tricky sharps and flats, some low notes and a few shrill high ones. Teresa knew them all.

"Perfect," Mr. O'Malley said at last. He opened the door and waved Papa in. "You spoke correctly—your daughter didn't miss a single note." He turned to her. "What do you think, Miss LeClair? Are you interested in working here? It's a good living, and you'd bring joy to the people who play our organs."

Teresa turned away. A cardinal flew past the long window, a flash of red against the gray slate of the next building.

"Resa—answer Mr. O'Malley's question," Papa said.

"I'm still in school," Teresa said at last.

Mr. O'Malley nodded. "Of course." He winked at her—winked! Teresa felt sick, but Papa didn't seem to notice.

"Your father tells me—how shall we put it—that you don't exactly *enjoy* school," Mr. O'Malley said.

Teresa's eyes burned. Papa had betrayed her, but she wouldn't cry in front of this man. "I plan to finish the year," she said.

"That's admirable," Mr. O'Malley said. "But summer will be here soon. Come see me some afternoon and we'll see how you might work with the reeds. If your hands are as adept as your ear, we could use you here."

Adept with her hands? Hardly. The cardinal flew into an elm tree beyond the next building. It threw back its head and opened its beak, but Teresa couldn't hear its song. She tried to picture herself alone in this room, wrestling with the reeds and hand tools. She could sing all day to the four walls and no one would notice or care. "I'm sorry, sir—but I can't," she whispered.

Papa flushed. "Resa. Don't be rude." His voice softened. "You don't know what it's like until you try. You'll come in to watch Mr. O'Malley. I insist."

Mr. O'Malley put up his hands. "We wouldn't force you," he said. "Go home and talk things over with your parents. I hope you'll have a change of heart."

The men discussed her pay, as if she weren't even in the room. Teresa watched the cardinal through the glass. When it flew off, she sent a message to the bird. *Take me with you*, she begged silently. *We'll fly away. Down the river and then to New York City and the Great White Way. We'll fly—and we'll sing.*

9.

Teresa avoided Papa that night and the next day. She practiced her songs in front of her mirror when Papa was home, and at the piano after school. She let Nonnie in on her secret, but told no one else. On Friday night, she tapped on Nonnie's door and slipped into the musty room, carrying her great-grandmother's clean laundry. Nonnie stood by the window, her nose pressed to the glass. "Nonnie—what are you doing?"

"I can't open the window," Nonnie said. "I want to smell the lilacs."

The window was stiff and swollen. Teresa banged and jiggled the frame until she was able to lift it. The lilac was in full bloom, its purple blossoms weighing the top branches down. They both breathed in the sweet scent. "Lovely," Nonnie said. "Nothing like it, is there?"

"Nothing." Teresa took Nonnie's stockings and underthings from the basket and set them in the top drawer. Something glinted in the pile of handkerchiefs. Teresa pulled out a gold locket, the size of her silver dollar. A curlicue design was etched into the metal, which felt smooth and warm on her palm. "Oh," she whispered.

"What have you found?" Nonnie asked.

"A gold locket." Teresa set it in Nonnie's hands.

Her great-grandmother slid her fingers across the surface. "I remember this. It opens on the side. Go on, you try."

Teresa wiggled a fingernail under the cover and found a heart-shaped photograph. She stepped to the window and held the picture to the light. It took her a moment to realize she was looking at a faded photograph of her family—or rather, her family as it used to be. "It's Mama, Papa, and me—and Pascal, when he was a baby. I'm wearing that dress you made, with the smocking across the top."

"The little blue dress," Nonnie said. "It took me days to do those stitches. You looked so sweet in that frock." She sighed. "Those times are gone now."

Teresa agreed, although she and Nonnie had different "times" in mind. She studied the photo. Mama and Papa stood together, their shoulders touching. Papa's fiddle was tucked up under his chin. His beard covered his mouth, but his eyes were smiling. Mama's cheeks were round and full. She cradled Pascal in her arms. He was just an infant, with a smooth bald head. The three of them faced the camera, but Teresa's face, half hidden by her knotted curls, was turned up to Papa.

She had adored him. Once.

Nonnie's voice broke into Teresa's thoughts. "Your papa was so proud of his little family," Nonnie said. "He took you downstreet to the photography studio." She smiled at Teresa. "The locket should be yours. Wear it tomorrow, for good luck."

"Thank you, Nonnie." Teresa slipped the locket, on its chain, into her pocket. As she helped Nonnie back to her chair, she noticed the mannequin her great-grandmother had used when she still made dresses for women in Brattleboro. When Teresa was little, the mannequin—with her pretty chest, slender waist, and plump hips—seemed real. Teresa had named her Ethel. Nonnie stopped sewing when her eyes went bad, and usually the mannequin was bare—but today, Ethel wore a taffeta dress with ruffles across the bust. "Why is Ethel dressed up?" Teresa asked.

Nonnie turned her milky blue eyes on her. "You need to wear something fetching tomorrow, but I don't think this will fit you. If only I could still sew."

"The judges didn't like my new shirtwaist. What should I do?"

"Come closer." Nonnie reached up to Teresa's shoulder and ran her hand down to her waist. "You're taller than I am, but we're both busty on top. Leave my closet door open and hand me my cane, will you? Who knows what I'll find in there. Come see me in the morning."

"Thank you," Teresa said, though she guessed that nothing in that crowded closet would fit her—or look right. "Did you hear me practicing?"

"I did." Nonnie laughed. "What silly lyrics—*heaven will protect the working girl.*" She tapped her own chest. "Heaven didn't protect *this* working girl."

Teresa was quiet a moment. She hadn't thought of Nonnie as a "working girl"—but of course she was, all those years stitching clothes for Brattleboro women. She felt a pang as Papa's words rang in her head. If they went back on the road—what would happen to Nonnie?

"Go along, angel. You need your beauty sleep."

Teresa kissed Nonnie's forehead and left the room. She was no "angel," but why spoil Nonnie's sweet trust?

10.

Teresa woke before dawn, pulled on an old dress, and hurried downstairs to do her chores. Papa barely looked up from the newspaper when she went by. "You're an early bird," he said.

"Are you going to work?" she asked, as if she didn't know what Papa did on Saturday mornings.

"*Bien sûr*," Papa said. "Of course I'm working. Would you like to visit with Mr. O'Malley today?"

"I can't." Teresa grabbed the egg basket. "I'm busy." True enough.

By the time she had watered and fed the chickens and collected the eggs, Papa was gone. Mama stood at the stove, frying bacon. Fire crackled in the wood stove and sweat trickled down her face. "We might have a new guest tonight," Mama said. "You can make up the bed in the room next to Mr. Jensen."

Teresa's hands shook. "Mama," she said. "I have to tell you something."

Mama flipped the bacon strips and wiped her hands on her apron. "You sound so serious. Is it the sick headache?"

If only it were that simple. "Remember that contest I won, on choir night? I agreed to sing for them this morning. I have to be at the theater at nine o'clock." Before Mama could argue, Teresa explained what the judges had asked her to do. "I *promised* I would come," she said. "And they're holding a ticket for me to this afternoon's show. Mama, please. Let me go."

Mama slid the frying pan to the cool side of the stove. "Of course you will keep your promise. And what a nice compliment." Mama's dark eyes twinkled. "It sounds like fun. What will you wear?"

"I don't know. They asked for something—'sophisticated.' Nonnie said she might find something." She clutched Mama's hand. "What if Papa finds out?"

"Don't worry. Nonnie and I will fix it."

"Thank you." Teresa hugged her mother tight and wiped her eyes. Nonnie *always* came through—and sometimes Mama did, too.

❧

Half an hour later, Teresa stood in front of Nonnie's full-length mirror, dressed in a burgundy skirt with buttons on the side and a cream-colored silk blouse with a high collar. The skirt skimmed her ankles. It wasn't the latest fashion, but close enough. "I made the blouse for a woman who never picked it up," Nonnie said. "And the skirt was your grandmother's. She was your height." Nonnie laughed. "She'd turn over in her grave if she knew you were singing on the street."

Mama tied Teresa's curls back with a pale blue ribbon and settled the gold locket around her neck. Teresa stared at the stranger in the mirror.

Nonnie touched Teresa's hair and ran her fingers over her shoulders. "It fits you nicely. Not too tight? Does the skirt clash with your curls?"

"No. It's perfect," Teresa said. "And so is the blouse."

"How does she look?" Nonnie asked.

"Beautiful," Mama said. "I only wish you could see her, too."

Pascal poked his head around the door. "Resa, why are you dressed up? Are you going to church?"

"I'm a song plugger today."

"What's that?"

"I sing on Main Street so people will buy tickets to see the shows at the Princess."

Pascal's eyes lit up. "Is it vaude, with dumb acts? Mama, can I go too? *Please?*"

"We'll see," Mama said. "I'll bring you downstreet later, when I go to Miss Wilkins's for bread. Now run along, Resa, or you'll be late."

Teresa patted her pocket to make sure she had the vial with Nonnie's rouge. She would put some on at the theater.

"You'll wow them," Nonnie said.

"Let's hope."

Pascal followed Teresa down the hall and out the door. "Does Papa know?" he asked.

She turned on him. "No. Don't you dare tell."

"I won't—if you get me a ticket to the show."

"You're a pest." When his face crumpled, she ruffled his hair. "I'll try," she said. "Find me when you come with Mama."

Butterflies fluttered in her belly as she climbed onto the trolley, gave the conductor her nickel, and found a clean seat, careful not to wrinkle her skirt. Even though Pascal would be a nuisance, she almost wished he had come with her. How could she do this alone?

11.

Teresa stood on the sidewalk outside the Princess clutching her music. She breathed deeply, as Mr. Tish always urged them to do at the start of choir practice. A sign under the theater's marquee boasted that the Princess was *Brattleboro's Finest Place of Entertainment, a Place for Ladies and Gentlemen as well as Children.*

The marquee itself gave Mr. Jones and Pietro top billing, in bold capital letters: "MARVIN JONES AND SON, A FIRST-CLASS SONG AND DANCE ROUTINE!" Their names were above the "ROSE OF ABILENE, THE KANSAS FLOWER WHO PLUCKS YOUR HEART STRINGS."

What a silly slogan. The empty theater seemed even bigger than it had on Tuesday night. Teresa rouged her cheeks and lips in the washroom before walking down the center aisle. Her footsteps echoed on the wooden floor. She stopped, halfway to the stage apron, when a familiar tune sounded from the orchestra pit: the opening phrase of the "Working Girl" song. Mr. Quincy came out onstage, peered into the pit, and clapped his hands. The music stopped in the middle of a measure. "First band call!" he bellowed. "Everyone on stage." He waved to Teresa. "That includes you."

Teresa glanced at the empty rows of seats. Was she the only one here?

"Come along," Mr. Quincy said. Teresa climbed the stairs and stood uneasily near the footlights. "Nice." Mr. Quincy nodded. "You look like a young lady this morning."

A rhythmic scuffling sounded from behind the scrim. Mr. Jones and Pietro danced onstage from the wings. They wore shiny shoes with spats, straw hats, and matching navy-blue suits with white flowers in their buttonholes. Mr. Jones brandished a cane, and Pietro snapped a silky red scarf in front of Teresa as he danced past. Teresa felt dowdy next to the dancers, in spite of Nonnie's fancy clothes. The men clicked their heels and drew up beside her. Mr. Jones was breathing hard, but Pietro looked cool and calm.

Mr. Jones waved his gloved hand. "The girl with the fine set of pipes. You ready?"

"I guess." Teresa lowered her voice. "Actually, I'm nervous."

"Everyone gets stage fright," Pietro said. "Even song pluggers." He tapped out a short, syncopated riff, his shoes clattering on the wooden stage apron.

"What makes your shoes so loud?" Teresa asked.

"Metal plates." Pietro's shoes beat out a complex rhythm that took him across the stage, behind the curtain, and back out again. He drew up in front of her and gave her a bow. "You learn your music?" he asked.

"Of course," Teresa said.

Mr. Quincy bustled across the stage and exited into the wings. "Enough chit-chat," he said. "Miss Stanton! We're waiting on you."

"Coming! Coming!" a high voice trilled. A short blonde woman appeared at stage right. She wore a pink dress that showed most of her legs. Her curls bounced as she minced to the edge of the apron. "Who turned off the heat?" she demanded.

Mr. Quincy tugged his mustache. "We don't heat our dressing rooms in May," he said. "Now, if we could get started—"

Miss Stanton rubbed her bare arms and puckered her mouth. "Mr. Quincy. I've played Hammerstein's Victoria *Theatre*, in New York *City*. I'll have you know I am not accustomed to this sort of treatment."

Teresa glanced over Miss Stanton's head in time to see Pietro imitating her, tipping his head back and forth in a simpering way. Teresa bit the inside of her cheek and studied the floorboards to keep from laughing.

"I'm sorry about the dressing rooms." The manager rubbed his bald head. "I'll see what we can do."

"That's the least of your problems." Miss Stanton flicked her hair off her collar and turned to stare at Pietro and Mr. Jones. "I'm used to top billing. Taking second place to white minstrels is bad enough. But billing me after two—" she swallowed. "After two men of inferior race. I simply don't see how you can expect me to perform under these circumstances. Why—they're not even wearing cork!"

"We know who's inferior here," Pietro muttered.

Mr. Jones sent Pietro a warning look and Mr. Quincy sighed. "This is only the rehearsal, Miss Stanton. They'll be in blackface later; don't worry. And we billed you as your agency suggested."

"Excuse *me*. Mr. Keith would *never* put me second to . . . to these . . ."

Before she could finish her sentence, the bandleader rapped his baton on a music stand. "Time's a-wasting, Ma'am. We're only paid for an hour's rehearsal."

"Right." Mr. Quincy loosened his tie and pointed at Teresa. "This young lady is going to plug your songs around town this morning. We need to be sure she knows the tunes before we send her out."

Miss Stanton stared at Teresa. "This *child*? Can she even sing?"

"Like a nightingale," Mr. Jones said quietly.

"Enough!" Mr. Quincy shouted. "Get to work, or you'll all be fired." He stomped offstage and into the orchestra, where he took a seat a few rows back.

"We'll start with 'Cousin of Mine,'" the bandleader said. He raised his baton and nodded to Miss Stanton. "Ready? You first, and then Miss LeClair."

The bandleader had upstaged Miss Stanton! Teresa grinned, and edged closer to Pietro and Mr. Jones as the orchestra ran through the tune. Miss Stanton insisted that the band start over until the tempo was the way she wanted it.

"Fussbudget," Pietro said under his breath.

"She's a little flat," Teresa whispered. Even worse, the woman's voice was breathy and small.

After the third time through, Miss Stanton turned to Teresa. "*Your* turn," she said in a nasty tone.

Teresa moved close to the orchestra pit, took a long breath, and nodded to the bandleader. She felt as stiff as Nonnie's mannequin and she missed the first note. The bandleader stopped the piano player. "Try again," he said. "Pretend you're singing at home, for your mama."

Or for Nonnie, Teresa thought. She took a deep breath and felt her voice fill the theater on the second verse. A rollicking beat sounded behind her in the final chorus. It was Pietro, keeping time with his feet. "*He's mother's*" (*tap tap*) "*sister's*" (*tap tap*) "*angel child*," she sang (*tappity tap*); "*He's a cousin o' mine.*"

"This is outrageous!" Miss Stanton strutted toward them like one of Mama's banty hens. "Boy—if you dance behind me in *my* numbers, I'll send you back where you came from."

"My name is Pietro Jones," he said. "And going back won't bother me. Harlem's the best place in the world."

Mr. Jones gripped Pietro's elbow, and Mr. Quincy opened his palms, as if begging for pennies. "Please calm down. Don't worry, Miss Stanton. No one will interrupt your act."

Miss Stanton tapped the toe of her silver shoe. The bandleader peered up at Teresa from the pit. "The dancer has a good idea," he said. "Give the tune a little more oomph. Remember, this is a funny song. The boy's not really her cousin—he's a beau. Could you belt it out, be a bit saucy?"

Saucy? Teresa blushed. She'd never had a beau, so how would she know how to act? Papa used to sing this song on the train, when they were on their jumps between one town and the next. She'd never thought about its meaning. "All right," she said. Maybe she *was* too young and innocent.

Mr. Jones pointed his cane toward the back of the theater. "Someone you know?"

A yellow head popped up from behind the last row, and three red balls spun above the seats. Teresa sighed. "My brother. He's not supposed to be here."

"Never mind," Mr. Jones said. "Sing it to him. Be yourself caught out, making excuses to your mama 'bout something you done wrong."

More like excuses to Papa, Teresa thought. She cleared her throat, signaled to the bandleader that she was ready, and imagined her voice carrying over the empty seats to Pascal.

I ain't seen Jerry in about ten years
You know that's a mighty long time—
He's mother's sister's angel child—
Why, he's a cousin of mine.

Pascal clapped, and Mr. Quincy called, "Good, good," from the first row. "Try the next one."

Miss Stanton and Teresa took turns on the "Working Girl" song, and Teresa managed to avoid meeting the woman's eyes. Instead, she imagined that Mama was the woman in the song, who warned her daughter about the dangers of the city; that it was Mama who prayed that heaven would protect her from the city's *"temptations, crimes, and follies/Villains, taxicabs, and trolleys . . ."*

When Miss Stanton sang, she put on an act, as if she were a yokel from some no-count town. She refused to run through it a second time. "I need to save my voice for the performance," she said, and disappeared into the wings.

The bandleader shook his head, Mr. Quincy threw up his hands, and Pietro danced a slow jig across the stage. Teresa guessed they all felt the same way: The so-called "Rose" of Abilene was more like the thorn than the flower.

12.

"All right, Miss LeClair," Mr. Quincy said. "Davey's waiting for you in the lobby; he'll go with you to Fenton's. I'll find you as soon as I get the next act started."

Teresa hurried up the aisle. Too bad she couldn't see Pietro and Mr. Jones dance. A tall young man with a sweeping mustache, a fiddle tucked under his arm, greeted her in the lobby. "I'm Davey." His hazel eyes twinkled as he and Teresa shook hands. "You sure got that Rose Stanton het up."

"What did I do wrong?" Teresa asked.

"Nothing, lass. You just sing better than she does."

"He's right. That dumb lady sings like she's out of breath!"

"Pascal!" Teresa whirled around.

Her brother peered through the small hole inside the box office window. "Tickets?" he asked.

"How did you get in there?" Teresa opened the ticket booth and yanked him out. "You nearly spoiled my rehearsal."

Pascal twisted from her grip. "Did not. You sang better after I waved to you."

"The boy's right as rain." Davey pointed at Pascal's trousers, bulging at the hips. "Rocks in your pockets?"

Before Pascal could answer, the door to the theater swung open and Mr. Quincy appeared. Pascal froze. "So *you* were the one making the ruckus," Mr. Quincy said. "You know this boy, Miss LeClair?"

"My brother. I'm so sorry. Pascal—please go home."

"Can't. Mama said to meet her at Miss Wilkins's Café." Pascal pulled the three red balls from his pockets. "My sister sings, and I juggle. Want to see?"

"Not now." Mr. Quincy mopped his mottled cheeks with a kerchief. "Maybe never." He nodded at Davey. "Take Miss LeClair to Fenton's to see if folks will buy the sheet music, then work your way up and down Main Street. Don't forget the café—and finish at Mann's. They should have a good crowd by lunchtime."

Lunchtime? Teresa bit her lip. "Excuse me, Mr. Quincy—I thought we'd be done by noon."

"Then you'd best move along."

Mr. Quincy turned on his heel, but Pascal blocked the door. "Could I see the show with my sister?" He danced from one foot to the other. "Resa promised me a ticket."

Teresa was on thin ice. She gave Mr. Quincy a little curtsey. "Excuse me, Mr. Quincy, sir. You did say I could come to the first house."

"All right, all right. Two tickets. They'll hold them at the box office. But young man: keep those hands in your pockets and get out of my sight before I lose my temper." Mr. Quincy flung the door open and disappeared into the theater.

Teresa gripped Pascal's shoulder and steered him through the door. "Go to Mama," she whispered in his ear, "or I'll tell Papa what you've been doing. How did you get juggling balls, anyway?"

Two red spots appeared on Pascal's pale cheeks. "With Nonnie's money. She gives me pennies when I help her find things. Anyway, *you're* the one keeping secrets from Papa." He ducked under her arm and was gone.

"Little brothers. Bane of me existence when I was young." Davey opened the door for her. "Drove me quite mad, they did, when we were boys in Ireland." He pointed at Pascal, who was running up the hill, his arms pumping. "Love 'em while you can. That's my advice."

13.

The store was crowded. Mr. Fenton greeted Teresa as if they were old friends and cupped his hands around his mouth. "Laa-dies and gentlemen!" he called out, and the crowd quieted. "We have a special treat this morning. A local girl with a golden voice will plug two songs for today's show at the Princess. If you enjoy her tunes, we have the sheet music right here." He pointed to a stack of music on the front counter. "Ready, Miss LeClair?"

Teresa cleared her throat. Davey bowed the *A* string and twisted the tuning pegs. Teresa winced. She didn't dare tell him that one string was flat. Her stomach felt like jelly that hadn't set.

Davey raised his eyebrows and gave her a small nod.

Now or never. Teresa took a deep breath, Davey played two measures of "Cousin of Mine," and she jumped in. Davey's quick tempo made it easier to take the bandleader's advice and give the song more bounce. When she came to the punch line—"*ain't no harm for to hug and kiss your cousin*"—she winked, and the crowd laughed. By the end of their second number, the stacks of sheet music were dwindling, and one woman called out, "Is she the one performing this afternoon?"

"No," Mr. Fenton said. "She's too young to be onstage. She's plugging for the 'Rose of Abilene.' But we'll see her name in lights someday. Give her a hand."

The strong applause sent Teresa out onto the sidewalk with her head in the clouds. For the rest of the morning, she sang up and down Main Street while Davey played for her. They stopped at DeWitt's grocers, at Houghton and Simond's dress shop, even at the automobile repair shop. The last stop before Mann's was Miss Wilkins's Café. It was steamy inside, and the smell of sage and fresh bread made Teresa's stomach grumble.

No sign of Mama or Pascal.

Miss Wilkins greeted Teresa with her wide smile. "Why, if it isn't Teresa LeClair. Don't you look fine. That must be your great-grandma Aurelia's handiwork." She clapped her hands. "Listen up, everyone! You have a treat in store."

The café went quiet and Teresa and Davey dove in. By this time, Teresa had learned that her audiences liked "Cousin" the best, so she sang the silly "Working Girl" number first, then livened things up with the second tune. The customers laughed and clapped, and a few people slipped coins into her pockets. "Give them a nice bow," Davey whispered in her ear.

Miss Wilkins wrapped two warm biscuits in a napkin and handed them to Teresa. "Thank you for sending those nice gentlemen to me last night," she said, her voice low. "Knowing what life can be like for them on the road, I hope I gave them a good rest. I plan to see them dance later." She cupped Teresa's elbow. "Take care of that voice. It's going to carry you somewhere."

"Thank you." If only her voice *could* take her far from here. But what did Miss Wilkins mean about the Joneses and their life on the road? She felt ignorant.

"Let's go." Davey beckoned to her from the door. "We're due at Mann's at noon."

Mr. Quincy was right: The department store was crowded. Davey spoke to one of the sales girls, who cleared a spot for them at the notions counter. "We'll give them the one song, leave them wanting more," Davey said. He launched into the first few measures of "Cousin." A small crowd gathered, and they were well into the second verse when the bell on the door jingled behind Teresa. She stepped to the side without missing a note, and sang out to the crowd: "*I ain't seen Jerry in about ten years . . .*"

Teresa felt the crackle of tension before she noticed the sales girls frowning. She'd lost the crowd. Davey's fiddle faltered and his bow suddenly screeched. "Put that thing down! You can't even play."

Papa stood in the open door, holding Davey's fiddle high above his head. "*Mon Dieu!* You call that fiddling?" His voice was wound up tighter than the top string on Davey's fiddle. "What are you doing with my daughter?"

14.

Papa gripped Teresa's wrist and yanked her out onto the sidewalk. "Papa, let go! You're hurting me."

Davey followed close behind. "My fiddle, sir! Take care."

Papa shoved the fiddle at Davey. Women shoppers peered through the door and Teresa twisted away from Papa's grip. "People are staring."

"Let them," Papa said. "You have disgraced our family."

"Why?" Teresa demanded. "Because I can sing?"

Before Papa could answer, Teresa heard Mama's voice. "François! *Arrêt*—stop!" Mama bustled down the hill, her basket over one arm. Pascal jogged along beside her. Everyone was suddenly talking at once. Teresa tried to explain the song plugging while Papa let loose a string of French swear words and Pascal tugged at Teresa's skirt. "What happened?" he asked. "What did you do?"

"I sang," Teresa said.

Davey stowed the fiddle in its case and turned to Mama. "Your daughter sings like an angel, Ma'am. Been my privilege, it has, to play for her this spring morning." He dug into his pocket and handed Teresa a silver dollar. "This is from Mr. Quincy, for your good work." Davey shook Teresa's hand. "Take care of that voice. Fenton's right: Your name will be in lights one of these days."

"Your playing helped me sing better," Teresa said.

"Ta." Davey touched the brim of his cap and strode away, whistling a B-flat tune.

"Angel my foot." Papa cleared his throat. "Are you quite done making a fool of yourself?"

"François." Mama's voice was fierce. "If I may say so—*you* are the fool. Creating a scene; shaming Teresa in public. It's not right."

Teresa gave Mama a grateful smile. She felt warm inside, in spite of Papa's rage. She held up the silver dollar. "See, Papa? There are other ways to make money. Just like you did once, on the road."

Papa shook his head. "Enough of this talk. There's much you don't know about that life. Anyway, you have chores to do at home—in case you've forgotten."

"Hush." Mama pulled Papa aside to let people pass on the sidewalk. "Chores can wait. Don't deny Teresa her success. We get little enough in our lives."

"*Eh, bien.* Very well; have it your way," Papa said. "If you want to slave away all day without help, that's your choice."

He strode across the street to the trolley stop. Mama sighed. "I'll go with him," she said. "Maybe I can calm him down. Teresa, take Pascal to the theater."

"I'm hungry," Pascal said.

Teresa patted her pocket. "I have two biscuits from Miss Wilkins." She held up her coin. "And I'll buy us something else to eat."

Mama put her hand over Teresa's. "Save that." She gave her a few coins. "Get some treats at the theater." She hoisted her basket.

"Come with us," Teresa said. "Please? We could get you a ticket."

Mama hesitated. Her brown eyes were soft with longing—but she shook her head. "Not this time. It will only make me sad." Before Teresa could ask why, Mama had hurried across the street to catch the oncoming trolley.

"*Please* can we go to the Princess now?" Pascal begged. "I want to watch them set up."

Teresa grabbed his hand. "Run! It's about time we saw a proper vaudeville show."

15.

The theater was full for the matinee. Mr. Quincy rubbed his hands together when he spotted Teresa. "Good job, good job. You really brought them in." He led them to seats in the third row, where Pascal swung his legs and bounced on the wooden seat with excitement.

"Calm down," Teresa said, though she felt the same way.

The show began with a boring silent film, followed by a dark-haired man with *NICO THE GREEK!* stitched on his striped shirt. He pedaled a unicycle and juggled red bowling pins as he wheeled around the stage. He dropped one pin, then another, and lost his balance. The audience booed and catcalled, and someone threw a raw egg. It caught in the spokes of the cyclist's wheel and spattered all over his pants. "Look." Teresa nudged Pascal as a shepherd's crook poked from the wings. "He's getting the hook."

The cyclist wheeled away before the manager could catch him. "I could do better than *that*," Pascal said.

"Hush," Teresa said. Lively music rose from the pit as Pietro Jones and his father danced onstage. The audience quieted immediately. Miss Stanton must have won her battle; Mr. Jones and Pietro no longer had the headliner's spot near the end. But it didn't matter: "MARVIN JONES AND SON" stole the show.

Both dancers were elegant, their long legs slicing and flashing as they echoed the band's rhythm on the wooden floorboards. In spite of his graying hair, Mr. Jones was as athletic as his son. They danced in perfect tandem, then apart. Pietro used his scarlet scarf as if it were his partner. He swept it through the air, snapped it when his feet tapped loudest, then used it to trap his father, wrapping it around him twice before he pulled on it to spin him away.

But Teresa couldn't stand to look at their faces. Thick black cork covered their skin from the hairline to the tops of their collars. Even worse, their mouths wore fake, exaggerated smiles that made them look foolish. Pascal nudged Teresa. "Are those the colored men we saw this afternoon?" he whispered. "Why do they wear that goop?"

The woman on the other side of Teresa gasped. "You must be joking!" she cried. "Why—they dance so well, I thought they must be white."

Teresa squirmed. She'd seen blackface before, but she'd always assumed, as this woman did, that the actors were white underneath. Maybe Papa was right—there was a lot she didn't know about that life. But was that her fault?

The Joneses finished with a ragtime number and the audience called them back for an encore. Pietro came out alone. He danced up and down a small flight of stairs, making it seem as if he might take off at the top and disappear into the flies, high above the stage. Did he *like* wearing cork? How could he?

Rose Stanton's music came up next and the audience whistled and stomped when Miss Stanton found her place in the spotlight. Her breathy voice was as tight and flimsy as her dress; it barely carried to their seats in the third row. How had she ever played at a New York theater? Maybe audiences liked seeing her legs in those pink tights.

Miss Stanton performed four songs, ending with the "Working Girl" song. People started shifting in their seats, and the woman next to Teresa put on her coat and climbed over her to reach the aisle. When Miss Stanton took a bow, someone in the back shouted, "Give us the song plugger!"

"Yes!" someone else called. "Where's the girl from the shops?"

Pascal elbowed Teresa. "They want you."

"We want the plugger! We want the plugger!" another man chanted, and others joined in until the theater rocked with the beat. Rose Stanton hurried into the wings. The heavy curtains swung closed, but the audience kept on clapping.

Mr. Quincy stepped out onto the stage apron, his high forehead beaded with sweat. "Stop! Stop!" he called. "The show is over."

But the audience stomped and shouted until finally, Mr. Quincy squinted over the footlights. "Miss LeClair—are you out there? Could you give us a quick number?"

Teresa stood up slowly. Her heart skittered and she could hardly breathe. She edged her way out to the aisle while people around her clapped and whistled. Mr. Quincy hurried down the steps, grabbed her elbow, and steered her toward the stage. "Just sing one number, will you?"

"But what?" Teresa whispered. "Miss Stanton already performed the tunes I know."

"How about the song you did on Tuesday night?"

"'Hard Times?' That's so sad."

"Doesn't matter. Give them something—anything!"

The crowd was settling, but Teresa could feel their anticipation. She tried to catch her breath. A violinist's bow waved like a beckoning hand from the orchestra pit. She leaned over the edge. It was Davey, his smile as bright as the footlights. "What can we do for you?"

"Can you play 'Hard Times'?"

Davey glanced at the other musicians, who nodded. "'Course we can. Key of E-flat?" He played the chord.

"Perfect," Teresa said softly. "I hope I can sing."

"You'll be fine. We'll give you four bars. Watch Bert." Davey waved to the pianist, who was not—thankfully—the clumsy piano player from the other night. "He'll cue you in with a nod."

Teresa climbed the stairs with lead in her shoes. The audience cheered, then went silent so quickly, she wondered if they had all disappeared, or if this was one of those dreams where you suddenly can't hear anything. The apron seemed too narrow, the footlights blinding. Where should she stand?

"Find the spotlight," a low voice called from the wings.

Was it Pietro, or Mr. Jones? Teresa breathed deep and stepped into the yellow pool of light in front of the curtain. Davey played the first few measures. Teresa watched Bert, who cued her in. She sang of a poor family's sorrow, of the "*sigh that is wafted across the troubled wave,*" but the family she pictured was her own. She heard the *clackety clack* of wheels and the lonesome whistle of the train that snatched them away from the stage so long ago. She remembered Papa, his head nodding, his bow arm curved as his fiddle played this plaintive tune. As she repeated the final chorus, a sweet tenor added harmony from the wings, so faint she might have imagined it.

The last notes died away. The audience was silent for a long pause, as if everyone had inhaled at once—and then the clapping began.

She'd forgotten! Forgotten the thrill of that deep hush, forgotten the spine-tingling joy of holding an audience spellbound. Teresa smiled, bowed—once, then twice—and then, unsure of where to go, found the gap in the curtain and slipped through. She nearly collided with Pietro. His dark eyes twinkled with mischief.

"That was *you* singing harmony," Teresa said.

"Who, me?" Pietro's right eyebrow lifted. "Of course not." His face looked so strange, his painted smile so phony, that Teresa turned away.

"Ugly, isn't it?" Pietro's voice suddenly turned serious. "I hate cork."

"Do you have to wear it?"

He waved her toward the stage. "Listen—they're still clapping. Give them a curtain call."

Teresa went back out, bowed at the waist, and ducked behind the curtain again. Mr. Jones waited for her this time. "You sure did ruffle that Miss Stanton's feathers." He laughed. "Did she ever strut downstairs to her dressing room!"

As if she heard them, Miss Stanton's shrill complaints rose from the dressing rooms below.

"She's ignorant," Pietro said. "You won't catch me onstage again with her, ever."

"I'm sure Miss Stanton agrees with you one hundred percent," Mr. Jones said. He turned to Teresa. "Take care of that voice," he said. "You'll go far."

"Thank you," Teresa said. "I loved your act. You're such good dancers."

"I have to work at it," Mr. Jones said. "My boy here—he's got natural talent. He's the one persuaded me to add ragtime to our act."

"You just saying that, Daddy." It was hard to read Pietro's feelings above his phony smile, but he lifted his top hat and turned to his father. "How about we do the next shows without the cork? We've only got one day in this two-bit town—who's going to mind?"

Mr. Jones shook his head. "We've been through this, son. Even Bert Williams wears cork—and he's the best comedian onstage, anywhere."

"His partner, George Walker, was the finest dancer around. He never blacked up," Pietro said. "Maybe Williams is a coward."

"Or maybe smart," Mr. Jones said. "How many other colored men you see playing the Ziegfeld Follies, the greatest theater pageant in New York?"

"Could be me, someday." Pietro danced in place, his shoes ticking a lazy rhythm on the wooden floor. "Just you wait, Daddy. When I hit the big time, I'll go onstage wearing nothing but my own brown face." He pointed at Teresa. "Why should she go on as her own self when I can't? Is that fair?"

Teresa cringed. Had she done something wrong?

"Hush," Mr. Jones said. "You're too smart for your own good. Can't you see she's just a girl?"

"Never too late to get educated," Pietro said, and turned away without a word.

Teresa's cheeks burned. Probably she *was* dumb about many things—but he didn't have to rub it in! "I need to find my brother," she told Mr. Jones. "It was nice to meet you." She shook his hand. Pietro was bent over, changing out of his dance shoes. He didn't look at her.

"I expect to see your name on the marquee one of these days," Mr. Jones said.

Pietro's laugh was cold. "Daddy, you kidding? She won't see no lights, staying in this burg." He stood up, pulled the curtain open, and peered out. "You want this to be as far as you get?"

In spite of his taunts, Teresa followed the line of his hand. With the house lights dimmed and people's programs scattered on the empty seats, the Princess Theater did seem shabby.

"Everyone starts someplace," Mr. Jones said. "And look at us. We're performing in Brattleboro, aren't we? She's too young to think about leaving town."

"Is she?" Pietro turned to Teresa, his eyes challenging her above the mask of his corked face. "New York is where it happens," he said. "Where life begins." He danced in time with his words. "Where the cream plays the Palace"—*tappity tappity tap*—"and the dregs play the honky-tonks—" *tapetta tapetta tapetta.*

"You'll be dancing with the dregs yourself if you don't behave," Mr. Jones said. "Now hush. We have three more shows today, in case you forgot. Don't give this girl a complex."

"Last train to New York is at ten tonight." Pietro cakewalked sideways, flicked his scarf at her, and disappeared into the wings. For a moment, Teresa wanted to cry—though she couldn't say why.

Mr. Jones shook his head. "I apologize. His head's too big sometimes." He pointed toward the back of the theater. "Someone's got a show of his own going on."

Two, three, then four scarlet objects flew in wobbling circles behind the last row of seats. Had Pascal stolen bowling pins from the cyclist? Teresa groaned. "My brother juggles all the time."

"Looks like performing runs in the family." Mr. Jones touched the brim of his top hat. "I hope our paths cross again."

"I hope so, too. Thank you for helping me." Teresa lifted her skirts, descended the stairs, and ran up the aisle. But Papa's words in the café gave her a sudden chill: *Once he makes up his mind . . .*

16.

Pascal's bag of bowling pins, thrown away by the cyclist, bumped and clattered as they walked home from the trolley stop. "Wonder what chores Mama will make us do," Pascal said.

"Papa's going to punish me," Teresa said.

"I know." He wrapped one skinny arm around her in a quick hug.

Mama was in the front hall, hoisting a basket of clean sheets and towels. "Perfect timing," she said. "Papa killed an old hen. She's waiting for you to pluck her."

Pascal held his nose. "No fair! My job is drying the dishes."

"They can wait," Mama said. "First get the hen ready for the stew pot. I'll make up the bed for tonight's guest."

"Is it a new boarder?" Teresa asked. A permanent guest might save her from working at Estey. But Mama shook her head.

"She told Papa one night, maybe two. Still, every little bit helps."

Teresa and Pascal changed into old clothes and sat on the back porch, the chicken set between them on a packing crate. "Yuck." Pascal flicked a white feather into the bucket. "When I'm a famous juggler and acrobat, I'll never touch a dead chicken again. Even a cooked one."

"And when I'm a famous singer, I'll make sure Mama doesn't have to cook for boarders." Teresa dug her fingernails into the rubbery flesh and yanked another feather out. Pietro was right. She would never amount to much if she stayed in Brattleboro. Maybe it was better than a "two-bit" town—but the Princess wasn't a New York theater and never would be. Would she spend her days in the tuning rooms, her weekends plucking chickens and scrubbing pots until her hands were raw and chapped, like Mama's? She glanced at her brother. Would Papa drag him to work at Estey, too? Pascal chewed on his lower lip as he worked at the chicken. "Let's sing," Teresa said.

"What song?"

"*Down by the old mill stream*," Teresa sang, and Pascal joined in. If only they *could* travel down the stream, down the river—anywhere—to find their place in the big time.

Mama waited on supper, serving it later than usual, but their new guest didn't show up. With Mr. Jensen at the table, Papa glowered, but didn't mention the song plugging—which only made Teresa more nervous. Her few bites of potato sat in her stomach like stones, and the old hen was too stringy to eat.

"We need spoons for dessert," Mama said. Pascal ran down the hall and came back with five spoons, which he tried to juggle as he walked. They fell to the floor with a clatter.

"That's enough!" Papa roared. Mr. Jensen pushed back his chair and left the table without a word. They waited as his cane tapped on the stairs. When his door shut with a soft click, Papa glowered at Teresa. "Singing up and down the street like a common urchin—why didn't you tell me?"

"I knew you wouldn't let me go." Teresa met Papa's eyes. "Did people call *you* an urchin, when you and Mama eloped?"

"Don't be fresh." Papa's Adam's apple bounced up and down.

"What's 'eloped'?" Pascal asked.

"Mama and Papa ran away to get married without telling anyone," Teresa said. "But don't worry. No one wants to marry me."

Papa spoke through gritted teeth. "As long as you are in our house, eating food your mama cooks and my hard labor pays for, you will ask permission to go out. You will tell us where you are going—and not lie about it. You will—"

"François." Mama set a hand on Papa's shoulder. "Calm down. Teresa won a singing contest. She sang on the main street. People enjoyed it. Don't spoil her happiness."

"Resa will not sing in public again. She will try her hand in the tuning rooms after school on Monday. If all goes well, she starts work when school ends." He glared at Teresa. "This is for your own good. You can't count on marrying a rich husband, and school doesn't agree with you. Your history teacher told me you are failing. He said you didn't know basic facts—about when the Civil War began and ended, or that Vermont was once an independent republic that forbid slavery . . . You are always somewhere else, he says."

Somewhere else indeed. Teresa put her hands under the table to hide their shaking. She couldn't speak.

Mama laughed. "Easy, François. Did *you* know the answer to those questions when you came down from Québec?"

"I knew my Québec history." Papa punched his fist on the table, making the glasses bounce. "It was hammered into us. And that has nothing to do with Resa now."

"Do you *want* to work at Estey?" Pascal asked.

Before Teresa could answer, Papa said, "She needs to. Then your mama won't have to toil away here. Mama deserves a better life—don't you agree?" He touched Mama's hand, but she shrank away, as if he had burned her.

"I will have no part in this," Mama whispered. "It's a crime for you to take her out of school so young. Have you thought of that?"

"Is it criminal to provide for my family? To give my daughter a trade that pays well? You believe in working women—*c'est vrai?*"

"Yes, it's true," Mama whispered. "But not when it could ruin her health."

Papa pushed back his chair so hard that it toppled over, and left the room. They sat, not moving, listening to the thump of his boots as he crossed the hall and slammed the back door.

No one spoke until Mama scraped the plates. "Pascal, go to Nonnie. See if she wants pudding."

Pascal disappeared. Teresa sat still. "How can you let Papa do this to me?"

Her mother's face twisted. "I'm sorry," she whispered. "I tried everything I know."

Teresa jumped up. "That's not true! You could go to Mr. Estey, tell them Papa lied. He said that I'm sixteen! If you won't do it—I will!"

"It's not so easy," Mama whispered. "Resa, think. If they realize Papa has lied—they might fire him. And then, where would we be?"

"Back onstage," Teresa said.

"Please. Not that again. You heard your father," Mama spoke quietly. "Anyway, we can't abandon Nonnie."

Mama's words stung, but Teresa couldn't think about Nonnie now. She gripped Mama's arm. "Guess what happened today? The audience at the Princess wanted *me* to sing. They clapped and shouted until Mr. Quincy begged me to come onstage."

Mama wiped her eyes with the hem of her apron and gave her a tiny smile. "And did you?"

"Yes. I sang our song—'Hard Times.'" Teresa hugged herself. "Mama, I know I shouldn't brag—but people whistled and stomped when I was done. I *loved* it." She lowered her voice. "You loved performing, too. Didn't you? Admit it."

"Yes. But my voice was never as strong as yours." Mama cupped her elbow. "I need to show you something. Bring the plates."

Teresa followed Mama to the kitchen and set the dishes in the sink. Mama shut the kitchen door softly and pushed a chair up against the dish cabinet. She pointed to the big soup tureen sitting above the cupboard. "Climb up and reach inside."

Teresa lifted her skirts, scrambled onto the chair, and took the lid off the tureen.

"Here, give me the top," Mama said.

Teresa handed down the round lid and reached inside the big pot. She found Mama's china piggy bank inside, so heavy she nearly dropped it. "Wow—it's full." Teresa held the bank in both hands. The pig's green half-shut eyes seemed to smile at her. She looked down at Mama. "Is this all from your egg money?"

"Yes—and some of Mr. Jensen's rent. Your papa doesn't know," Mama said. "Put it back and climb down."

Teresa gave the pig a farewell pat and set it carefully inside the tureen.

"This will be yours when you're sixteen and finish school, Resa. In the meantime, maybe we can find a way out of this Estey mess." She raised her eyebrows. "Perhaps you won't pass your next test at the organ works?" Mama gave her a tiny wink.

"Mama—what—?"

"Shh," Mama touched her finger to Teresa's lips, silencing her.

The doorbell rang. Mama didn't finish her sentence. She brushed Teresa's forehead with a kiss. "That's the new guest. Will you greet her? I must look a fright."

17.

Teresa hurried to the front hall as the doorbell shrilled again. "Coming!" Teresa opened the door—and nearly fell over. Miss Stanton stood on the doorstep, her blonde ringlets plastered to her forehead. A long coat covered her legs, although her pink tights showed at the ankle, and two leather valises leaned against the porch railing. Miss Stanton gasped and dropped a round hatbox. "You!" she gasped. "What are *you* doing here?"

"This is my home," Teresa said.

Miss Stanton fumbled in her pocket and brought out a piece of paper. "I must have the wrong address," she said. "I was *told* this was a nice place to stay . . ."

Papa clattered downstairs. "Miss Stanton, is it? Come in, come in. I was just fixing your room. Teresa, where are your manners?"

Miss Stanton pulled herself to her full height—which wasn't much—and puffed out her chest like a bird showing off its plumage. "I'm Miss Stanton. I thought I had a reservation here tonight. I must be mistaken. The 'Rose of Abilene' doesn't stay in seedy hotels." She bent to pick up her hatbox.

Teresa bit her lip to keep from laughing. She couldn't decide which was more amusing—watching Papa's discomfort or Miss Stanton's temper tantrum.

"Papa!" Pascal leaned over the banister above them. "That's the lady from the vaudeville show. What is *she* doing here?"

"Enough, Pascal." Papa cleared his throat. "Are you looking for LeClair's boardinghouse?"

"That's what it says here." Miss Stanton jabbed the piece of paper. "I sent you a note, asking for a place to stay."

"Indeed you did." Papa passed a hand over his hair. "I'm sorry for the confusion." He picked up her luggage. "Pascal—show Miss Stanton to her room."

Pascal slid down the banister and dropped to his feet with a little bounce. "But Papa—you said you'd never rent rooms to people in vaude."

"Don't be rude," Papa said. "Miss Stanton is our guest."

Miss Stanton jabbed a painted finger at Teresa. "Is this hussy your *daughter*? She owes me an apology—showing me up in the theater this afternoon."

Now it was Papa's turn to look confused. "Teresa—what is this about?"

"The audience wanted to hear me sing, and Mr. Quincy brought me onstage," Teresa said. "I can't help it if they liked me better than Miss Stanton." Teresa turned on her heel and ran down the hall to Nonnie's room—the one place in the house where Papa wouldn't bother her.

Nonnie's shadowy form stirred in the armchair. "Resa? I was expecting you. Pascal tells me you were a star today."

Teresa ran to Nonnie and put her head in her lap, as though she were a little girl again.

Nonnie stroked her hair. "Angel, you're trembling. What happened?"

Teresa perched on the footstool at Nonnie's feet. In a rush, she told Nonnie about the song plugging, her surprise performance—and Papa's threat to sign her up at Estey. "He lied," Teresa said. "He told the man at Estey that I'm already sixteen. Mama says Papa will lose his job if I tell them the truth." She went to the window. The lilacs were fragrant in the dusk. "He can't make me. I'll die in there."

Nonnie sighed. "We'll think of something."

Nonnie was ninety-five, frail, and nearly blind. How could she save Teresa from the organ works? "Shall I help you to bed?"

"Not yet, Resa dear. I'm listening to the sounds of springtime. Do you hear the veery? Like a flute, with the notes descending."

She cocked her head, looking like a bird herself. "And so ethereal—as if the bird calls to us from another world."

Teresa pressed her ear against the screen until she picked out the soft trill of birdsong over the rush of the Whetstone Brook. "Your hearing is so good," she said.

"Beautiful sounds make my blindness bearable. Give me your hand, child."

Teresa took Nonnie's small, dry hand in her own.

"Hold on to your dreams," Nonnie said. "Reach for the stars—no matter what happens. Promise."

"Yes," Teresa said. "I will." She kissed Nonnie's soft forehead.

As she closed Nonnie's door she heard Mama and Papa arguing in the kitchen. Teresa held still. "She's on a bad path," Papa said. "Lying to us, insulting our house guest, doing badly in school. Working at Estey will teach her obedience. Otherwise—*j'ai peur*, Alice."

"Afraid of what?" Mama said. "She's a child, François. She has big dreams. You did once, too. Have you forgotten so quickly?"

Teresa couldn't hear Papa's reply. Never mind. She knew what she had to do.

A few hours later, Teresa sat on her bed, fully dressed in her shirt-waist dress, the locket on its chain hidden beneath her high collar, her cloak buttoned. Her silver dollars, from the contest and the song plugging, clinked in one pocket. The card from Miss Connover was tucked in the other. Her small valise held the fancy skirt and blouse she'd worn to plug songs, her dressy choir shoes, a picture of Nonnie as a young woman, and a stack of sheet music for the songs that she and Mama used to sing together.

She had also packed another change of clothes, some socks, and underthings. She went to the window. A streetlight burned a circle of light under the elm tree and moonlight cast shadows across the floor. No time to waste.

Teresa slipped downstairs. She stopped a minute at Pascal's door, but forced herself to keep going. She couldn't lose her nerve. No light shone under Mr. Jensen's door or Miss Stanton's. Teresa held her breath going past Mama and Papa's room. Their voices muttered, and Papa said Teresa's name in a growl. She grabbed the railing and tiptoed down the next flight, avoiding the creaky boards.

As quickly and quietly as she could, Teresa climbed onto a kitchen chair, lifted the heavy piggy bank from its hiding place, and set it on the kitchen table. She wrapped it in a napkin, stowed the bank in her valise, and unfolded the note she'd written to Mama. She scanned it in the moonlight. *Mama, I'm sorry. I couldn't wait another year. I hope you understand. I'll write soon. All my love, Resa.*

She grabbed a pencil and added, in a scribble, *Kiss Nonnie for me and tell her I'll keep my promise.*

The grandfather clock chimed in the music room. Teresa climbed back onto the chair, tucked the note into the soup tureen, and slipped out the back door. When she crossed the front yard, she thought she heard a whistle. It must have been the neighbors calling their dog. She pulled her collar up and ran.

18.

Teresa smashed the piggy bank on the curb outside the railroad station, scooped the coins into her valise without counting them, and left the pottery shards in the street.

"One way, Miss?" the stationmaster asked.

She nodded. He was patient as she counted out the coins. "It's late at night, for a young girl traveling alone," he said.

"My friend is joining me in Greenfield." Running away from home, telling lies—it was all so easy—but her hands trembled.

The stationmaster didn't notice. "Move along, please."

Teresa stood at the far end of the platform, away from the gaslights and the few other passengers. Was that Mr. Jones and Pietro, near the station door? She turned her back and waited, ashamed to speak to them. If they knew Miss Stanton was staying at her house tonight, would they think she'd lied about Papa's rules?

The train's mournful whistle sounded from north of Rattlesnake Hill and the engine's acrid smoke made her eyes smart. She climbed aboard, found an empty seat, and pressed her face to the glass. She remembered train rides with Mama and Papa and their troupe, sharing stale sandwiches and stories. Conroy, the magician, would pull coins out of Teresa's ear. Mama would make a bed for her on the hard seat and Teresa would fall asleep with her head in Mama's lap.

Now she was on her own without Mama. She was much too excited—and frightened—to sleep.

An hour south of Brattleboro, she felt a tap on her shoulder. "Resa, help! The conductor's coming."

She twisted in her seat, her heart racing. Pascal crouched beside her, his cap pulled low over his eyes. The train leaned into a curve and he was thrown against her. "*Pascal!*" She wanted to scream. "What are *you* doing here?"

"I followed you. I thought you were going to the last show at the Princess—but then I saw your bag. Are you running away?"

"Tickets please!" A man's voice bellowed from the back of the car.

Pascal gasped. "I don't have a ticket. Buy me one. Please?"

She wanted to slap him. "You're an idiot! I'll throw you off at the next station."

His eyes welled with tears. "You can't! How would I get home?"

"You should have thought of that before you got on the train." Of course, she couldn't drop Pascal off in the middle of nowhere at this hour. The clicking sound of the conductor's punch came closer. Teresa fumbled in her pocket for her own ticket, then opened the valise and grabbed a handful of coins.

Pascal peered over her shoulder. "Where'd you get all that money?"

"From Mama." Almost the truth. Teresa's throat closed in panic. If she sent Pascal home in the morning, would she have enough money to stay in New York? "You've spoiled everything!"

Pascal pouted. "I thought you'd be glad to see me."

"You thought wrong."

The conductor peered at them over the top of his glasses. "You young ones traveling alone?"

"Yes—" Pascal began, but Teresa jabbed him with her elbow. "Our parents sent us to meet our aunt in New York," she said.

"That so?" The conductor took Teresa's ticket, as well as money for Pascal's. "Where does this 'aunt' live?" he asked.

"Gramercy Park," Teresa said, without missing a beat.

"Nice neighborhood," the conductor said. "But the train arrives before dawn. You'd best be careful."

"She said she'd meet us at the station," Teresa said.

The conductor frowned. "You don't fool me. Why would your parents only buy one fare?" Still, he handed Pascal a ticket, then passed through to the next car. Pascal edged away from her on the seat. "Liar," he whispered. "Our only aunt is Papa's sister in Québec. And you stole Mama's money."

"I don't steal," Teresa said. "Mama told me it was mine." She didn't tell Pascal that Mama expected her to stay home until she turned sixteen.

Pascal stared at her as if she were a stranger. "Are you going with those two dancers?" he asked.

"Of course not," Teresa said, although she remembered Pietro's challenge. She grabbed Pascal by the shoulders. "Listen. You heard Papa. He was going to make me work at Estey. I couldn't stand to be locked up there for the rest of my life."

"I know. I heard them fighting through the wall," Pascal said. "They scared me. Mama was mad at Papa. They were so loud, they didn't hear me leave."

"Mama tried to change Papa's mind—but he's too stubborn. I want to sing, just like you want to juggle."

Pascal sat up and pointed at the lumpy sack, stuffed under the seat in front of them. "I brought my juggling balls, and the bowling pins, in case you were going to the Princess. I can help you make money."

She wanted to shake him! But Pascal was too young to understand. What could she do? If she sent him home, he'd tell Papa where she'd gone. But he was too young to run away. He'd need food and a safe place to stay. "You're impossible," Teresa said.

Pascal blinked back tears. She took his hand. She could never stay mad at him long. "It's all right," she said. But it wasn't. The train chuffed on. "We'll figure it out in the morning. Let's try to sleep."

Pascal leaned to the right, ever so slightly, until his head rested on her shoulder. "Where's Gramercy Park?" he asked.

"I haven't a clue," Teresa said.

The train rattled and shook on the straightaway. *In the morning, in the morning*, it sang. The whistle blew, a shrill D-sharp that made her ears ring. The Connecticut River gleamed in the moonlight and sparks trailed out over the water. They hurtled past lit buildings and angled slashes of trees. The wheels chattered and clacked, and the last lights of town flickered and disappeared as the train sped through its dark corridor. Teresa was headed south, with almost no money, to a city she'd never seen. Terror clutched her belly with its sharp claws—but she'd made a promise to Nonnie. She'd reach for the stars—or die trying.

THE CURTAIN FALLS. END OF ACT ONE.

ENTR'ACTE 2

Setting: A fall evening in a Vermont boardinghouse. The action takes place in a front parlor that serves as a music room. An upright piano stands at stage left, next to an Estey pump organ. Double glass doors open onto the front hall. Faded wallpaper covers the walls. A maple tree with bright orange leaves is visible outside the window. The year is 1908.

CHARACTERS:
TERESA (RESA) LECLAIR: age ten. She is tall for her age, with a mane of twisted orange curls that give her the look of a young lion.
FRANÇOIS LECLAIR: Teresa's father.
PASCAL LECLAIR: Teresa's brother, age four.
ALICE LECLAIR: Teresa's mother.
NONNIE: Teresa's great-grandmother. She is losing her sight but not her smarts.

As the curtain rises, François perches on a stool at the piano, tuning his fiddle. The case sits open on the floor. Nonnie sits in an upholstered chair near the window. She appears to be asleep.

TERESA: (*Enters through the glass doors, carrying Pascal. She sets him on a stool at the organ.*) Papa, play us a song.

PASCAL: (*Clapping.*) Play! Play the song!

FRANÇOIS: Not tonight. *Je suis fatigué*—so tired. Too much work at Estey. Besides, the fiddle is out of tune. (*He plucks a string, frowns, twists the peg.*)

TERESA: Let me tune it.

FRANÇOIS: That's a job for grownups.

TERESA: Please, Papa?

NONNIE: (*Rousing herself.*) Let her try, François.

FRANÇOIS: (*Fusses with another string and its peg, scowls, and shoves the fiddle at Teresa.*) *Eh bien*, you're so smart—show me.

TERESA: (*Clutches the fiddle to her chest.*) If I tune it, will you play for us?

PASCAL: Play, Papa! Play *my* song!

FRANÇOIS: *Oui, oui*, I'll play. Pascal, stop bouncing. You'll break the stool. Resa, be careful with the fiddle, *d'accord*? She's traveled many miles since *my* papa gave her to me in Québec City. You treat her right.

TERESA plays an A on the piano and plucks one string, then another. She twists the knobs, listens, plucks each string again. Papa stares, astonished. Pascal sucks his thumb, his eyes wide. NONNIE listens, her head cocked to the side, nodding when Teresa gets it right. TERESA smiles, hands the fiddle back to FRANÇOIS. He takes the bow from its case, runs it over the strings, plays a few bars of a haunting melody.

FRANÇOIS: (*To TERESA.*) Who taught you to do that?

TERESA: No one. I listen until it sounds right.

FRANÇOIS: (*Plucks a string.*) What note is this, Resa?

TERESA: A.

FRANÇOIS: How do you know the names of the notes?

TERESA: Nonnie taught me.

FRANÇOIS plays more notes, first on the fiddle, then on the piano. TERESA names each one accurately, including sharps and flats. Papa plays the notes faster and faster, until Teresa claps her hands over her ears.

TERESA: Stop, Papa! *C'est assez*—it's enough!

NONNIE: For heaven's sake, François—don't torture the child.

FRANÇOIS: (*To Nonnie.*) Why did you not tell me—that she had this talent?

NONNIE: I thought you knew. She always sings on key.

TERESA: Can we go onstage again, Papa? Like we used to do? Remember how you and Mama and me sang together?

NONNIE: Mama and *I*.

FRANÇOIS: Of course I remember. But we got in big trouble. They gave me the hook!

TERESA: You liked being onstage, Papa—didn't you?

FRANÇOIS: I did, *ma chérie*. Very much. (*He goes to the window, his fiddle tucked up under his arm, and stares at something unseen beyond the maple tree.*) Our life is different now.

TERESA: Because of Pascal?

PASCAL: Me? What did I do?

FRANÇOIS: *Rien, mon petit*. You did nothing.

TERESA: Nothing except being born.

FRANÇOIS: (*Angry.*) Resa—don't ever speak that way about your brother.

NONNIE: Remember, François—you always said you would play New York's Victoria. Wasn't that the name of the theater? When you and Alice eloped, that was your plan.

FRANÇOIS: *C'est vrai*. It's true I had big dreams: to see our names in the lights of Broadway. Instead, they called me a "catgut scraper" and we played only small-time theaters. We practiced in cramped dressing rooms, slept with the fleas, traveled on cold, lonesome trains. Our pockets were always empty. And it was no life for a child, living on the road: bad food, no school, up all night. But then . . .

FRANÇOIS tucks the fiddle under his chin, sets his feet wide, draws himself up tall and looks over their heads, as if facing an audience. He doesn't notice that ALICE has entered from the hall. She leans against the wall, listening.

TERESA: Then what, Papa?

FRANÇOIS: Then the crowd cheers and throws you pennies. People stomp and call you back for one more song. When that happens—there is nothing like it in the world. *Rien.*

Long pause. They all seem to hear the unseen audience clapping.

PASCAL: (*Tugs at his father's shirt.*) Play, Papa. You said . . .

FRANÇOIS: *Très bien.* Okay. I play a song for Resa, whose ear is so smart, and for Pascal, who loves to dance. (*He notices ALICE, gives her a wink.*) And for your *maman*, who taught you both to sing—*and* to dance.

FRANÇOIS tucks the fiddle under his chin and plays an Acadian reel, then a jig, keeping time with the heel of his boot. NONNIE finds her way to the piano, sits down, and adds rhythmic chords to Papa's tune.

ALICE: Nonnie, play "The Sidewalks of New York!"

NONNIE: What key, François?

FRANÇOIS: In G.

NONNIE feels for the keys with her fingers and they play the waltz together. PASCAL slides off the stool, grabs ALICE by the hand, pulls TERESA in. They dance around the room, laughing and swaying to the beat of the waltz. FRANÇOIS plays the tune on the fiddle while NONNIE's chords provide the rhythm and harmony.

ALICE AND TERESA: (*Singing, in unison. On the word "fantas-tic" they all jump into the air and kick their heels.*) East side, west side, all around the town . . . We'll trip the light fan-*tas*-tic! On the sidewalks of New York.

Fade to black.

ACT TWO

THE GREAT
WHITE WAY

NEW YORK CITY
MAY 1913

19.

The train shuddered to a stop before dawn. Pascal and Teresa climbed a granite stairway, their footsteps echoing on the cold stone, and entered a cavernous station with a ceiling as distant as the sky. Teresa felt small. Even though she didn't know what on earth to do with Pascal, she was glad when he took her hand.

"Where are we going?" Pascal asked.

"To Miss Connover's house. The judge who invited me to stay with her and take voice lessons." Teresa fingered the worn calling card in her pocket. She had memorized the address—but where was Gramercy Park? And how did you get there in the middle of the night? What if Miss Connover wasn't home? And what would she do with Pascal? Teresa stood, frozen, as a few travelers straggled past, headed for the stairways.

"Look." Pascal tugged at her sleeve. "The dancers are here!"

Pietro Jones hurried across the marble floor, a bulky bag on his shoulder, a newspaper rolled up under his arm. His father lagged behind, talking to a man in a railroad uniform. Pascal waved and Pietro stared, shook his head in disbelief, and hurried over. "Well, well," he said. "If it isn't Miss LeClair. Didn't think you had it in you." He nodded at Pascal. "You two related?"

"I'm Pascal. Her brother."

"Pleased to meet you." Pietro glanced over his shoulder as if someone were after him. "Where you headed?"

"We're not sure. Pretty crazy, I guess." Teresa tried to sound confident, but her voice shook.

Pietro shrugged. "You have to be a little nuts in this business. Too early in the morning for The Beach," he said.

"What beach?" Pascal asked.

"Not the sandy kind. Talking about The Beach outside the Palace Theatre. Thin piece of sidewalk where everyone goes looking for work. Some folks call it Panic Beach. You stroll up and down, keep your eyes and ears open, find out what troupe needs a dancer, who's looking for a dumb act . . ." Pietro tapped out a rhythm that echoed in the vaulted chamber. "We got our own version of The Beach in Harlem. Call it the Tree of Life." He set his bag down. "Watch this a minute, will you?" Pietro went to help his father with his valise. When they returned, Pietro said, "Daddy, look what the cat dragged in."

How rude! Pietro's moods were as unpredictable as March weather. Still, they must look a mess with their wrinkled clothes and uncombed hair. Pascal's face was smudged with soot. Teresa gave Mr. Jones a shy wave as he set his bag down.

"Fancy meeting you here." Mr. Jones wiped his brow with a handkerchief, although it was chilly in the station, and looked around. "Where's your mama and daddy?"

"At home." Pascal's voice was small.

Mr. Jones frowned. "New York's no place for young ones. They know you're here?"

"Not yet." Would Mama find the note Teresa had left behind? Would Papa blame Mama? What would they do when they found Pascal was gone, too? A cold fist grabbed hold of her belly.

"This city ain't easy on runaways," Mr. Jones said. "You gotta be careful."

"Listen to you, Daddy!" Pietro nudged his father's foot with the toe of his shoe. "How old were you when you left Tennessee? Twelve going on eleven?"

"Going on thirteen." Mr. Jones shook his head at Teresa. "It's different for girls. And this little one, not even out of short pants—"

"I'm almost nine!" Pascal said.

"That so?" Mr. Jones held out his hand. "Saw you juggling in the Princess the other day, but I don't think we've been properly introduced. I'm Mr. Jones. And this is my son, Pietro."

Pascal shook Mr. Jones's hand. "I know. I'm Pascal. I juggle." He wrinkled his nose at Pietro. "Where'd you get that funny name?"

"Pascal! That's rude," Teresa said.

"No funnier than your name." Pietro winked at Pascal. "My name comes from my ancestor who discovered America."

"Christopher Columbus was your *ancestor*?" Pascal asked.

"His pilot was an African man named Pietro," Pietro said. "He helped Columbus find his way here. Right Daddy?"

"That's right." Mr. Jones rubbed his eyes. "Instead of a history lesson, why don't you pilot us out of the station. You find that *Amsterdam News*?"

"Right here," Pietro said, waving the rolled newspaper. "Got all the news we need about our part of town." Pietro and his father picked up their bags and headed for the end of the room. Teresa and Pascal followed. Pascal's sack rattled as he dragged it up the stairs. Teresa pushed the heavy doors open and stood outside under a protective roof. The pavement was wet with rain; it was cold, for May. When Pascal shivered, Teresa opened her cloak and pulled him close.

Mr. Jones frowned at Pascal. "Where's your coat, son? The wind howls through these city canyons."

"I didn't bring one." Pascal's face was blotchy with cold.

Pietro reached into his pocket, pulled out his red silk scarf, and wrapped it around Pascal's neck. "Every juggling act needs a bit of color." He pretended to cinch it tight.

"But the scarf's part of your dance routine," Teresa said.

Pietro shrugged. "More where that came from."

"That's very kind," Teresa said.

"You have someplace to go?" Mr. Jones asked.

"We're headed to Miss Connover's, the lady judge from the contest." Teresa pulled the card from her pocket.

Mr. Jones examined it under the gaslight and whistled. "Gramercy Park—that's high tone. She know you're coming?"

"Not exactly." What a fool she was! "She wanted to give me singing lessons."

"Lessons!" Pietro laughed. "You already know how to sing—you just got to put some jive in it, add a little movement . . ." He stopped, picked up their bags, and whispered to his father. "Man in blue, Daddy. Better move on."

Mr. Jones glanced toward the street corner. A burly policeman stood under the light with his back to them. "Some white folks don't appreciate colored men talking to you, at this hour of the night," Mr. Jones said softly. "You got any money?"

Teresa nodded. "Very well," Mr. Jones said. "We'll set off down the street. You follow, a half block behind. No way you can get safely to Gramercy Park before morning, and that lady won't be happy, you ring her doorbell at dawn. I'll show you some friendly rooming houses. The officer asks you anything about us, say you needed directions." He touched the brim of his cap.

Pascal started after them, but Teresa held him back. "You heard him. Not yet." Mr. Jones's warning made her feel as if they were doing something criminal. She hoisted her valise and waited a few minutes before they followed the Joneses at a safe distance. Tall buildings loomed above them on both sides of the street. Teresa nearly tripped on a rat that skittered across the sidewalk and down the alley. She stifled a scream and Pascal jumped. "Did you see that rat? It was bigger than a dog."

Teresa pulled her brother close, grateful for his presence. What if she were dodging rats—and unfriendly policemen—by herself? She kept to the center of the sidewalk. In a few more blocks, the tall buildings gave way to row houses with shuttered shops on the ground floor. She heard the familiar sounds of a neighborhood waking up. A milk wagon passed, its glass bottles jingling, and newsboys called out to one another as they bundled their papers on the curb, but these "newsies"—as Mama called the boys who sold papers at home—were barefoot, dressed in shabby clothes, and pale—as if they hadn't eaten in days.

Mama. She pictured Mama tying up her hair, cinching her clean apron around her waist, grinding coffee beans at the hand grinder on the wall beside the sink. She'd make the coffee, set the table, slice the bread—and then set out the yellow bowl to beat the eggs. Would Mama climb the attic stairs and find the pillows that Teresa had slipped under the blankets to fool her? Would she first notice that Pascal was gone—and call the police? Would she look for her piggy bank—and discover the note? Nonnie had told Teresa to follow her dreams—but not with Pascal. Could she help it that he'd followed her?

A low whistle brought Teresa back to the empty streets of New York. "Resa, look." Pascal let go of her hand and hurried to Mr. Jones, who beckoned to them from the next intersection. "Down there's Broadway," Mr. Jones said, when they caught up. "West of here is the brand new Palace Theatre Pietro was telling you about."

"Papa always wanted to play Hammerstein's Victoria," Teresa said.

Mr. Jones nodded. "The Victoria's in the same neighborhood. But now the Palace is queen of them all." He glanced over his shoulder, keeping his voice low.

"Avenues go north and south, numbered streets east and west," Mr. Jones said. "The street numbers get higher as you walk north. Once you know that, you can't get lost. We'll leave you off in a few blocks, point you to the rooming houses. You may have to wait until daylight to get in."

How could you tell north from south, when buildings blocked the sky in every direction? Teresa clenched her jaw. She couldn't give up now.

The sky began to turn gray and steam rose from grates next to the buildings. As they crossed another intersection, Mr. Jones stopped in front of a three-story brick building. The sign in the window read *Mrs. O'Donnell's Theatrical Boardinghouse. Actors Welcome.*

Teresa's shoulders slumped. Had she come all this way to stay in another boardinghouse? But Pascal perked up. "See, Resa—'Actors Welcome.'" He turned to Mr. Jones. "Will you stay here too?"

Pietro's laugh was harsh. "Coloreds and whites don't stay in the same places."

"Where will you go?" Pascal blinked back tears.

Mr. Jones squeezed his shoulder. "Don't you worry about us, young man," Mr. Jones said. "Friends take care of us. We'll be just fine."

"*Fine*—if you don't mind sleeping on the floor," Pietro said.

"Hush. Etta's been good to us." Mr. Jones pulled a pencil from his pocket and jotted an address on the back of his train ticket stub. "You get stuck, we'll be here a few days, 'til we see what Toby's got."

"Toby?" Teresa's head felt fuzzy, as if she were trying to remember too many facts in school.

"Theatre Owners Booking Association," Pietro said. "We pronounce it 'Toby.' They manage us black actors. Some of us say the letters stand for 'Tough on Black Actors.'"

"Son—you just too cynical for your own good." Mr. Jones gave Teresa a sad smile. "Your mama and daddy must be worried sick about you," he said. "You send them a telegram in the morning."

"That's none of our business." Pietro pulled his father's sleeve. "We got a long walk ahead of us and plenty to do tomorrow—I mean, today. Good luck to you. Break a leg, wherever you end up."

Mr. Jones shook hands with Teresa, then Pascal. "Hold on to your wallets. This city burns up hard cash like tinder."

"We don't have much money to worry about," Teresa said. Twenty-one dollars and thirty-six cents, to be exact. She'd counted it on the train.

"Miss! Young man! You all right there?" A man's voice called out. Four heavyset white men carrying lunch pails stood on the opposite corner. "Those boys bothering you?" another man yelled. "Need help?"

Teresa shook her head. "We're fine."

"What'd I tell you?" Pietro's face hardened. He motioned to his father and they took off at a fast clip, their satchels slung across their shoulders.

"Mr. Jones isn't a 'boy,'" Pascal said.

"Hush," Teresa said, though he was right. She took her brother by the elbow and steered him up the stairs to the boardinghouse. Pascal's lumpy bag knocked against his legs, then against her own.

"You're hurting me," Pascal said. Teresa ignored him and rang the bell, as if they already had a room. No one came, and she remembered that Mr. Jones had told her to wait until the sun was up. The men on the far corner taunted them with some nasty words, then strode off in the opposite direction. Was this what Papa meant, when he said vaude was "no place for a young girl"? Teresa sank down on the top step and set her head on her knees.

"What are we doing now?" Pascal asked.

"Waiting." She pulled Pascal close and leaned against the iron railing.

"I'm scared." Pascal's face was wet as he huddled close. "I miss Mama. Who will take care of me?"

"I will," Teresa said. But Pascal would need to leave soon. She couldn't support them both here. Yet how would she live, if she bought him a ticket home? She'd have almost nothing left. Maybe Mama was right—she should have taken the Estey job, or failed the interview on purpose and suffered another year at school. Teresa sighed. Too late now. Besides—even prickly Pietro had said she knew how to sing. She couldn't give up.

"What if they won't let us stay here?"

"I don't know." She took off his cap and smoothed his hair, the way Mama would. One of Nonnie's favorite expressions came into her mind: *The world always looks better in the light of day.* She hoped that would be true when this day dawned.

20.

"What is this? Waifs on my front stoop? Get off now. Away with you!"

Teresa woke with a start as a broom slapped her rump. She scrambled to her feet before she even remembered where she was. A stout woman glowered at them from the top step, swatting her broom. "This is a respectable neighborhood!" she yelled, in a thick Irish accent. "Away with you, you hooligans!"

"Wait! I can explain—oof!" Teresa jumped aside, dodging the bristles. Pascal cringed and leapt off the steps. The clatter of wooden balls and bowling pins made it sound as if he'd broken every bone in his body.

"Excuse me, Ma'am . . ." Teresa gulped, trying to catch her breath. She pushed her hair off her face. If only she didn't look such a mess. "We need a place to stay."

"And how do you plan to pay me? Gold dust?"

"We have money. I rang the bell earlier, but no one answered."

"Of course not. I was asleep. This is a respectable place. My boarders come in late. They don't expect to be jolted out of bed by some passing vagrant."

"I'm *not* a vagrant," Teresa said. "My brother and I are quiet. We just need a bed for the night."

"The night's over, in case you hadn't noticed," the woman said. "I rent by the week. Take it or leave it." Before Teresa could answer, the woman asked suddenly, "If you're so respectable, what does your mama say about you sleeping on doorsteps?"

"Not much," Teresa said, "since she's dead." Luckily, Pascal was out of earshot, scooping up his juggling balls. Then, piling on the lies, she said, "We're meeting our father in a few days. We need a place until he arrives."

"Likely story." The woman sniffed. "There's a tiny room in the attic. You'll have to share a bed. Five dollars for the week, payable in advance, board included."

It was more than Mama charged for a room at home, but Teresa told her they'd take it. She was used to attic rooms.

They followed their new landlady—who was, indeed, the Mrs. O'Donnell of the sign—into the boardinghouse. Familiar smells seeped from the walls: stale cabbage, strong soap, coffee boiled too long. Mrs. O'Donnell waited while Teresa slowly counted out five dollars in coins. "Humph," she said, pouring the coins into a dish. "Give me paper currency next time."

As they passed through the dining room, Pascal pointed at the ceiling. A rhythmic thumping made the glass chandelier swing wildly over the table. Tiny chips of plaster dusted the rug like snow. Teresa raised her eyebrows.

Mrs. O'Donnell pounded the ceiling with her broom handle, sending a second flurry of plaster to the floor. "That foolish song and dance team, Russell and Wiggins. They need to rehearse onstage, not in my bedrooms." Teresa winked at Pascal. The boardinghouse might *smell* like home, but otherwise, it was already very different.

Mrs. O'Donnell huffed and puffed up one narrow flight of stairs, then another. As they climbed, snatches of song burst from behind a few closed doors. On the second floor, a man with a heavy accent shouted lines from a play, repeating them over and over, and a flute's ethereal melody floated along the hall, where a line of sleepy men and women in dressing gowns stood outside a closed door.

"Washroom," Mrs. O'Donnell said, and hoisted herself up the last flight of stairs. She showed them into a tiny room with a steep roof and a window the size of a pocket handkerchief. The bed sagged in the middle, but Teresa didn't care. Her eyelids had never felt so heavy. "Here you are," Mrs. O'Donnell said. She squinted at them. "Vaude brats, are you?"

Pascal, who hadn't said a word since they'd come inside, stiffened. "We're not brats," he said.

"It's all right, Pascal," Teresa said. "I'm a singer," she told the landlady. "My brother juggles," she said.

"You'll run afoul of the Gerry Society, that you will, putting him onstage," Mrs. O'Donnell said. "'Course, that's your worry, not mine. Breakfast at eight o'clock sharp." She closed the door behind her.

Teresa dropped her valise and sank onto the bed. "We're in New York," she said. "Let's sleep a while, and then we'll start looking for jobs."

"Jobs? Why?"

"So we can live."

They used the washroom, then climbed into bed with their clothes on. The sunken trough in the mattress pulled them toward the center. They kicked each other as they tried to get comfortable. Pascal fell asleep immediately but Teresa stayed awake a while, listening to the city sounds: the steady clop of horses' hooves; the rumble of engines; a roar that might have been a train, mixing with the steady thump-thump-thumping from downstairs.

Teresa held still. She was in New York. Where real vaudeville happened. Where stars were born. Where Papa had always wanted to perform. And where—according to Papa—the lights burned day and night. Something had to go right for them here.

21.

Teresa dreamed that Papa was playing the fiddle and keeping time with the heel of his boot: *Thump, thump, thump*—and then someone whimpered.

"Who's there?" Teresa opened her eyes and gasped. A wiry gray dog, its paws resting on the blanket beside her chin, looked her in the eye. Its fur stuck out every which way. Teresa laughed. "Hello. Who are you?" She reached out and scratched the dog behind one ear. Its mouth curled up on one side, like a smile, and it made a happy grunting noise.

"You're all dressed up," Teresa said. An orange plume bobbed on the dog's back, attached to a shoulder harness, and a matching orange bow made a short ponytail on top of its head. The dog's tail swept the floor, and when Teresa smiled, its tongue rasped over her fingers.

Teresa climbed out of bed, careful not to wake Pascal. "Edna!" a woman's voice called from the landing below. "Edna, come! Has anyone seen my dog?"

Teresa clucked to the dog and led it downstairs. A young woman with long, jet-black hair dashed toward Teresa, gave her a sideways hug—as if they'd been friends forever—and cried, "You're brilliant! Edna, you naughty pooch—where have you been?"

The dog wagged its tail and gave the woman that half smile again. Teresa laughed. "I never saw a dog smile."

"Isn't she cute? Audiences love her for that, especially people in the front row. Can you spare a minute?" The woman didn't wait for an answer, but took off down the hall at a fast clip, the dog trotting at her heels. Teresa hurried after her. "You're obviously good at finding things—maybe you can help me. I've lost something even more valuable than Edna, but don't tell her I said so."

As if Edna understood, she gave a mournful howl. "Hush!" the woman cried. She hurried to the end of the hall, pushed open a door with a faded number 7 painted in the center, and pulled Teresa in after her. "Don't let them out."

"Them" turned out to be a pack of white terriers, all smaller than Edna. One dog slept at the foot of the bed, another was curled up on the room's only chair, while a third lay in a tangle of blouses, underclothes, and belts spilling from a steamer trunk. The smallest terrier, its tail wagging, wriggled all over as it wound itself around Teresa's ankles. Like the others, it was white with a brown splotch across its back, but it also had a furry black patch surrounding one eye. "You look like a pirate," Teresa said, scratching her behind the ears. Was that a nose, poking out from under the bedspread? The room smelled of animals, Sterno gas, and perfume.

"How many dogs do you have?"

"Six." The woman waved her hand around the room. "Meet 'Madame Maeve and her Marvelous Marching Dogs'—though I'm not 'Madame' since I'm eighteen and not married. Also, the dogs don't 'march.' Never mind. Silly details."

Maeve *was* "marvelous" looking: Her hair fell in glossy black ringlets down her back, contrasting with very pale skin. Her eyes were a bright jade green, matching some of the rings that glinted on almost every finger, and her dress was made of some sort of gauzy fabric that made her look as if she were floating. "What are the dogs' names?" Teresa asked.

"One for each of the first six letters of the alphabet," Maeve said. "Alix, Bronwyn, Cleo, Dixie—our pirate—and Edna, whom you've met. Fido is the only boy—every canine family needs a Fido. Woe to the man who tries any funny business with *me* when Fido is around. And Dixie runs the show, don't you, girl?"

The pirate-patch dog wiggled all over. "Poor gray-haired Edna doesn't match," Maeve went on, "but we started out together back in Illinois, so I have to keep her. Now please—help me figure out where on earth I've stowed my earrings." She rummaged through the mess on her dresser. "You'd think I could keep track of something as valuable as diamonds."

Teresa gasped. "You have *diamond* earrings?"

"I did. Don't worry; I won them fair and square. What did you say your name was?"

"Teresa. Teresa LeClair."

"What a great stage name. Are you on your own?"

Pascal! Teresa gasped and started for the door. "My little brother's sleeping upstairs. I'd better see if he's all right."

Maeve pulled her back. "Brothers are always fine; I don't know how they do it. Be a dear, won't you, and help me look for a few minutes? I have to wear my drops when I go to the Palace. It will make such an impression—"

"The Palace Theatre? But it just opened! Are you performing there?"

"If only. I've won some amateur nights lately, so my agent is meeting me at Keith and Albee's booking agency to see if they'll give me a route. I must look my best—now where *are* those jewels?"

Maeve seemed to know everything about getting onstage in New York. Teresa searched for the earrings on the rug and under piles of old newspapers. She moved a dog aside and looked through a pile of scarves and beads. She lifted a stack of bright-colored hoops, got down on her hands and knees, and looked under the bed. Edna licked the back of her neck and Teresa sat up quickly—knocking her head on a wobbly end table near the bed. "Ouch!" She caught the table before it fell, but a drawer opened, showering the rug with coins, hairpins, safety pins, a string of beads—and a pair of earrings.

"Brilliant! You're brilliant!" They knelt together, picking everything up, and Maeve helped Teresa to her feet. "Did you hurt your head?"

"It's hard as a rock," Teresa said.

"Does that mean you're as stubborn as I am?" Without waiting for an answer, Maeve wiped the earrings on the hem of her skirt and dropped them into Teresa's hand. "Hold them a sec. I don't want to lose them again." She brushed her hair with quick strokes, then pinned it up in a thick coil.

The earrings twinkled in Teresa's palm. "They're beautiful," she whispered. "I've never seen such big diamonds." She'd never so much as *touched* a diamond, for that matter.

"Go to Panic Beach and you'll see more diamonds than sand on a real beach," Maeve said. She clipped on the earrings. "Mine are in and out of hock, depending on my luck. It seems to be on the up and up lately." She glanced in the mirror, gave her reflection an approving nod, and turned to Teresa. "Now—how can I help *you*?"

"Could we go with you to the Palace?"

"Of course. You have an act?"

"Not yet. I'm a singer—I want to break in. I don't know where to start—"

"At the bottom, love, right where we all do." Maeve's smile lit her green eyes. "You'll try every amateur contest in town, until someone notices you." She squinted at her. "How old are you?"

"Fifteen. But—"

"'But' is right. As of today, you're sixteen; otherwise you'll have the Gerry Society after you."

"What do they do?"

"Enforce the rules; make sure child performers are sixteen."

"I was onstage when I was six," Teresa said.

"Not everyone obeys. And how old is this little brother of yours?"

"Pascal? Almost nine."

"Hmm. That's a problem."

"I need to send him home, somehow. He followed me here."

"Does he have a skill?"

"He juggles."

Maeve's wide smile was infectious. "Perfect! We'll take our chances." Before Teresa could ask how and why, Maeve threw the window open and waved her hand at the street below. "Wash your face, dress yourself up, and wake that brother of yours. Manhattan awaits you!"

22.

An hour later, Teresa, Pascal, and Maeve rushed downtown. The dogs strained at their leashes and held their tails aloft like proud flags. Maeve had lined them up in order, so that Edna (who seemed to have adopted Teresa) was on the outside, while Dixie, the smallest, pranced along closest to the buildings. Fido sported a purple silk jacket with Maeve's name—*Madame Maeve and her Marvelous Marching Dogs*—stitched onto both sides. Pedestrians laughed and pointed as they passed. "Perfect!" Maeve cried. "Two dogs per person—why didn't you show up sooner?"

Maeve held her leashes in one hand and carried a big canvas bag in the other. Her dogs never got tangled, but Edna and Bronwyn—Teresa's dogs—kept twisting up their leads. "Wait!" Teresa called. If she lost Maeve and Pascal, she'd never find her way back to the boardinghouse.

They fought horse-drawn carriages and motorcars to cross the street. Teresa wanted to grab Pascal's hand, but the dogs helped them thread their way to the other side without a hitch. The streets were mobbed compared to the night before. Motorbuses, horses, and delivery wagons took up the center of the street. Teresa had never heard so many different languages spoken, or seen so many stores. They twisted through the crowd, passing a button shop, barbershops with red-and-white poles twisting outside, and toy stores. A pair of giant wooden eyeglasses dangled next to an optometrist's sign. Open wooden stalls lined the avenues, where men and women sold puppies, hats, fresh flowers—and food. The scent of fresh-baked bread, wafting from an open stall filled with loaves and rolls, made Teresa's stomach growl. A woman in an apron, her face smudged with flour, called out to her in French, "Mademoiselle! *Avez-vous faim*? You hungry, Miss?"

"*Oui! J'ai faim!*" Teresa called, but she didn't dare stop, although they'd missed breakfast. The current of moving people pulled them along, taking them under a bridge that blocked the meager sunlight. Suddenly the metal struts above them began to vibrate, darkness fell on the sidewalk, and a horrible squealing noise sounded overhead. Sparks flew. A bright green train with angry red headlamps passed on the elevated rails. It swayed on the corner as if it might jump the tracks and crush them like ants under a boot.

"Watchit!" Teresa screamed, and pulled Pascal close against a building. He ducked his head. Teresa stared at the massive cars hurtling through empty space. The dogs waited patiently at their feet until the train had passed.

Maeve, who had rushed on without them, spun around and hurried back. "Goodness—you look as if you've seen a ghost!"

"What *was* that thing?" Pascal asked.

"The Sixth Avenue El," Maeve said, reaching down to untangle the dogs. "Where are you from, anyway?"

"Vermont," Pascal said, before Teresa could stop him. Maeve seemed trustworthy, but how did they know she wouldn't tell someone—like the police—if she found out they were runaways?

But Maeve just laughed. "So you're green," she said. "When I first came to town, I was so green you could have cut me like new hay. Come on, mustn't keep my agent waiting."

So Maeve and Pietro were both right, calling Teresa green. Never mind. She was here, in New York City. She had arrived.

Teresa craned her neck and looked up. The tops of tall buildings scratched the clouds like fingernails. She sniffed the air. An old woman with wizened brown skin and blackened palms sold hot chestnuts while a band of boys, no older than Pascal, hawked apples, peppermint candy, and matches, in at least three languages. Teresa listened to the city's music as she ran to catch up with Maeve. New York sounded like an orchestra playing out of tune with an offbeat, disjointed rhythm. Perfect pitch wouldn't help anyone in this town!

Maeve hurried them through the crowds. At last, they turned a corner and faced a tall white building on the other side of the street. "There she is." Maeve set her bag down and swooped her arm through the air, as if ushering in a famous personality. "The spanking-new home of our dreams. Meet the Palace."

The dogs sat on their rumps, panting, as if they were impressed, too. The stately building rose from the sidewalk. Stacks of billboards surrounded the Palace, advertising everything from the latest Stevens-Duryea car to hair cream. A flag swinging from the second-story windows promised "TEN STAR ACTS!" The curved marquee was studded with lights and boasted the names of acts and performers in giant letters. Crowds of people milled around on the wide sidewalk near the entrance. Surely this was the most elegant theater in the world.

Maeve nudged her. "She's something, isn't she?"

Pascal pointed to the crowd. "Is that The Beach?"

Maeve's eyes twinkled. "Aren't you smart? Who told you about that?"

"Our friend Pietro," Pascal said.

Was Pietro a friend? Teresa wondered. He was prickly and critical. On the other hand—he had challenged Teresa to come to New York. She looked down at Pascal, whose eyes shone like new coins. "Isn't it wonderful?" Teresa asked.

Pascal pointed to the tall letters on the marquee. "Will they write your dogs' names up there?"

"A dumb act will never be a headliner," Maeve said. "But I can dream."

"I'm working on a dumb act," Pascal said. "Someday, Resa and I will have our names in lights."

Teresa squeezed his shoulder. "Thanks." For a moment, she forgot that she needed to send him home.

"Who knows if we'll ever play the Palace," Maeve said. "Any old booking would be fine with me now. Just get me off these amateur stages and on the road with a real vaudeville troupe."

They led the dogs past groups of men and women who were laughing, arguing, and sharing stories outside the Palace doors. Teresa heard snatches of Spanish, French—and some very staccato language. Everyone seemed rushed, as if they had just come from someplace or were about to run off somewhere. "Excuse us!" Maeve sang out. People parted to make room for the dogs, and Teresa noticed a man with a diamond stickpin in his tie. Another wore diamond cufflinks even though his coat was shabby. "*Bella! Bellissima!*" he cried in Italian, and whistled as she walked by. Teresa ducked her chin and hurried after Maeve into the lobby.

"Look at you," Maeve said. "Your cheeks are burning."

"That man whistled at me."

Maeve laughed. "*And* he called you beautiful! Get used to it— you'll turn heads here. That's why I've got Fido. Just ignore them. Now: What do you think?" She opened her arms and twirled around the lobby. It was a vast open space surrounded by sparkling mirrors, an arched ceiling, and so many doors that Teresa felt as if she were in a castle where a queen might appear any minute. Maeve herded them toward the elevator. "Sit!" Maeve told the dogs as the golden doors swished closed behind them.

Teresa held her breath as Maeve asked for the sixth floor. Her stomach fell while her body soared. The dogs sat in a row, ears pricked, tails wagging. Teresa laughed.

"What so funny?" Maeve asked.

Teresa pointed to the dogs. "If I had a tail, I'd be wagging it, too." Then she caught sight of herself in the shiny brass walls, which reflected their images like warped mirrors. Even though she'd changed into her new shirtwaist, Teresa felt dowdy compared to Maeve, who used the reflection to adjust her green felt hat, tipping it cockily to one side. Teresa turned away. She was ashamed of her hair, in its usual snarl, and her carpet of freckles. She couldn't imagine anyone "turning heads" to look at her now.

"Are we almost there?" Pascal's voice sounded small at the back of the elevator. Teresa sighed. How could she enjoy the city if she had to worry about her brother all the time? She'd have to get him home somehow.

"Sixth floor," the elevator operator announced. The elevator swooshed to a stop and they piled out. Maeve led them to an enormous room filled with desks. Men and women hurried back and forth, carrying papers, sheet music, and instruments. Every now and then, someone shouted out a name to the lines of people waiting near the elevators.

"The people at the desks are booking agents," Maeve explained. "And all these scared-looking folks are like me: searching for a gig." She straightened her shoulders, tipped her head to the side, and batted her long eyelashes. "The secret is *looking* like you're a success, before you even start." She waved to a man in a straw hat. "There's my agent. Wish me luck." Maeve unhooked the dogs and gave their leashes to Teresa. "Hold these for me, will you?" Before Teresa could protest, Maeve told the dogs to heel and took off.

The dogs lined up and followed her like obedient soldiers. Where was Pascal? Teresa panicked for a moment, until she noticed a small brown orb, followed by another one, flying through the air near the elevators. She hurried over. Pascal had left his bag of balls and bowling pins at the boardinghouse—so what was he juggling? She pushed through the small crowd. The brown orbs circled fast—too fast. One fell to the floor, followed by another. Chestnuts.

Teresa grabbed one. "Pascal, did you steal from that woman?"

"They were just lying on the ground," he said.

Teresa was ready to scold him when Maeve reappeared, her eyes bloodshot. "What happened?" Teresa asked.

"*No interest*; that's what they said. It doesn't matter how many contests we've won." Maeve's voice shook.

"I'm sorry." Teresa loosened the knots in her handkerchief, which she'd used to tie up her money this morning, and handed it to Maeve. "It's kind of dirty," she said.

Maeve tried to smile. "That's okay, hon," she said, and wiped her tears. "Back to the amateur circuits. And that's where you and your brother need to start. We'll go together." She gestured to the dogs. "Sit, all of you."

Teresa helped Maeve snap on the leashes and handed two dogs to Pascal. He hardly seemed to notice. "You all right?" Teresa asked.

He didn't answer. They crowded into the elevator again, and Maeve nudged Teresa. "The Loew's Royal Theatre has a contest tonight. Shall we give it a try? I could get you on the list."

"All right." Teresa's mouth was suddenly full of cotton wool. An amateur night in New York would be a thousand times scarier than a children's singing contest. And what would she do with her brother?

Something thumped behind them and the dogs whimpered. Teresa whirled around. Pascal lay in a crumpled heap on the floor, his face white as paste. The dogs circled around him like a crowd of doctors, licking his face and wrists. Dixie set up a howl.

Teresa dropped to her knees beside him. "Pascal! Wake up!" He didn't move.

23.

"Stop the elevator!" Teresa cried. The operator pulled the elevator up with a shudder and bent to touch Pascal's neck. "Poor kid's fainted. Get those dogs out of the way; give him some air." He took the elevator to the ground floor without stopping and helped them carry Pascal to a plush couch in the lobby. "Water fountain over there," he said, pointing, and disappeared.

Maeve loosened Pascal's collar and fanned his face with her hat. "When did he last eat?"

"Yesterday?" Teresa's face burned with shame. Her own stomach cramped with hunger, but being in the Palace had made her forget about food.

Pascal's eyes fluttered open. "What happened?"

"You fainted," Teresa said. "Can you stand up?"

He wobbled to his feet and leaned against her. "I want Mama."

Maeve glanced at Teresa across Pascal's head. "We need to talk. You help Pascal; I'll take the dogs. Get him some water at the drinking fountain—and then we're on our way. Next stop: Kellogg's Cafeteria."

Maeve begged bowls of water from the management at the restaurant, herded the dogs into a corner, and helped Pascal to a table behind the dogs. "Keep an eye on the pooch patrol—we'll get you some food." Maeve stationed Fido at the door, where customers could read the sign on his purple jacket as they came in. People laughed and bent to stroke the dogs as they waited for seats.

"Best advertising I'll ever have," Maeve said. She led Teresa through the cafeteria line. "This meal is on me. You can take me out after you win your first amateur night."

"You haven't even heard me sing," Teresa said. "What if I'm terrible?"

"Well then, enjoy your only free lunch."

"How much can you win, in these contests?"

"It depends. Five, ten, fifteen dollars, depending on the theater."

Fifteen dollars? She could send Pascal home and still have enough to stay in New York—at least for a while.

Teresa and Pascal devoured chicken potpie, mashed potatoes with gravy, and milk. Maeve went to the counter for a second glass of milk for Pascal, and he drained it as fast as the first one. The color came back into his cheeks. He slipped away from the table and sat on the floor with the dogs, scratching them in turn behind their ears.

Teresa swallowed hard. "Mama would never have let him go hungry," she said. "And Papa will kill me when he finds out we're here."

"Truth time," Maeve said.

"What do you mean?" Teresa shifted uneasily.

Maeve cupped a hand over Teresa's. Her eyes were warm. "Trust me," she said. "I won't give you away. I assumed you were runaways. If we're going to be friends, we need to be honest with each other. And maybe I can help you."

Friends. Even though Maeve was a few years older, Teresa felt as if she'd known her forever. "I had to leave home," Teresa said.

Maeve nodded. "I understand. I was sixteen when I ran away from our Illinois farm. Go on."

Teresa told her everything: how her parents had eloped before she was born; how they raised her on the vaudeville circuit, putting her to bed in the top drawer of a steamer trunk as they traveled the small-town circuits; how she performed with them before they moved back to Vermont, where her parents worked at Estey and ran the boardinghouse. "It's hard on Mama," Teresa said. "She can't work at the factory anymore. And Papa—"

She stopped.

"Tell me." Maeve tipped her head to the side, listening, in a way that reminded Teresa of Nonnie.

"Papa changed," Teresa said. "He stopped playing the fiddle and he won't sing with Mama. Even worse, he planned to shut me up in the tuning rooms at the organ factory. I'd rather die than work there." Teresa twisted her napkin in her lap. "I thought I was running away alone, but Pascal followed me. Mama will never forgive me if something happens to him. I need to send Pascal home."

"It's not your fault that he followed you," Maeve said. "We'll think of something."

A burst of applause made them turn around. Pascal had pushed some furniture aside and was juggling a bruised apple and three chestnuts. His cap sat on the table next to him and his hair fell down into his eyes, but he never missed a beat. He even tossed a chestnut under one leg and caught it while keeping everything else in the air. Maeve elbowed Teresa. "He's good!"

Pascal threw the apple too far to the side, just missing it. As if they'd planned it, Dixie leapt high, caught the apple in her mouth, and brought it to Maeve, her tail wagging. The restaurant erupted in laughter and the chestnuts rattled onto the wood floor. Pascal scooped them up, looking flustered.

"Keep going, lad!" a man called, and a coin flew through the air, just missing Pascal's cap. Maeve tossed him the apple and

Pascal started up again. This time, he whistled to Dixie before throwing her a chestnut. Dixie stood up on her hind legs, caught the chestnut, and tipped her head as if she were bowing. The customers whooped. Two women leaned over to drop more coins into Pascal's cap. Pascal grinned and waved.

Maeve nudged Teresa. "He's got the magic touch. And we've just added a new trick to my routine." She put on her hat and grabbed her bag. "Time to practice. We're going to have a terrific night."

We? Teresa couldn't help smiling.

24.

Teresa and Pascal sat at the upright piano in Mrs. O'Donnell's boardinghouse. Teresa set her sheet music on the piano, blew dust from the keys, and played a few chords. "Ouch," she said. "Out of tune. Never mind—I can still practice." She glanced at Pascal. "Are you excited about tonight?"

"I guess." Pascal's voice sounded as flat as the piano keys. "Maeve says I can be part of her act."

"What's wrong with that?"

He shrugged. "I don't like it here."

"But you said you wanted to perform onstage."

He sniffled. "Not without Mama and Papa. I want Papa to come get me."

"He'd force me to come home and shut me up at Estey. Listen." Teresa cupped his chin in her hand, forcing him to meet her eyes. "I've paid Mrs. O'Donnell for a week's lodging. When we win some of these contests, I'll have money for your ticket. Remember, you didn't have to follow me."

"I know." Pascal fidgeted on the piano bench. "What if you don't win? I mean—you're a good singer, Resa, but people might be better here."

"You're right. I could 'die,' as Mama would say. But look: You earned some money yourself this morning. And there's always Miss Connover, the lady judge. She might take me in and give me lessons."

"You mean—you won't go home? Ever?"

"Not now." Teresa pulled Pascal close. "I'm not leaving *you*. But I need to sing."

"What if Mama and Papa think we're dead?"

He *would* bring that up. "I left Mama a note."

"About me?"

"Of course not. I didn't know you would follow me! Please don't cry." She stroked his head. "Six more nights. If I haven't earned enough money by then, I promise we'll send Papa a telegram."

"Promise?"

"Of course. I need to practice my songs. Now go to Maeve and learn your part."

Maeve helped Teresa dress for her first night on the town. Teresa wore the skirt and blouse that Nonnie had made. The gold locket shone against the creamy fabric. Maeve clucked her approval as she clipped some silver barrettes in Teresa's curls.

"Your hair shines like a bright light when you come into a room," Maeve said. "And those golden eyes make you look like a young lion."

Maeve, with her silky tresses, thought Teresa's twisted curls were pretty? "The boys in school said my eyes were witchy," she said. "They call me 'carrot top,' and 'freckle face.'"

"That just shows they like you," Maeve said, rubbing rouge on Teresa's cheeks. "You'll make a grand entrance, show them you're on top of the world."

The world sat heavily on Teresa's shoulders that evening as they rode the El to Brooklyn. She glanced at Pascal. He pressed his face to the window, his eyes wide with astonishment. He wore a green jacket with gold braiding that Teresa had bought in a secondhand clothing shop with some of Mama's coins. His juggling bag bulged with his bowling pins, a set of new juggling balls that Maeve had found, and apples for his trick with Dixie.

As the train hurtled past apartment windows, Teresa felt as if she were watching a moving picture show at the nickelodeon. People ate, read newspapers, yelled at one another, or just stared at the walls. They didn't seem to notice the train, even though it seemed as if it might smash right into their flats. The train rounded a sharp curve and Teresa nudged her brother. "Look—you can see the engine." But Pascal covered his eyes. He was as green as his jacket.

Their next train lumbered across the Brooklyn Bridge. Teresa gasped. Great cables swooped down from twin towers like filaments of thick silk. "We're so high!" she said. "Pascal, look!"

He glanced down, then away. Teresa couldn't take her eyes off the view. A steamer, its giant smokestack belching smoke, passed beneath them, reflected in the dark water. Behind them, strings of white lights blinked on all over the city, speckling the skyscrapers like stars.

Maeve smiled at her from across the aisle. "Isn't it gorgeous? I never get tired of this view."

Teresa gripped her seat. If only her clutch of coins were bigger. She'd sing her heart out so she could stay forever.

The Loew's Royal Theatre had two balconies and so many seats that Teresa's hands went clammy with fear. The stage manager, a large man with even more freckles than Teresa, was happy to see Maeve and her dogs. "Welcome back," he said, rubbing his hands. "You were popular last time."

"I have a helper tonight." Maeve pointed at Pascal. "He juggles. You'll love our new tricks."

"A little young, isn't he?" The stage manager twisted his handlebar mustache between the tips of his fingers. "Never mind. The Gerry Society leaves us alone—but if there's any trouble—" He crooked one arm into a hook shape, then peered at Teresa through thick glasses. "And who have we here?"

"I'm Teresa LeClair." If only her voice would stay steady! "I'd like to sing tonight. I won a singing contest a few weeks ago."

The stage manager shook his head. "Sorry, Miss—but I've got sixteen acts already. I'm not sure I can fit you in."

"Oh, but she's wonderful!" Maeve set a hand on the stage manager's arm and gave him a pretty smile. "You won't be sorry, I promise."

"All right, all right." He pulled out a crumpled sheet of paper, scribbled something and squinted at it, as if he couldn't read his own writing. "Miss Cullen, you and the dogs will be third; we have another dumb act going on first." He crossed something out. "Miss—LeClair, is it?" Teresa nodded. "You'll be eighth. Give your music to a stagehand and he'll pass it to the orchestra. No stage hogging—two songs are enough." He cleaned his glasses on the hem of his coat and raised his bushy eyebrows at Teresa. "Tough audience here. Tomatoes if you bomb, coins if they love you." He stomped into the wings.

"Phew!" Maeve said. "We passed one hurdle."

"Tomatoes?" Pascal asked.

"Not at us, silly," Maeve said. "Everyone loves dogs. Now, let's talk to the prop man. I have to change, and I need Edna's big hoop. Oh dear, why do dumb acts always go on so early in the lineup? Here, Pascal, hold the leashes. And don't worry about our tricks; if Dixie doesn't catch the apple, just keep going . . ." With a flurry of props, wagging tails, and scarves, Maeve and Pascal disappeared into the wings.

Teresa gave her music to a stagehand and stood in a corner, humming to herself. She should sing scales to warm up her voice. Was that allowed? Other performers came and went, some silent, others as restless as Maeve. "*Nyet! Nyet!*" someone grunted behind her, followed by scuffling, then silence. Was that Russian?

"Curtain in five," a woman's voice called.

Teresa backed into the wings and pulled the heavy curtain aside to peek at the audience. A raucous crowd filed in, looking for seats. Teresa swallowed once, twice. The pure sound of an oboe playing an *A* floated from the orchestra pit, followed by a violin tuning up.

"Well, well." A muffled but familiar voice sounded behind her. "If it isn't Miss Teresa LeClair."

Teresa whirled around. "Pietro! What are you doing here?"

"Shh," he warned. "Trying to win some money, make myself famous."

She couldn't help staring. "You look so—so fancy." She was going to say "handsome" but stopped herself. Pietro wore tails with a starched white collar, a red bow tie, and a top hat. A scarlet flower bloomed in his buttonhole. And he *was* handsome, without the burnt cork. "Where's your father?"

"In Harlem. Thought I'd branch out on my own. I'm seventh, my lucky number. And you?"

"Eighth."

He shook his head in mock sadness. "Mmm, mm. That's a doggone shame. I'm a tough act to follow."

"We'll see," she said, trying to sound cocky. "After they hear me, they'll forget they ever saw *you*."

"So the Princess Theater gave you a swelled head." Pietro scraped the soles of his shoes, one at a time, into a pot hidden in the corner.

"What's that?" she whispered.

"Rosin. Gives me traction so I won't slip on this smooth floor." He pulled on his white gloves.

"Curtain!" a woman bellowed from the bowels of the theater.

The house lights dimmed. Horns played a fanfare, and a drumroll sounded as the announcer stepped out in front of the curtain. "La-a-a-dies and gentlemen!" he cried. "Welcome to another amateur talent night, the night when *you* decide who the next big stars will be! We have seventeen acts lined up. We have comedy, we have animals, we have soulful singers and dancers with flying feet. Give them a big hand. If you like them, shower them with favors. If you don't . . ." He didn't finish his sentence, but the audience laughed, and someone shouted: "Rotten eggs!"

"Let the music begin!" the manager cried.

25.

The show opened with a short film, followed by a flourish of horns and violins. A pair of male acrobats, dressed in pink satin suits studded with silver beads, turned cartwheels onto the stage. They vaulted over bicycles and each other, twisted themselves into contorted positions, did flips, walked on both hands, then on one. The audience was lukewarm, and when the two men dashed into the wings, they just missed Teresa. "We died," one whispered. The other muttered something she couldn't understand.

Teresa took a deep breath, then another. Could you "die" for real, if your heart was beating like a drumroll?

"Don't worry." Pietro's voice came from right behind her. "You'll be fine."

How did he know what she was thinking?

A comedian came on next. He made fun of himself and of anyone with a foreign accent, and he used a bad word for Jews. Papa hated it when people called him "Frenchie" or "Frog," so he and Mama had forbidden those words, and all other insults, in their house. Teresa was glad when the audience booed at the comedian. An egg splattered on the stage, then a tomato, followed by a barrage of spitballs. Suddenly, a long hook, like a shepherd's crook, snaked from the wings, grabbed the comedian by the waist, and yanked him offstage. He scuttled sideways like a crab and the audience went wild. Stagehands hurried out to clean up the mess with mops. Teresa shuddered. Would she get the hook?

Too late to back out now. The stage manager announced Maeve's act. She and Pascal hurried onstage surrounded by the dogs, their tails wagging as they pranced on their hind legs. No wonder Maeve hadn't worn her costume on the train! She had poured herself into a slinky, low-cut green blouse, satin shorts with slits up the sides, and black tights. The outfit matched her green eyes as well as the ribbons on the dogs' collars. The audience cheered, whistled, and clapped.

"Nice scarf," Pietro murmured. "What's your baby brother doing out there?"

"He's not a baby now." Pascal was transformed, and not just because of Pietro's scarf, fluttering from his neck like a flag. It was the way he saluted the audience and began to juggle the wooden balls, as confident as if he'd been onstage all his life. How did he *do* that?

The audience loved Maeve's act. The dogs caught tiny hoops on their noses. They "spoke" with yippy barks when she asked them questions, jumped over and on top of each other, and walked across each other's backs like acrobats. Pascal's trick with Dixie worked perfectly. He tossed an apple out to the right, keeping the others moving, and Dixie snatched it up and set it at Maeve's feet. Pascal pretended to count the remaining apples and made a puzzled face, as if he couldn't figure out where the apple had gone. He kept going until he only had one apple left, which he threw over his head in disgust. When Dixie caught the last one, the audience roared their approval and rained a torrent of pennies onto the stage.

"A natural comic," Pietro said. "Who would have thought?"

Maeve's last number had the audience gasping: With gloves on her hands, she held a flaming hoop near her body. She kept it low at first, then raised it higher and higher as the dogs jumped through, first singly, then in pairs. Pascal zigzagged across the stage, scooping up pennies, as Maeve curtsied and made a fiery exit into the wings. Teresa turned to Pietro. "They're good, aren't they?" she whispered.

Pietro's face looked frozen. His stage fright made Teresa feel even worse and she hardly noticed the acts before Pietro's turn. He stepped in and out of the rosin one last time, and waited, bouncing on his heels, for the music to begin.

"Good luck," Teresa whispered.

He recoiled as if she'd spit on him. "Good luck is *bad* luck," he snapped. "For dancers, you say *merde*."

Teresa raised her eyebrows. Papa would wash her mouth out with soap if she said that word at home, but she blurted it out anyway.

"Welcome Pietro Jones, of Marvin Jones and Son!" the stage manager called. "He's dancing on his own for the first time tonight!"

Pietro entered tap dancing, his body loose yet controlled. He sashayed into a strutting cakewalk, followed by a ragtime number. His feet moved faster and faster, even though his upper body stayed still. Finally, he danced up and down a small set of stairs and ended with a flourish of his top hat, his feet clicking like castanets.

Pietro danced into the wings and nearly knocked Teresa over. He bent over at the waist, breathing hard. "Get ready," he said. "They're handcuffed. Sittin' on those hands." He raised a finger. "Listen. There's your call."

The music was familiar, but Teresa couldn't move, and her name drifted from someplace far away. Pietro gave her a small shove. "Break a leg."

How did she get onstage? Somehow, she found herself in a hot spotlight while the band played the opening bars of "Cousin of Mine." Teresa missed her first cue. The bandleader coughed, pointed his baton in her direction, and played the first four bars again. Teresa began to sing, but the audience grew restless.

A woman's whisper came from the wings. "You can do it!"

Was that Maeve? Teresa tried to ham it up and put some bounce in it, but she felt clumsy. She struggled on and was relieved when she reached the end of the last chorus. *"He's Mother's sister's angel child . . . he's a cousin of mine."*

The band played the introduction to "Hard Times" and she launched into the first verse. She remembered how Mr. Jones had told her to pitch her voice to the last row at the Princess. She opened her throat and let her voice soar, hoping they'd hear her in the second balcony. The audience stopped whispering. A good sign? Pietro hummed some harmony from the wings on the final chorus, just as he had done in Brattleboro. Teresa tried not to notice; she didn't want to lose the beat.

At last, it was over. Teresa let the last note drift away. The audience threw a few pennies—hardly enough to pick up—but at least people clapped. Teresa took a quick bow before running offstage.

"Hurrah!" Pascal's high voice piped up from the wings at stage left.

"I died," she said to Pietro when she could catch her breath.

"They liked your second number," Pietro said. "Must be my harmony." He raised his eyebrows, teasing.

"What's the matter—think I can't sing on my own?"

"Hssst. Quiet over there." The stage manager gave them a warning look as he came off from announcing the next act.

Teresa leaned against the wall and waited for her heart to stop thumping. She'd just had her New York stage debut. Not a success, but not a complete disaster. No hook, no rotten eggs, she hadn't missed a note—and she hadn't fainted. *So there, Papa. Try to stop me now.*

26.

When the show ended, everyone who had escaped the hook lined up on stage. "Laa-dies and gentlemen, you pick the winner!" the stage manager cried. He started down the line, dangling a five-dollar bill over each performer's head, and waited for the audience to respond.

Five dollars would give her another week at the bed and breakfast. Teresa crossed her fingers behind her skirt, though she knew she couldn't win. But perhaps Maeve and Pascal could? The dogs sat in a circle around Pascal and Maeve, their ears pricked, tails wagging, looking as hopeful as Teresa felt.

Teresa received polite applause, as did Pietro—in spite of a few boos. The crowd gave Maeve, Pascal, and the dogs a big hand, but saved their loudest cheers for a young English couple who had performed the death scene from *Romeo and Juliet*. The manager gave the winners the five-dollar bill and paid the other acts fifty cents apiece.

It wasn't much. Maeve had told Teresa that the famous risqué actress Eva Tanguay made thousands of dollars in one week. Still, fifty cents would buy lunch.

Pascal and Maeve hurried across the stage, beaming, with the dogs fanning out around them. "I have 75 cents!" Pascal announced. "Maeve gave me half the money, and I picked up so many pennies."

Maeve hugged Teresa. "You were wonderful!"

"I wasn't. My songs are boring."

"So change them! That's what amateur nights are for. You find out what works, what flops. The first time is the hardest. You're on your way."

"Was someone speaking Russian?" Teresa asked.

"Probably." Maeve laughed. "The whole *world* is in New York!" She turned to Pietro, who was taking off his tap shoes. "Young man, you are a terrific dancer. Have you tried the Lincoln, in Harlem?"

Pietro looked up. "Why, what's there?"

"A Saturday-night dance competition. Six colored dancers compete against six whites. The winner takes a twenty-dollar gold piece. I'm sure you could lick them all, especially if you work on that ragtime number. You'd slay them."

Pietro smiled. "Thanks for the tip, Miss—"

"Cullen. Maeve Cullen. And you are Mister . . . ?"

"Pietro Jones."

"Pietro. A wonderful stage name. But Jones is a bit ordinary; you might think of dropping it. No offense. Teresa and Pascal, be angels and hold the dogs while I change into my street clothes." Maeve hurried offstage, pins flying from her hair, leaving them to untangle dogs and leashes.

"Tells you what she thinks and then some," Pietro said in a dry tone.

"She has good ideas," Teresa said. "What about that contest?"

"Depends." Pietro tucked his tap shoes under his arm and tugged at Pascal's red scarf. "Guess this brought you good luck. You're on your way. Your sister should hustle to keep up."

Pascal scowled at Pietro. "Resa was good," he said. "So were you."

"Not what the audience said." Pietro stowed the top hat in a hatbox and pulled on his felt cap. "This crowd won't give me the time of day." He unbuttoned his gloves, tugged them off one finger at a time, and held up his hands. "How many faces my color you see out there?" He pulled the curtain back a few inches so Teresa could watch people filing out.

"None," Teresa admitted. "It looks like Brattleboro. Your friends can't come to watch you?"

"We're not welcome in most white theaters, unless we sit in the balcony." Pietro's voice was cold. "And you won't find coloreds without cork on Broadway. This manager is better than most; said I could go on without blacking up, long as I was alone onstage. Those are the rules."

"That's stupid!" said Pascal. The dogs sat up expectantly, as if they thought he might do another magic trick, and Dixie whined.

"Are your theaters different?" Teresa asked.

"Is night different than day? Summer than winter?" Pietro tapped out his questions with one foot.

Teresa turned away, stung. "Is it my fault that I don't know everything?"

"Like I said once: It's never too late to learn."

"If you know so much, why don't you teach me?" When Pietro didn't answer, Teresa tugged on the dogs' leashes. "Come on, pups. Let's find Maeve."

Pietro did a quick two-step and landed in front of her. "Don't go off in a huff, Miss LeClair. You want to get educated, come to Harlem's Lafayette Theatre on amateur night. Then you'll see different."

"Why?" Pascal asked. "What happens?"

Pietro's eyes danced. "Doesn't matter if you're black, white, or purple. They love you, they tear the place down. You die, Puerto Rico shoots you dead."

"Dead? Who's Puerto Rico?" Pascal's eyes bulged.

"A funny Puerto Rican man. He runs onstage with a popgun, makes a shooting sound, and you're gone." Pietro shaped his thumb and forefinger into a pretend gun. "Pop! That's the Lafayette's hook. It's the only theater in New York where my people can sit in the orchestra. They put on classic plays there, too, starring colored actors." He raised his eyebrows at Teresa. "What about it? Want to try?"

Teresa shook her head. "Not after tonight."

"Guess I figured you different."

"What do you mean?"

"Didn't take you for a coward. After all, you *did* run away from home."

Teresa put both hands on her hips. "So what if I'm afraid. You were nervous tonight—weren't you?"

Before Pietro could answer, the stage manager strode out from the wings, his face red beneath its freckles. "What's going on here? You giving this lady a hard time?"

Pietro looked at his feet. "No, sir."

"We were just talking," Teresa said quickly.

"Pietro's our friend!" Pascal said.

The manager grabbed Pietro's arm and twisted it behind his back. "Don't get uppity in my theater, think you can socialize with a white girl. Didn't I go out of my way to help you tonight?"

Before Pietro could answer, Fido scrambled to his feet, the fur on his shoulders bristling. He stalked toward the stage manager.

"Call off that dog!" The stage manager let go of Pietro and stumbled backward.

Pascal pulled on Fido's leash, but the dog's legs were locked in place and he quivered all over. Edna lifted her head and howled like a hound dog while the other dogs milled around the stage manager, growling. "Naughty dogs," Teresa crooned in a sweet voice.

The stage manager trembled with rage. "Get out of my theater. All of you. Right . . . this . . . minute. And don't you ever come back." He backed away slowly, his eyes on the dogs, his hands protecting his neck. He glared at Teresa. "I thought you had promise. Instead, I see you've got no sense." The stage manager tripped over Pascal's juggling bag, caught himself, and hurried into the wings.

"Pick up your things—we need to find Maeve." Teresa's hands shook as she untangled the dogs.

"Where's Pietro?" Pascal asked.

They turned around. The stage door stood open to the night. The dogs whined as Teresa and Pascal peered outside. Rain lashed the dark alley. Pietro was gone.

27.

Three days later, Teresa sat at the breakfast table, so tired she could hardly see. Every night, she and Maeve and Pascal had entered one amateur contest after another. The day before, they'd competed in the afternoon and again at night. Now Teresa had a sore throat and a froggy voice. If Mama were here, she'd make her a soothing hot drink, with honey and gingerroot. Nonnie would pull out some of her special throat lozenges, even give her a sip of her special evening "medicine." Instead, Teresa was forced to sip Mrs. O'Donnell's lukewarm tea.

Maeve and Pascal had nearly won last night, and Teresa hadn't done badly. Yesterday she'd sifted through some discarded sheet music on Mrs. O'Donnell's piano and found a copy of "When Irish Eyes Are Smiling." In a rare moment of friendliness, their landlady had come into the dining room to listen as Teresa tried singing the tune. "Not bad," she'd said, and corrected Teresa's pronunciation. "Give it a bit of a lilt and belt it out. The Irish in the audience will love ya." And they had. Last night's crowd had peppered the stage with coins—Teresa even had some nickels and dimes in her pocket—but it was barely enough to keep Pascal in food; it was not enough to send him home.

What would Nonnie tell her to do? Teresa reached into her cloth bag and pulled out the photo of her great-grandmother that she kept with her. Nonnie wore a beautiful, brocade dress with a high neck and long sleeves, one she'd probably stitched herself—and her eyes were clear and full of mischief. "Reach for the stars," Nonnie had said. "I'll try," Teresa whispered. She slipped the photograph back in the bag. "No tuning rooms for me."

She went to the piano and studied another song: "By the Light of the Silvery Moon." Pietro had danced to that number at the amateur night. It had a nice bounce with room for a quick tap shuffle at the end of each phrase. But her body felt awkward on stage. She'd probably trip over her feet if she tried to dance.

Teresa glanced at the newspaper lying open on the table and flipped to the classified section at the back, where Maeve often found news of amateur nights and other contests. A bold headline jumped out at her: "INFORMATION WANTED." Underneath, small box advertisements asked readers for information about runaway wives, and husbands who had abandoned their children. One ad wanted "News Of Owen Harte, Last heard from lying sick at St. Louis, Missouri." Another asked: "Of Peter Gier, once of Manhattan. The undersigned sent him money and had it returned."

Teresa was about to put the paper away when she spotted her own name at the bottom of the page. Her hands shook so hard, she could barely read the notice, set off from the rest of the page in a box:

> INFORMATION WANTED: Of our children, Teresa and Pascal LeClair, of Brattleboro, Vermont. Last seen by station master in company of two dark-complexioned men on New York–bound train. Teresa age 15, redheaded singer. Pascal age 8, blond, slight. Reply to this office. Handsome reward provided by the undersigned. F. LeClair.

Teresa tasted bile. "*Idiote*," she whispered in French. Of *course* Papa would look for them! What was she thinking—that Mama and Papa would do nothing when their children disappeared? She had imagined Mama frantic with worry about Pascal, and Papa raging—but she hadn't thought beyond that. Teresa read the ad again. At least Papa called her a singer. But how could he give away her age? What if some stage manager realized she wasn't sixteen?

Worse, Papa made it sound as if Pietro and Mr. Jones had kidnapped them. Teresa hadn't even spoken to them on the train. Would this get them in trouble? Mr. Jones was right: She should have sent Papa a telegram right away. But then he'd come find them. Teresa felt dizzy.

Metal crashed on the ceiling above her head and the chandelier swung wildly. Teresa tossed the newspaper onto the table as Mrs. O'Donnell strode through the door, brandishing her broom. She thumped the ceiling hard, adding pockmarks to the circle of bruises on the plaster. "That brother of yours," she said. "Thinks I wouldn't notice that my table knives are missing." She glared at Teresa. "He's up with that juggling team that came in last night. I'm going to speak to him now."

"I'll go," Teresa said.

"Do it right away, then." Mrs. O'Donnell gathered up the newspaper and tucked it under her arm. "No one cleans up their mess around here. Where's that father of yours?" When Teresa didn't answer, she said, "Humph. Thought so." She headed for the kitchen. "Rent for next week is due Saturday," she called over her shoulder.

"Yes, Ma'am." As if she could forget. Teresa stared at Mrs. O'Donnell's retreating back, willing her to drop the paper, but she shut the door firmly behind her. Teresa ran upstairs.

"Pascal!"

Metal crashed again, a door opened, and Pascal stuck his head out. "What?"

"Mrs. O'Donnell wants her knives back."

Pascal squinched up his nose. "Your voice sounds funny."

"Something wrong, Miss?" A young man with pinkish eyes, white hair, and skin the color of paste peered around the door.

"I need—" Teresa caught her breath. She'd seen an albino squirrel once—was this an albino man? Whatever he was, he had a friendly smile. She looked past him into the bedroom. The floor was covered with props. Juggling balls, huge rings, and unlit torches were stacked in neat piles on the rug. A pair of stilts leaned against the dresser, and a second man, with olive-colored skin, stood in the middle of the room, juggling four white balls as naturally as if they were part of his breathing. The balls flew in lazy circles, singly, then in pairs, behind his back, over his head. He nodded at Teresa but never lost his rhythm.

Pascal stepped closer, knocking the knives together at his feet. "They're good, Resa. They're teaching me things. *Please*, let me stay?"

"We won't hurt him, Miss," said the pale man. "He's no bother. We'll keep the door open, if it makes you feel better."

"*Sí*," said the second man. "*Amigos*," he said, pointing at his chest, then at Pascal.

Friends already? Was this safe? She thought of Papa's warning, that vaude was "no place for children." Still, the jugglers seemed kind and this was her last chance. "Thank you," she said. "Pascal, I'm going out for a few hours. Return the knives to the kitchen, and don't bother these men. If you need anything, ask Maeve. Don't leave the boardinghouse, no matter what."

Pascal's shoulders slumped and he suddenly looked small and frightened. "Where are you going?"

"To see about your ticket home," she said.

Which was almost true. That would have to do for now.

28.

An hour later, Teresa stood outside an ornate, cast-iron fence, looking through the grillwork at a leafy park. She had found her way there by train and on foot, with a lift at the end from a kind man in a milk cart who said, "Sure, I know Gramercy Park. That's where the rich folks live. They're so fancy dancy, you can't get in without a key."

Teresa pulled out Miss Connover's card. *Gramercy Park #3*— were the houses inside the garden? She put a foot on the bottom rung and hoisted herself up, gripping the spiked bars at the top of the gate. It was hard to see beyond the curtain of new spring leaves. Teresa dropped to the sidewalk. The milkman was right: The gate was locked and no one was inside.

The sound of children chattering made her turn around. Two little girls, dressed in buttoned coats and felt hats, were skipping toward the gate, followed by an older woman whose face was as white as her starched cap. Was she a nursemaid? The woman strode to the gate, slipped a key into the lock, and let the girls through. Teresa hurried over before the gate swung shut. "Excuse me, Ma'am? I dropped an earring in here the other day—when I was walking with Miss Connover—I wonder if I could go in and look for it?" She edged into the space opened up by the gate—and now she could see, quite plainly, that there were no houses inside, just trees with the blush of new leaves, a planting of tulips, and some shrubs pruned into stiff shapes.

The nurse waved Teresa away and pulled the gate closed with a heavy clang. "No strangers in the park—those are my orders. If Miss Connover took you in here once, I'm sure she'd do it again. Why don't you ask her? She's home this morning; I saw her in the hallway."

"Thank you!" As the nurse turned away, Teresa called, "Sorry to bother you again. It was raining the day I came. I'm not sure which house is Number Three."

"Why, the brick one." The woman pointed toward a street beyond the park. "The number's hidden behind the shrub. I keep telling the missus she should prune it back so's people can see." She hurried after her charges.

Teresa followed the street around the back of the park to a row of elegant houses. As the nursemaid had said, a lilac bush concealed the number on the brick building. Teresa entered the front door and stood in a small entryway in front of a second door—which was locked. Three metal plates were screwed onto the wall, beneath three buttons. *L. Connover*, read the fancy script on one plate. Teresa cleared her throat and screwed up her courage. She'd come this far; she couldn't turn back. She pushed the button. A bell sounded, then silence.

She waited: nothing. Pushed the button again. This time, a door opened on an upper floor and she heard the faint sound of piano music. "Who is it?" a high-pitched voice called.

Teresa took a deep breath. "Teresa LeClair. I'm here to see Miss Connover."

"She's giving a lesson. Do you have an appointment?"

"She asked me to visit her." Teresa climbed the stairs to the first landing, her heart pounding like her footsteps.

"Just a moment."

The music stopped. Teresa wiped her damp palms on her skirt. What was taking so long? Finally, the same woman's voice said, "Come up. But you'll have to wait."

Teresa hurried up the stairs, expecting a grown woman. Instead, a girl about her own age stood in the doorway. She wore a maid's uniform, her sandy hair tied back in a bun under a starched cap. She showed Teresa into a small room, pointed to a straight-back chair, and said in a clipped voice, "Miss Connover will be with you shortly."

Teresa's palms were damp. She wiped them on her skirt. The maid raised an eyebrow. "Miss Connover wonders if your parents are with you?"

None of your business, Teresa thought, but she said, "Not yet."

The maid made a small, disapproving noise and left the room.

Teresa wiggled in the hard chair, trying to get comfortable. A china bowl filled with wrapped toffees sat on a small table beside a love seat, just like Mama's candy basket in the front hall. Teresa's stomach growled and her throat burned. Surely Miss Connover left these for visitors? She quickly tucked three candies into her pocket.

Bookshelves lined the walls of the room from floor to ceiling. Their leather bindings, nestled against the paneled shelves, made the room feel warm. Chintz fabric covered the loveseat, and a lamp lit the room with a golden glow. Even though she'd worn her best skirt and blouse, and wiped her boots clean, Teresa felt shabby next to these fine things.

Low voices sounded in the next room and the piano music started again, an odd melody in the key of E-flat. The dissonant chords grew so loud and angry, Teresa wanted to clap her hands over her ears. She tiptoed into the hall and peered into the most magnificent space she had ever seen. A row of floor-to-ceiling windows looked out over the trees in the park below. Oil paintings in ornate frames hung on the walls, which were painted a soft yellow. A red-and-gold carpet covered the floor, and a real piano—a shiny, black, *grand* piano—stood in the middle of the room, its lid propped open. A young man with slick brown hair sat at the keyboard. Miss Connover leaned over him, pointing at the sheet music. "Try that phrase again," Miss Connover said. "Ives wants you to feel what he's seeing."

Who was Ives? The scene was beautiful, elegant—and all wrong. Teresa edged away from the door. She thought of Maeve's laugh, more musical than anything this man was playing. She thought of the dogs, prancing along New York streets as if they owned the world. Finally, she pictured herself, wedged into a tight starched uniform, taking orders from a prissy maid no older than herself, trying to learn opera—while the hurly-burly, gritty life of variety went on without her.

Teresa turned, tripped on the edge of the carpet, and caught herself just in time. Her boots clattered on the stairs. The music came to a sudden halt.

"Teresa?" Miss Connover's clear voice rang out in the stairwell, but Teresa threw open the door. She left it open behind her, dashed past the park, and ran down a long block until she'd left the fancy houses behind. She plunked down on a stone wall to catch her breath.

Papa was right. Opera was for fancy folks. No matter how hard she tried, she'd always be Teresa LeClair, daughter of a vaudeville singer and a catgut scraper. And proud of it.

Teresa glanced at the street sign. Twenty-first Street—more than thirty blocks to Mrs. O'Donnell's. She unwrapped a toffee and let its sweetness soothe her throat. Pietro's words from the other night suddenly echoed in her head: *I didn't take you for a coward.*

"I'm not," Teresa announced to the empty sidewalk. She took a deep breath and began to walk.

29.

When Teresa finally arrived at the boardinghouse, her legs ached from the long walk, but her head felt clear. Dusk was falling, and the house was quiet. This was the hour when performers would be walking up and down on The Beach, or traveling to an amateur night. The lucky ones would be applying their makeup in a dressing room, in a real theater.

The dining room was empty. An envelope was propped up against the sugar bowl. She bent over to look at it. Her name, Pascal's, and Maeve's were scrawled across the envelope in a bold, unfamiliar hand. She tore the letter open and carried it to the window, reading in the fading light.

Miss Cullen, Miss LeClair, and Pascal. Amateur Night, Lafayette Theatre, Thursday at seven. 7th Ave. and 132nd St. Mr. Pantages is coming. Learn any new songs? New juggling tricks? Pietro Jones.

Tomorrow was Thursday. If she won some money, she could send Pascal home. But who was Mr. Pantages?

Teresa folded the note. Pietro was being friendly again. After that awful night when the stage manager drove Pietro out, she assumed they'd never see him again. She rushed upstairs to Maeve's room and knocked. Silence. She hurried to her own room. A note was pinned to the door: *We're trying again. Pascal is safe with me. See you at breakfast. Maeve.*

The tiny room felt lonesome and dark under the eaves. Teresa picked up the sheet music for the "Silvery Moon" song. The song only had one real verse. She hummed the tune and went over the words, singing each line over and over to memorize it.

Amateur night at the Lafayette. Where "Puerto Rico" would "shoot" you if you "died"—could she do it?

Teresa clenched her jaw. She'd said no to Papa and Estey; today, goodbye to opera. If she wanted to make it in vaudeville, it was now or never.

"*By the light . . . of the silvery moon . . .*"

Teresa was waiting in the dining room the next morning when Maeve dragged in, long after everyone else had eaten breakfast. She looked pale and worn. She poured herself a cup of coffee, spooned in three heaping teaspoons of sugar, laced it with cream, and sipped it slowly, propping her chin up with one hand.

"Where's Pascal?" Maeve asked.

"Still sleeping. You came in late."

"A terrible night," Maeve said. "I'm ready to go back to Illinois."

"Not yet." Teresa passed her Pietro's note.

Maeve read it, rubbed her eyes, read it again. "Pietro? Oh, that boy who likes you—"

"He doesn't!" Teresa slopped coffee on the table and blotted it with her napkin.

Maeve rolled her eyes. "Could have fooled me."

"He's much older and he thinks I don't know anything. Besides . . ."

"I know. But you must be careful." Maeve lowered her voice. "Colored men in the South get lynched if they *look* at a white girl. There are crazy places in this country—including my hometown."

"Why? What happened?"

Maeve inched closer. "Five years ago, in Springfield, Illinois, near where I grew up, a white woman claimed she'd been raped by a colored man. She lied—but the city went crazy. People killed innocent Negroes, burned their homes and stores, drove the rest out of town. It was horrible." Maeve picked at her napkin. "After it happened, my father . . ." She cleared her throat. "He didn't say he *approved* of the riots. But there were strange meetings at our house. You know about the Klan?"

"Sort of." Papa had told Teresa about white men in white robes who burned crosses and terrorized and killed colored people— and sometimes even Catholics. That made Papa very nervous, though he hardly ever went to church. "I thought they were only in the South."

"I'm afraid not. A crowd of men came to our house, carrying their robes and pointed hats—and my daddy *knew* them all. I couldn't believe it. I had to leave." Maeve gave Teresa a wan smile. "But I found my dogs, created my act. Now I've met you and Pascal. But yes—you and Pietro should be careful."

Teresa looked away. A car sputtered past a horse and carriage on the street. The horse shied and whinnied. Pedestrians hurried past, some dressed in finery, others in ordinary work clothes. Many faces were white, but some were brown. Everywhere in New York, she heard languages from all over the world. Had she lived in a dream, back in Vermont? She thought of Miss Wilkins and her popular café. Everyone loved her pies and breads—but was Miss Wilkins ever afraid?

"A penny for your thoughts," Maeve said.

"I never knew what it was like for people like Pietro and his father," Teresa said. "We didn't know about those riots."

"You were just a little girl then."

"But my parents must have been onstage with people wearing blackface. They never talked about it."

Maeve shrugged. "It probably seemed normal to them. Just the way things are."

"Pietro hates wearing cork."

"Who can blame him?" Maeve lathered jam on a biscuit and ate it, brushing the crumbs off the tablecloth. When she looked at Teresa this time, her eyes twinkled again. "Pietro has laid down quite a challenge. A Lafayette audience could be tough. And we'd perform for Mr. Pantages!"

"Who is he?"

"Alexander Pantages, born Pericles Pantages in Greece—imagine a name like that! Anyway, he runs the Western Circuit. He must be looking for new talent." Color rose in her cheeks. "Well?" Maeve asked.

"Well what?"

"I'm game if you are."

Teresa buttered a biscuit and nibbled at the edges. "What if we're the only white people in the theater?"

"Then we'll know how Pietro feels at *our* amateur nights."

Teresa hadn't thought about it that way. "Pietro said the Lafayette has a man with a toy gun who 'shoots' the worst acts."

Maeve laughed. "Then we'll collapse onstage and play dead."

Teresa picked at her biscuit. "It could be my last chance. If we don't win anything, I'll have to go home. And I still owe you money."

"You'll pay me back someday." Maeve grabbed Teresa's hand. "You can't leave now. You don't know how good you are. You need to strut a little, show some stage presence."

She pushed her chair back. "Let's line the chairs up." She drew the chairs into two rows, making an aisle beside the table and the sideboard, and pointed to Teresa. "You're in the wings, stage left, about to make your entrance. The audience is out there." Maeve waved toward the windows. "The spotlight tracks you as you come onstage. You're going to slay them."

Maeve tossed her hair back and pranced along the aisle she had made. "You're as regal as the Queen of England. Come on!"

Teresa went to the door, pulled herself up to her full height, and tried to walk on as Maeve had. But her hand knocked against the table, and she tripped on the edge of the carpet, nearly falling down. "I'm too big and clumsy," she cried.

"Nonsense. Most women would kill to be as busty as you are—and many would buy a sheath dress to show it off. Try again."

Teresa caught sight of her face in the mirror over the sideboard. Her cheeks were so scarlet it looked as if her freckles ran together. "How does the Queen of England walk?"

"Like she owns the world. As if she's better than anyone else around."

Teresa went to the door again. This time, she held her head high and snapped her fingers to an imaginary beat, adding a little bounce in her step. When she reached a spot that could be center stage, she planted her feet like a dancer, one foot in front of the other, and nodded toward Maeve. "Music, please."

Maeve laughed. "Excellent! Now do it again. And again."

30.

Teresa, Maeve, and Pascal practiced for the Lafayette all day. While Teresa went over her songs, Pascal and Maeve worked on a new trick. Finally, at Maeve's insistence, they all took naps. "We've got to be rested and ready," she said.

The Lafayette was as elegant as any theater on Broadway, with bright lights blazing on the marquee. Teresa's palms were damp and her throat was scratchy and dry. She watched Maeve dress in a crowded dressing room below the stage while questions swarmed like bees in her mind. Why had Pietro asked them to come? He read newspapers all the time—had he seen Papa's ad? He wouldn't turn her in—would he?

Floorboards rumbled above them as the audience filed in, and stagehands rushed up and down the stairs, carrying props. Teresa snapped her fingers at Edna. "You go on for me, pooch." The dog set her head in Teresa's lap, waiting for an ear rub. Maeve stood with her back to Teresa, putting on her makeup. She wore a tight red skirt and a low-cut blouse. "You look nice. But I can't do this," Teresa said.

"You don't have a choice, doll. The orchestra has your music— you're going on." Maeve opened her lipstick. "My hands are shaking. You trust me to make you up?"

"Do what you want," Teresa said. "They'll hate me."

With their makeup in place, they combed each other's hair. Pascal brushed the dogs. "Ready, Pascal? We're on second," Maeve said.

Pascal nodded. Teresa glanced at her brother. His face was pale and his eyes seemed dull. Guilt twisted in her belly. She gave him a quick, sideways hug. "Just one more night," she said. "You'll be great."

He shrugged her off and lifted his juggler's bag. It rattled and clanked as they started up the stairs.

"Brattleboro meets Harlem."

Teresa recognized Pietro's voice before she turned around. He was dressed in the cutaway suit and white starched shirt he'd worn in Brooklyn. His flower was the only change: a white carnation in his buttonhole. "Nervous?" he asked. Before she could answer, Pietro reached for Pascal's bag. "That's heavy, young man," he said, and hoisted it over his shoulder. "You have new tricks up your sleeve?"

Pascal finally smiled. "Maybe," he said. "Don't look in the bag."

"Wouldn't dream of it," Pietro said. "You're smart not to give your secrets away, even to your friends."

Friends. Teresa flushed, embarrassed that she'd thought badly of Pietro. "Is your father here?"

"Right behind you." Teresa glanced down the stairs. Mr. Jones tipped his top hat to her but didn't smile. He looked as nervous as she felt. They climbed to the stage together. The wings were full of performers, some in fancy dress, others wearing acrobats' costumes. Except for a blonde woman in a ball gown, every other face was brown or black. She and Maeve and Pascal pulled the dogs into the wings on stage left. Edna licked Teresa's hand. "Thanks, girl," Teresa whispered. "That helps."

"When do you go on?" Maeve asked Mr. Jones.

Pietro held up seven fingers.

"How did you get your lucky number again?" Teresa asked.

Pietro shrugged. "Someone wants us to win." He danced a lazy soft-shoe pattern in the wings.

"Curtain in five," a man called from behind the scrim.

They waited in the shadows. Pietro adjusted his tie, smoothed his hair, replaced his hat, fiddled with his carnation. Knowing that Pietro was nervous only made Teresa feel worse. She peeked around the curtain. The theater was enormous, with tier upon tier of seats. The audience was the most elegant of any she'd seen, with only a few white faces. The women wore ruffled dresses of silk or organza, more elegant than any party gown Nonnie had made. If only Nonnie could see this finery! A few even sported fur coats on this warm night. The men paraded down the aisle in stylish suits, carrying canes with carved handles. "Everyone looks so dressed up," Teresa whispered.

Pietro nodded. "High tone. You watch out for that Foster tune—might be a problem here."

"Why?"

Pietro shook his head. "For someone so smart, you don't know much. In his other songs, Foster celebrated slave life. You think we like that stuff? 'Massa's in de cold cold ground'—'My old Kentucky home'—worked by *slaves*?" he said, nearly spitting the word "slaves."

Teresa's eyes burned. "Those words aren't in my song," she said. Pietro was the most confusing person she'd ever met. He called her smart but criticized her in the same breath. Some *friend*!

"Pietro, watch your mouth," Mr. Jones said. "Don't spoil Miss LeClair's act—pay attention to your own. We don't want to end up on the Death Trail."

"Where's that?" Pascal asked. His voice trembled.

Pietro tightened Pascal's scarf. "Up north in Canada, where it's so cold you freeze your nose off."

"I'm going home," Pascal said.

Pietro glanced at Teresa. "That so?"

Teresa didn't answer. Her stomach was playing tricks on her. She swallowed hard, determined not to throw up.

"Curtain in two!" the voice called. And then: "Places, first act!"

With a roll of the snare drum, amateur night at the Lafayette began.

31.

As Pietro predicted, the audience was hard to please. They hated the first dumb act. They shouted, threw things, and stomped their feet, until Puerto Rico, the man with the toy gun, "shot" the acrobats. They crept offstage to boos and catcalls.

Maeve was next. Her face was pale against her dark hair, her lips tight with fear as the announcer called their names. "Please welcome Madame Maeve, her Marvelous Marching Dogs, and a surprise guest!" he cried.

Pascal clung to Teresa's waist. "I can't do it."

"Too late now." Maeve put on a shiny smile as if it were a piece of clothing, and Teresa gave Pascal a tiny shove. "Break a leg."

At Maeve's command, the dogs reared up on their hind legs and trotted out from the wings. The audience roared with delight, and the applause continued right through their act. The dogs hopped up and down off their little stands, lined up in a row of five so that Alix could trot across their backs, and jumped through Maeve's hoops.

Pascal juggled with kitchen knives as the dogs trotted in circles around him. Had he stolen the knives from the boardinghouse? The cutlery spun and glittered above Pascal's head, just missing his eyes and bitten fingernails. He looked small and vulnerable, with his hair falling into his eyes, but the audience loved him. At the end of Maeve's act, the prop man appeared with a burning hoop and the dogs jumped through, one at a time, making a small pyramid with the biggest dogs on the bottom and tiny Dixie on top. Cheers erupted around the theater and coins rained onstage. Pascal zigzagged across the stage gathering pennies, but dropped them quickly, his face twisted in pain. "They're hot!" he cried.

The audience roared with laughter. A stagehand grabbed the flaming hoop and Maeve peeled off her gloves, handed them to Pascal, and strutted onto the apron, arms held high, her red skirt shimmering in the gaslight. She signaled to the dogs. They lined up and raised their rumps in the air, tails wagging, to take their own bows. More coins clattered onto the stage. Pascal pulled on a glove and dashed to and fro, picking up pennies, until the stage manager signaled them off.

They ran into the wings, the dogs milling about. "They loved you!" Teresa cried. She hugged Pascal. "What's wrong with the pennies?"

"They're burning hot!" he said.

"They heat the coins with matches—that means they love us." Maeve was gasping for breath.

The next few acts came and went. Teresa barely noticed. Her insides were jelly. When Pietro and Mr. Jones went on, she forgot to send them off with the French swear word, and the roar of applause, when they came offstage, only made her more nervous. When it was her turn, her teeth chattered, though she was drenched with sweat after standing in the stuffy wings. "Help," she whispered to Maeve.

"Queen of England," Maeve said.

The announcer called Teresa's name. He even pronounced it correctly. Maeve gave her a little shove. "Breathe."

She took some deep breaths. In her head, she heard Nonnie telling her to sing like an angel. All right, Nonnie, she told herself. This one's for you.

The audience settled down. Teresa took a step forward, then hesitated. "Hsst." She looked across the stage. Pascal, Pietro, and Mr. Jones were signaling to her from the wings, urging her on. She strode out, swinging her arms as if she had all the time in the world. What if her voice squeaked?

She took another breath while the band played the first few bars, and launched into "Silvery Moon." She dipped and swayed from side to side along with the beat, tapping her toes. The crowd didn't cheer, as they had for Maeve and then for the Joneses, but they were polite. She went straight into "Hard Times," giving it a bit of bounce. When she reached the first chorus, Pietro's tenor floated from stage left, adding harmony.

Was he crazy? Teresa rolled her eyes and shrugged her shoulders, as if to say: *He's impossible—what can I do?*—and kept on singing. She twirled her hand to speed up the tempo, and the band followed along. A solo banjo accompanied her on the next verse. Instead of bemoaning her fate, Teresa sang as if she dared the hard times to come back. "*Many days you have lingered around my cabin door—oh! Hard times, come again no more!*" She belted the last chorus to the last row in the balcony, and raised her hands in triumph, as if she'd beaten those hard times to the ground.

A hush fell over the audience; silence hummed in her ears for a few long, terrifying seconds. Then the applause began. Teresa bowed, ran offstage, and returned for a curtain call. She glanced toward the wings, to see if Pietro would join her, but he had disappeared.

"You were wonderful!" Maeve wrapped her in a tight hug. "When did you and Pietro practice?"

"We didn't." Teresa leaned over, trying to catch her breath. "It was just like that other time, in Brooklyn. I guess he helps."

32.

The next act—colored twin sisters with a song and dance routine—hurried onstage to perform a ragtime number. Teresa, Pascal, and Maeve took the dogs downstairs to wait for the final curtain call. Pietro was perched on a tall stool in the corner, reading that book he carried around. Mr. Jones leaned against the wall nearby, flipping through a newspaper.

Teresa stopped in front of Pietro. "Thanks for singing with me," she said.

Pietro looked up. "Who, me? I'd never do that. You must be hearing things."

Was that the hint of a smile? "What are you reading?" she asked.

He slipped a finger between the pages to mark his place. "*The Souls of Black Folk.* I was looking at the last chapter, where Du Bois writes about the 'Sorrow Songs.' *Those* are the songs we need to hear."

Mr. Jones lowered the newspaper. "Son, be gentle. She's not the one to sing those tunes. And isn't 'Hard Times' sorrowful enough? You're much too cocky." He gave Teresa a nod. "Pay him no mind. That song suits you."

Teresa thanked him and hurried down the hall to the dressing room, where Maeve and Pascal were resting with the dogs. Pietro had told her not to sing a Foster song—but then he'd joined in. He'd called her ignorant—but he'd just made her act a success. He talked about this writer named "Do—boyss" as if she should know who he was. She didn't understand Pietro at all.

Seven acts to go. Pascal fell asleep wrapped in Teresa's cloak, his head on Edna's scratchy fur. Teresa rested her arms on the vanity and tried to sleep, but the floor above them shook with stomps, bumps, scrapes, and shuffles, and the audience countered with its own rough music of jeers or applause. Finally, the stage manager called, from the top of the stairs, "Places, everyone!"

Teresa slipped into the end of the line and waited while shoes traipsed above her on the stairs: dance shoes, spats, floppy clown shoes, spiked heels. Her own Sunday choir shoes were shabby in comparison. Why had she entered this contest, anyway? She'd never win.

As they filed out through the wings, Maeve nudged her. "Strut onstage, remind them who you are." She clucked to the dogs. They pricked their ears and raised their tails into *C* shapes. The acrobat ahead of them entered with a backward flip, bouncing on his hands and landing on tiptoe, his arms in the air. Teresa followed Maeve and Pascal onstage, but the most she could manage was a small wave.

The audience gave her a nice hand and they also had hearty cheers for Maeve and Pascal, as well as for the Joneses. But they saved their loudest roar for the comedian who had closed the night. Even the orchestra had laughed at his jokes—"a really good sign," Maeve had told Teresa. He took the five-dollar bill from the stage manager, kissed it with a loud smack, and bowed low. The curtain swung closed for the last time.

Five dollars. With that five-dollar bill, Teresa could have sent Pascal home. What would they do now?

The performers hurried away in pairs or alone. Teresa and Pascal huddled with the dogs on the empty stage while Maeve talked to a man in an usher's uniform. She ran over and tickled Pascal under the chin. "An usher says there's a message for me in the lobby—hold the dogs, will you? And don't look so blue. You were both terrific. Just think: Puerto Rico didn't shoot us!" She parted the curtain, giving them a quick glimpse of the theater as she headed for the lobby. The seats were nearly empty and ushers were cleaning up.

Pascal and Teresa untangled the leashes and hooked them onto the dogs' collars. Pascal leaned against Teresa. "We didn't win anything. How will I get to Vermont?"

"We'll figure something out. We have lots of coins—we can count them when we get home."

"Mrs. O'Donnell's boardinghouse isn't *home*."

"You're right." The stage felt vast and lonesome with everyone gone and Teresa was relieved when Maeve reappeared, her cheeks as scarlet as her blouse.

"Resa! Pascal! Mr. Pantages wants to see me! He's talking to Mr. Jones and Pietro now—and Resa, he wants to speak to you, too." The dogs leapt up and nipped the hem of Maeve's skirt, their tails wagging like tiny whips. Teresa's heart thumped as she followed her up through the curtain and up the aisle to the lobby. Was this her lucky break?

The lobby was full of people talking, laughing, and pushing through the doors. Maeve led them to Mr. Pantages. A white man with narrow eyebrows and oiled hair, he was talking to Mr. Jones and Pietro in the corner. He consulted a small notebook and glanced at Maeve as they approached. "Our animal act on the Western Tour has an injured horse. Miss Cullen, you and the dogs would do nicely in their place. I've told Jones and his son that we can also use a dance routine." He peered over his glasses at Pascal. "You've got talent, son—but the Gerry Society will shut me down if I put you onstage. Come see me in a few years."

Pascal nodded and plopped down on the floor, sitting cross-legged. His face was blank. "Stand up," Teresa whispered, grabbing his arm, but Pascal wrapped his arms around Dixie.

"The boy needs his mother," Mr. Pantages said, narrowing his eyes at Teresa.

As if she didn't know! Teresa listened as Mr. Pantages turned to Mr. Jones. "You and Miss Cullen will join the tour in Denver. Come into the office tomorrow and we'll go over the route. Of course—western towns expect blackface."

Pietro scowled, but Mr. Jones nudged him and said, "Yes, sir."

Teresa couldn't hear Pietro's response. Her pulse swooshed in her ears as Mr. Pantages approached her. "You're a bit green, but you've got a strong voice. No openings for singers on that western tour, but I do need song pluggers here in town. Come by tomorrow and I'll get your information." Teresa's eyes burned, but she wouldn't cry. A song plugger in New York was a step up from plugging songs in Brattleboro—but how could she manage on her own?

Mr. Pantages handed out business cards. Pietro and his father took one and headed for the door, greeting people with smiles, waves, and tips of their hats. They slipped outside without saying goodbye. So much for being friends.

"Watch yourself," Mr. Pantages told Teresa as he gave her his card. "You're lucky this is a friendly audience. You'll be in serious trouble if you sing with that boy again, unless he's in blackface."

"Yes, sir." She'd never asked Pietro to sing with her—so why was it her fault? Teresa didn't dare protest. Mr. Pantages put on a bowler hat and left the theater. A crowd of eager performers trailed after him, like children after the Pied Piper.

"Teresa, do you know what this means?" Maeve clapped her hands, startling her. Dixie and Edna barked and yipped. "No more amateur nights. No more scrambling for money to pay the rent. Four shows a day on the road. My own route at last." She hugged Teresa, then Pascal, and handed out biscuits to the dogs. Fido and Bronwyn balanced on their hind legs, their tongues wagging, and the few people left in the lobby clapped and laughed.

Teresa tried to smile. She should be happy for her friend. But who would keep her company now? Who would encourage her, push her onstage when her heart was quailing? As if she knew that Teresa was upset, Edna trotted over and leaned against Teresa's leg. Her warmth was a comfort—but even Edna would be gone soon.

Maeve slapped herself on the cheek. "What a fool I am! To boast like this—when you won't be with me. You're like my sister now. What will I do without you?"

Pascal was petting Dixie, his face buried in her fur. "That's okay. I want to go home." Tears streaked his wan face. "Don't you miss Mama and Papa, Resa? What about Nonnie?"

Did he have to bring up Nonnie? Teresa couldn't speak.

Maeve ruffled Pascal's hair and pulled him to his feet. "We'll get you home soon, though my act won't be the same without you. Leash the dogs, will you?" They gathered dogs and props and headed for the stage door. Maeve gave Teresa a sad look before they went outside. "You look like you just lost your best friend."

"Maybe I did."

"Don't be silly. We never say goodbye in vaude. Just *arrivederci*, because we always meet again." She kissed Teresa on the cheek and hoisted her prop bag. "Song plugging is a good way to get started. They might even give you a car of your own, so you can zip from one theater to the next."

"I don't know how to drive," Teresa said.

"So—you'll learn! I can see you now, touring around town in your Tin Lizzie." Maeve put two hands on an imaginary steering wheel, squealed, and leaned to one side, as if taking a corner too fast. The dogs yipped and tugged at their leashes. Teresa knelt beside Edna and buried her face in the dog's fur. "I might have to steal you," she whispered.

Although it was late, the sidewalk outside the Lafayette teemed with people. Maeve raised her voice above the hubbub. "You've been here a week and you haven't seen the Great White Way. That means you haven't lived. Follow me."

An hour later they stood at the corner of Broadway and Forty-second Street. Teresa felt breathless. Had someone plucked the Milky Way from the sky and draped it over Manhattan? Lights winked, shimmered, and beamed in all directions. Strings of electric lights spelled words; poured champagne into a glass as tall as a building; flashed the names of stars on theater marquees.

"Look at the kitty!" Pascal cried. A giant white kitten, electrified from the tip of its nose to the end of its tail, played with a silken ball of yarn. Nearby, the figure of a white woman, outlined in lights, danced with open arms above the crowded street. Although it was after midnight, crowds streamed past: men sporting bowlers and walking sticks, women in wide-brimmed hats so laden with feathers, it seemed as if the women might topple under their weight.

When Maeve said it was time to go, Teresa lagged behind with Edna and Cleo, humming Mama's favorite waltz tune. *"East side, West side . . . we'll trip the light fantastic on the sidewalks of New York."*

More like the *life* fantastic. Teresa finally smiled.

33.

They straggled up the sidewalk in the early hours of the morning, surprised to see the boardinghouse windows ablaze with light. Pascal was almost sleepwalking as Maeve and Teresa helped him up the steps. Maeve pulled out her key, but the door was unlocked. "How strange."

Teresa followed her inside—and nearly fell over. Mrs. O'Donnell stood in the entry in her dressing gown, her hair under a nightcap. "About time," she said. "Someone's waiting for you."

Edna growled low in her throat. Teresa looked past their landlady. Had someone died? She gasped. A florid-faced policeman stood in the corner, his arms crossed—

Next to Papa.

Pascal screamed. "Papa!" He threw himself into Papa's arms, sobbing.

"There, there, Pascal. *Reste tranquille.* Easy. Are you all right, *mon petit?*" Papa stooped to touch Pascal all over, like a father checking a newborn baby. He spoke to Pascal in French, his voice too soft and soothing for Teresa to hear his words, then set Pascal on the couch. At last, he turned to Teresa. "What can you say for yourself?"

Teresa's voice had flown. She was in one of those nightmares where you freeze in place, unable to speak or run. Papa made no move to touch her, to hug her—nothing. "Hello, Papa," she managed to squeak out at last.

Maeve came up with a pale smile. "We didn't mean to be so late." She put out her hand to Papa. "I'm Maeve Cullen," she said. Papa ignored her, and Maeve's face went scarlet as her hand fell to her side.

Teresa was blinded by tears. Everything was ruined. She started for the stairs, but the policeman—who had been still as a statue—was suddenly at her side. He set a heavy hand on her shoulder. "Not so fast, young lady. We need information about the men who kidnapped you."

"Kidnapped?" Teresa's heart raced. What had Papa said, in his ad? *Last seen . . . in company of two dark-complexioned men . . .*

Pascal leapt to his feet. "Pietro and Mr. Jones didn't do anything!" he cried.

"Hush, Pascal." Teresa remembered Pietro's warnings and the stories Maeve had told her. She faced the policeman. "I came to New York on my own. It's my fault. I paid my own way. Pascal followed me, but Papa is right: I should have told him we were safe." No matter what Papa said or did now, she would never admit that she'd stolen Mama's egg money—or that Mama had told her it would be hers . . . someday. "Mr. Jones is kind. He told me to send you a telegram, but I didn't listen. So if you need to arrest anyone—arrest me."

She pushed up her sleeves and held out her hands for the cuffs. The policeman glanced at Papa. "Sir?"

"Resa, don't be a fool."

Maeve cleared her throat. "Excuse me, Mr. LeClair. I'm at fault, too. I should have insisted they get in touch with you. But Pascal is talented—he added so much to my act. Maybe we can show you in the morning?" Maeve gave Papa her prettiest smile, but he didn't melt.

"We will be on our way before dawn." Papa pulled Pascal close. "This is a family matter."

Maeve turned to the policeman. "Teresa and Pascal are right, officer. The men you're accusing had nothing to do with any of this."

Papa grunted. "Officer, I'm sorry we wasted your time. I'll take care of them now."

"You have a telephone in Vermont?" the policeman asked. When Papa nodded, he handed him a card. "Anything makes you uneasy, call this number." No one spoke as he left the room.

Mrs. O'Donnell stood in the doorway, scowling. "I expect all of you out of here in the morning." She turned to Maeve. "That includes you. One of your mutts howled last night until I thought I'd lose my mind. I've had enough of you and your riffraff."

"They're not *mutts*," Pascal said. "They're terriers."

"It's all right." Maeve hugged Pascal and squeezed Teresa's hand. "Come see me later," she whispered, and hurried her dogs upstairs. Pascal curled up on the sofa and fell asleep, as if life were back to normal.

Teresa's knees suddenly felt wobbly. She leaned against the wall.

"Well?" Papa said. "Your mother has been crazy with worry. Nonnie paces up and down with her cane. I'm here in New York missing work; who knows what Estey will do to me. You owe me an apology. And you need to thank Mrs. O'Donnell. She saw my ad and was kind enough to call me."

"I'm sure she appreciated your reward," Teresa said.

Papa scowled. "I see New York has taught you more insolence."

"*You* told me New York is the best place in the world."

Papa scolded her in French and turned to Mrs. O'Donnell. "I apologize on my daughter's behalf."

Mrs. O'Donnell shook her head in disbelief. "Good riddance to you all," she said, and left the room, her mules slapping.

Teresa stared at Papa. Something swirled inside her, like an eddy in the Whetstone Brook that surged forward, then back, in a storm. If only she could be like Pascal, throw herself into Papa's arms, feel his rough beard against her forehead. Though Papa didn't speak, his eyes were sorrowful.

But she couldn't go to him. Something else called her. It wasn't music she heard, but that moment of deep stillness that fell over the Lafayette, when the final notes of "Hard Times" floated to the rafters. In that single instant, before the crowd began to clap, she had captured an audience. She wanted to hear that silence again, to feel it in her bones. If she went home with Papa, she'd be trapped in the eerie quiet of the tuning rooms forever.

She sank into a hard chair as far from Papa as possible. "I *am* sorry," she said. "I hope you won't lose your job. And I'm sorry we worried you and Mama."

"You will tell that to your *maman*, and to Nonnie," Papa said. "For now, we should sleep. We leave in a few hours."

Teresa followed Papa and Pascal up the stairs to their garret under the eaves. Papa bumped his head on the ceiling and swore. "How much are you paying for this dump?" Teresa didn't answer. Papa unbuttoned his coat and sat on the edge of the bed. The bedsprings groaned as he pulled off his boots. "I'll sleep on the floor."

Teresa stowed her few things in her valise, careful to wrap her blouse around Nonnie's picture. "What are you doing?" Papa asked.

"Packing," she said. "You said we were leaving soon."

Teresa bent to help Pascal with his boots. His face was pale and pinched in the wavering light. She pulled him close, breathing in his sour little-boy smell. "Be good," she whispered.

Pascal threw his wiry arms around her and hugged her so tight she caught her breath. "All that juggling has made you strong." Teresa kissed the top of his head. "Night night." She took off her shoes and climbed onto the bed, fully dressed, her head at Pascal's feet as usual.

"'Night, Resa," Pascal whispered.

Papa spread his coat on the floor and lay on his back. In a few minutes, he was snoring. Teresa waited until Pascal's steady breathing told her he was asleep, too, before she slipped out of bed. She picked up her shoes and stood over Papa a moment. She longed to give him a hug, to ask for his blessing, but he'd never let her go. Instead, she blew him a kiss. "*Á bientôt*, Papa," she whispered.

See him soon? She hoped not.

Teresa tapped on Maeve's door, expecting to find her friend asleep, but Maeve pulled Teresa into chaos. A valise sat open on the bed, its contents spilling onto the rumpled blankets. The dogs' leashes, costumes, and plumes littered the floor. Maeve herself was dressed for travel, and the dogs were lined up by the window. They wagged their tails when they saw Teresa. Edna whimpered.

"Good dogs," Maeve said softly. "Lie down."

They did, all except for Edna, who hurried over to Teresa, waiting for a head scratch.

"Sorry for the mess," Maeve said. "I didn't expect to leave so soon."

"It's my fault."

"Nonsense. Pantages wants us to head west tomorrow anyway." She pushed her clothes aside to make space on the bed. They sat cross-legged, skirts up, knees touching, whispering. "You're not going home, are you?" Maeve asked.

Teresa shook her head. "How did you know?"

"You've caught the bug. I can tell. Even if you got on that train, you wouldn't last long in that factory—what did you call it?"

"The Estey Organ Works."

"Exactly. You don't want to make organs so *other* people can sing. You need to sing yourself."

"Yes—but how?"

"We'll think of something."

"Papa had the bug," Teresa said. "So did Mama. They gave it up."

Maeve took her hand. "There's something you haven't thought of."

"What?"

"Maybe they lacked talent. Maybe they knew that they'd always be second string."

"That's what Papa says. And Mr. Pantages didn't pick me."

"Not yet. You're still young and green. There's always tomorrow." Maeve glanced at her pocket watch. "I mean—today. Right now, we need a plan."

Edna whimpered and leapt up beside them on the bed. She curled up and set her head in Teresa's lap. Maeve laughed. "Even fussy Edna has taken to you. Tell me what you're thinking."

"We have to leave before Papa wakes up," Teresa said.

"Of course. Help me pack. The world awaits us."

THE CURTAIN FALLS. END OF ACT TWO.

ENTR'ACTE 3

Setting: *The attic room of a Vermont boardinghouse, late at night. The room holds a single bed with a brass bedstead, a chest of drawers, and a coat stand. The staircase from the floor below opens into the center of the room. Moonlight pours through a single round window under the peak of the roof, lighting the wide chestnut floorboards. A dormer window is open to the cool night air, and a barred owl hoots in the distance: "Who cooks for you? Who cooks for you-awll?" It is the spring of 1911.*

CHARACTERS:
TERESA (RESA) LECLAIR: age thirteen.
ALICE LECLAIR: Teresa's mother.
As the scene opens, TERESA sits up in bed, dressed in a nightgown. She stares at the round window in horror. Her bright orange curls fan out from her face like flames.

TERESA: Mama! Mama! Don't go!

Sounds of a door opening and quick footsteps on the stairs. ALICE appears, dressed in her nightclothes. She hurries to her daughter and wraps her arms around her.

ALICE: There, there, child. It was only a dream.

TERESA: (*Turns to ALICE but still seems imprisoned by the dream.*) Don't leave, Mama! Don't leave me!

ALICE: (*Runs her fingers through Teresa's hair in a vain attempt to smooth out the tangles.*) Don't worry, my sweet. I'm not going anywhere.

TERESA: But you *did*. In my dream, you were leaving, like when you ran away with Papa.

ALICE: (*Strokes her forehead.*) I'm right here, Resa.

TERESA: (*Leans against her mother. She shifts from the world of the nightmare to the reality of her attic room.*) Your canary died when you left. Right?

ALICE: How strange that you think of that. Poor Lebo. My father found him when he uncovered his cage, the morning after I left.

TERESA: Why didn't you take him with you?

ALICE: How could I bring a canary in a cage? He would have died on the road. (*Pause.*) My mama, your Grandma June, said Lebo died of a broken heart.

TERESA: Did he?

ALICE: Who knows. Maybe he was just old. (*Pulls the covers up to Teresa's chin.*) Do you feel better? We should sleep now.

TERESA: (*Murmurs.*) Did Lebo sing for you?

ALICE: He was a funny canary. He wouldn't sing in his cage. But if we let him out, he would perch on a lamp, or on my shoulder, and sing like an opera star. I guess he was like that song about the rich lady in the gilded cage. (*Sings.*) *She's only a bird in a gilded cage/ a beautiful sight to see. / You may think she's happy and free from care; / She's not, though she seems to be . . .*

TERESA: Sing more!

ALICE: I don't remember the words. Time to sleep now. (*She stands up to leave.*)

TERESA: Mama, wait. Why did Grandma June hate Papa?

ALICE: (*Frowns.*) Is that what Papa says?

TERESA: Yes.

ALICE: My mother didn't approve of your papa because he was Québécois and Catholic. Silly reasons. And because . . . (*She stands and tightens the belt on her dressing gown.*) I think she knew he might steal me away.

TERESA: Are you glad you ran away with Papa?

ALICE: Of course! I'm happy we got married. How else would I have you and Pascal? I wish we hadn't eloped, but we knew my parents would never let me go. They said vaudeville was cheap entertainment. (*Her gaze drifts, as if she's back in the past.*) Grandma June called women in variety "hussies."

TERESA: What's a hussy?

ALICE: Enough talk, my sweet. (*She kisses Teresa.*)

TERESA: Did Papa like Lebo?

ALICE: He did. But he wasn't surprised that Lebo died.

TERESA: (*Snuggles under the covers.*) Why?

ALICE: (*Stands at the top of the stairs, her hand on the banister, listening. The barred owl hoots in the distance and ALICE shivers.*) "Let the bird go," your papa said. "A bird only sings when it's free."

Fade to black.

ACT THREE

THE WESTERN
CIRCUIT

NEW YORK TO DENVER AND LEADVILLE, COLORADO
JUNE 1913

34.

At four in the morning, Teresa, Maeve, and the dogs huddled in the corner of an all-night café, their luggage at their feet. They sat at the counter, hands wrapped around mugs of coffee. "It was nice of that milkman to bring us here," Teresa said.

"And he didn't ask any questions. I'm going to miss your brother," Maeve said. "He added so much to my act."

"Too bad I don't have his talents." Teresa couldn't think about Pascal. Or Mama or Nonnie, for that matter. She sipped her coffee. It was as bitter as her thoughts. "When Papa sees I'm gone, he'll probably take Pascal home and come looking for me again—or send the policeman after me."

"At least you have a family who cares enough to find you," Maeve said.

"What do you mean?"

"I'm one of nine children, smack dab in the middle. My mother only spoke to me when she wanted something, like a baby's diaper changed or a nose wiped. My father was like yours—he said vaude was only one step up from girly shows. And he was furious when I started teaching Edna tricks—he planned to use her as a cow dog. But she's too smart for that, aren't you girl?"

Edna hopped over Dixie and set her head on Teresa's lap, where she gave Teresa a soulful look. They both laughed. "She's adopted you," Maeve said. "She ignores me completely now that you're here. We have to find a place for you on the Western Circuit—otherwise, Edna will be heartbroken."

"So will I," Teresa said.

The door to the office building opened at nine on the dot. As the elevator doors slid closed, Maeve said, "Take the plugger's job if he offers it to you. You'll make enough to live on, and you can keep going to amateur nights. That way, you'll be in his system when he needs a singer for an act."

How could she stay in New York alone? Before she could ask, the receptionist called Maeve's name and Teresa waited with the dogs. She tried to doze, but the chair was uncomfortable and the people passing by were noisy: boasting about routes; complaining about their agents, bookings, and bad pay; cooing over the dogs. Teresa picked up a photograph album from the table. Magicians, acrobats, dancers, singers, strong men, and comics smiled up at her from the publicity photos. Most were white, but a few were colored men in blackface. All were members of the Western Circuit. Would Maeve, Pietro, and Mr. Jones have their pictures in here? Even Maeve's dogs would have their own page before she did.

Eva Tanguay lounged on the next page. The actress lay on a thick carpet, her arms stretched over her head, her long hair flowing over the rug. If only the photographs were in color. What color was Tanguay's hair? Or the beaded cups that covered her breasts? Her pale, bare belly gleamed against dark, silky pants pulled tight at the cuffs. Teresa remembered a sign she'd seen backstage at an amateur night, which said, in huge, hand-printed letters, "VULGARITY, SUGGESTIVENESS, AND CUSS WORDS MUST GO!" Eva Tanguay must not have read that sign. In fact, the caption under Tanguay's photograph called her the "I Don't Care Girl."

Teresa had closed the album and was trying to get comfortable when two girls burst from an office door, followed by a third girl on crutches, who wore a cast below her knee. All three girls looked alike, with yellow curls, blue eyes, and matching shirtwaist dresses. Were they sisters?

"What will we do now?" one girl wailed.

The other girl—taller than the first—turned on the girl with crutches. "It's all your fault, Lydia. If you hadn't been showing off for that boy, we'd be headed west tonight."

Teresa sat up. Even Edna pricked up her ears.

"I wasn't showing off!" said the girl on crutches. "It's not my fault the stage had such a narrow apron. I'm lucky I didn't break my neck. Anyway, Mr. Pantages is wrong. I broke my *ankle*, not my voice. I could still sing with you, if he'd let me."

"You've ruined it for us," the taller girl said.

"Sorry." Lydia hobbled toward the elevator. "You'll be fine without me."

"But we're called the Singing Toronto *Triplets*!" the shorter girl cried.

"So now you're twins. Just think about me—going back to Great-Aunt Adelaid and her bland vegetarian cooking." The elevator doors opened, the girl hobbled in, and the elevator swept her away.

"How do you like that?" The taller girl crossed her arms and tapped her foot. She glanced at Teresa and frowned. "What are you staring at?" she said.

"Excuse me," Teresa said. "I was just—"

"Oh, look! Are these your dogs?" The shorter girl knelt down next to Bronwyn and scratched her under the chin. Bronwyn stretched out her neck and grunted happily. "They're so cute. Look, Julie—they all look alike—except for one."

The girl patting Bronwyn seemed younger than the other girl—and she wasn't as pretty, except for her cornflower-blue eyes.

Teresa stood up and faced the girl called Julie, who seemed to be the boss. "Excuse me. I overheard you talking. Mr. Pantages has invited me to be a song plugger, but I'd rather go west. If I joined your trio, you could keep singing."

Julie squinted down at her. "Is that so? You think you could step into Lydia's place just like that? You don't exactly look like us. Besides—we're not an *animal* act."

"Neither am I." Teresa struggled to keep her temper. "The dogs belong to my friend. And you're not triplets, are you?"

"Of course not. We just happen to look like sisters. Mr. Pantages prefers it that way—and our voices blend nicely."

"Twins and triplets don't always look alike." Teresa waved at the dogs. "Edna's different, but no one minds. Do they, Edna?" She snapped her fingers and made a whirling motion with her hand that she'd seen Maeve use. Edna leapt up, stood on her hind legs, and crossed the lobby with her tongue out. When a few people clapped, Edna dropped to all fours, wagged her tail, and snuffed at Teresa's pocket. "No treats today." Teresa turned back to the girls. "What do you sing?"

The younger girl put her arms around Edna, letting the dog lick her face. "Lots of songs. Why not let her try, Jules? We're all washed up without Lydia to sing lead. Besides, Mr. Pantages said his posters advertise the 'Singing Toronto Triplets.'" She smiled at Teresa. "She's Julie and I'm Catherine. Most people call me Cat— but don't tell the dogs," she said, with a wink.

"I'm Teresa LeClair." They shook hands. "Let's try a song, just for fun," Teresa said, although Julie didn't look like she did anything for the fun of it. Teresa pointed to the end of the hall beyond the elevators. "It's quiet over there."

"Pantages said he'd look for someone else," Julie said.

Cat ignored her and followed Teresa to the window. Julie lagged behind and leaned against the wall, her arms crossed.

"Can you sing 'After the Ball'?" Cat asked.

"Do you have to sing that one?" Julie asked, but Cat ignored her.

"I know the tune," Teresa said, although she wasn't sure about the words.

Cat clapped a hand to her mouth. "Lydia has the pitch pipe— we let her go off with it."

"What key do you sing in?" Teresa asked.

"G," said Cat. "But—"

Teresa closed her eyes, heard the note, and sang the three notes of a G chord.

Cat stared. "How do you do that?"

Teresa shrugged. She was putting on an act, but wasn't that what vaude was all about? "Let's try the chorus first," Teresa said. Maybe she would remember the words to the verses that way. She launched into the tune. Cat joined in, while Julie stared out the window, as if she weren't interested. *After the ball is over, after the break of morn . . ."*

Cat and Teresa were out of sync when they started, but their voices began to merge halfway through the first verse. Cat's alto was warm and rich, although she didn't have much power. "I've forgotten the words to the next verse," Teresa said.

Julie rolled her eyes but finally chimed in from her place against the wall. Her voice was breathy and a little sharp. Teresa didn't dare correct her. They sang the chorus together, and a soft-shoe beat sounded from the other side of the waiting area.

"Many a heart is aching," they sang. *"If you could read them all . . ."*

The click and sandpaper slide of tap shoes kept time to the waltz. Pietro? Teresa didn't dare turn around. The rhythm added bounce and caused Cat to shuffle into a few dance steps herself. Teresa swayed and snapped her fingers. Julie's smile seemed pasted on, but she kept singing.

A small crowd gathered, the dogs sat up, and the receptionist clapped in time. A man stepped off the elevator, and when the operator heard them singing, he held the doors open and sang along himself. Maeve appeared during the last verse, with Mr. Pantages right behind her. Cat beckoned desperately to Julie, who finally sidled over, as if they'd been singing together all along. Mr. Pantages squinted at them over his glasses and waved them on. "Keep going," he said.

They sang the final chorus again, and their audience broke into applause. Out of the corner of her eye, Teresa saw Pietro and Mr. Jones duck into the elevator as Mr. Pantages strode over. He looked them up and down, as if they were cattle at an auction. He peered at Teresa. "Haven't I seen you before?"

So he'd already forgotten her. "I was at the Lafayette, last night. You told me to come in today." Teresa pulled his card from her pocket.

"Right, right. The carrot-top girl with the strong voice. What was it you sang?"

Carrot-top? Teresa forced a smile. "'Hard Times.'"

"Ah, yes. Your delivery needs work, but you had nerve, trying out in Harlem. I'll give you that."

No need to tell him she'd nearly vomited before going onstage. "Julie and Cat need a singer," Teresa said. "If I joined them, they'd be triplets again."

Mr. Pantages glanced around the lobby, where the waiting performers were growing impatient, and ran his hand over his hair. "It would save me finding another singing group. What do you girls think?"

"It's fine!" Cat said quickly. "Isn't it, Jules?"

Julie's eyes were cold. "I guess. But only until Lydia comes back."

"Of course," Cat said, and Teresa echoed, "Of course."

"You have some rehearsing to do, Miss—" Mr. Pantages tugged on his mustache.

"LeClair."

"Right. These girls are experienced—and you're still green." He glanced from Teresa to the other girls. "You don't exactly look like triplets."

Teresa blushed. Bad enough that her hair was the color of fall pumpkins. Julie and Cat were thin-hipped, with nearly flat chests, and Julie was extraordinarily pretty.

As far as Teresa could see, neither girl had a single freckle.

Maeve spoke up. "If I might interrupt—they could dress alike, and wear the same cloth hats. I'll help Teresa sew a new costume."

Mr. Pantages squinted at Teresa. "How old are you?"

Teresa didn't miss a beat. "Sixteen." Julie rolled her eyes, but Teresa held Mr. Pantage's gaze. In her mind, she heard Nonnie say, *Mind your manners.* She crossed her toes, inside her shoes, for good luck. "I'd be honored to join your tour," she said.

"All right. Check in the office for your schedule," he said. "Be sure to have your picture taken before you leave. You all need to hurry to meet up with the rest of the troupe—so we're sending you on the 20th Century Limited."

"On that fast, fancy train? Hurrah!" Maeve clapped. Edna answered with a howl, Dixie yipped, and the other dogs burst into a chorus of barking.

"Just because it's fast doesn't mean you have luxury seats, and you'll need to pick up passes for your menagerie. Now get those animals out of here," Mr. Pantages demanded. "I didn't come all the way from Greece to run a circus!" He pointed at the receptionist. "Next victim," he barked, and disappeared into his office.

"Isn't vaudeville a kind of circus?" Cat asked Teresa.

"It is!" Teresa couldn't stop laughing. Maeve grabbed both her hands and swung her around in a circle. The dogs tottered behind them on their hind legs, as if they were on stage. "Western Circuit, here we come!" Maeve cried.

35.

When Teresa and the two girls emerged from the office with their touring papers and money for tickets, Julie pulled them to the side of the lobby. "Look," she said. "It's all very well, your joining us—but we don't know a thing about you. You could be a thief, for all we know."

"Jules—" Cat protested.

Julie ignored her. "And who was that—that ugly colored boy—who had the nerve to dance with us?"

Pietro, ugly? Hardly. Teresa felt her neck grow red. Thank goodness the Joneses had already left.

"He's a good dancer," Cat said. "Maybe he could help our act."

"Cat." Julie's voice was full of scorn. "You have no brain sometimes. Whites don't perform with coloreds—and that's that."

Julie was the brainless one. Teresa tried to keep her voice steady. "His name is Pietro Jones," she said. "He and his father have a dance routine. They're on the Western Circuit, so you'll meet them later."

"Not if they keep to themselves, as they should. Or maybe you and this Peter—or whatever his name is—can join forces in six weeks, when Lydia comes back. Assuming you like egg on your face."

Teresa tried a trick Mama had taught her, when the boys teased her at school: counting slowly backward from ten to zero before she spoke. *Ten . . . nine . . . eight . . .*

"Jules!" Cat looked ready to cry. "Don't you want to go on the road? If you don't, maybe Teresa and I can find a third singer. You said you'd never go home again, after what your fiancé did—"

"*That* is none of her business." Julie's cheeks turned bright pink as she turned to Teresa. "Look. All I'm saying is, you're lucky we agreed to this. Dressing alike isn't going to turn us into triplets. The doctor said Lydia will be out of the cast in six weeks."

Three . . . two . . . one . . . Teresa took a deep breath. "Fine." Six weeks with this ignorant girl might feel like an eternity. But with luck, she could get to Denver, sing at a few theaters along the route, and convince some manager to let her perform on her own. "We'll practice on the train."

"Right," Julie said. "And you'll learn *our* songs." She looked at Cat. "I've sung backup long enough. My turn to sing lead. You and *Terry* can sing harmony."

Two contraltos singing backup would sound strange, and they'd probably drown out Julie's weak voice, but Teresa was too tired to argue—or to correct Julie's butchering of her name. Luckily, Maeve burst out of the office with the dogs, their claws scritch-scratching on the smooth floor. "Hello, girls! You're so lucky to have Resa join your group." Maeve introduced herself and linked arms with Teresa. "We need to buy fabric for Teresa's costume. What color are your dresses?"

"Yellow." Cat reached into her valise and held up a yellow blouse with a matching ruffled skirt.

"Perfect," Maeve said, fingering the material. "See you tonight."

How would they buy fabric? Teresa's pockets were nearly empty, and she couldn't imagine shopping with six dogs in tow. But she waved goodbye to Cat and Julie. "See you on the train!" Cat called, as Julie pulled her into the elevator. They stepped inside and let the doors close without telling the operator to wait.

"Phew," Maeve said. She untangled the leashes and hoisted her bags. "That girl will be a challenge."

"She wants to sing lead."

Maeve shook her head. "She can't sing worth a darn."

Teresa nodded. "She's a little sharp. But maybe when we have an orchestra or even a piano—"

"Let's hope. Pretty is as pretty does, as my grandmother used to say."

"As my *great*-grandmother still says."

"There you go. I told you we were sisters."

They took the next elevator to the crowded lobby. As the dogs pulled her toward the door, Teresa gripped Maeve's arm. "This is crazy. They gave me money for my ticket, but nothing else. How will I buy fabric, or food on the train?"

"You'll see very soon." Maeve whistled. "Tally ho, dogs!"

Maeve led Teresa and the dogs on a fast clip down Broadway and onto a side street. Maeve stopped in front of a shop with a grimy window. A sign in faded gold letters read *Giardino and Sons, Pawnbrokers. Fine Jewelry, Precious Gems, and Knick-Knacks Bought and Sold.*

"Just what we need." Maeve pulled Teresa inside. The shadowy shop was filled with an odd mix of coins, jewelry, clothing, and furniture. A short man wearing a leather apron and a small-brimmed hat scowled at the dogs. "No pets," he grumbled.

Maeve gave the man her most dazzling smile. "This will only take a minute, I promise. Dogs—sit—and stay."

The dogs settled beside the door. Maeve reached up under her hair to unclip her earrings and held them out on the palm of her hand. "What will you give me for these?"

"Maeve, don't!" Teresa was horrified. She felt for her locket, hidden beneath her cloak, and unhooked it. "Take this instead. Please." She fumbled with the clasp, tipped out the tiny picture, and set the locket on the counter.

The man—who must have been the pawnbroker, Teresa realized—glanced at the necklace and shook his head. "You won't get much for this keepsake, miss. The diamonds, however . . ." He held a tiny magnifier to his eye and studied the diamonds. "Very nice."

"Maeve, please—"

"Shh."

The pawnbroker pulled a black cloth from beneath the counter and set the diamonds on it. They winked like ice crystals on the velvet. "Fine craftsmanship." The man handed Maeve some gold pieces, wrote out a receipt, and wished them luck. Teresa slipped the tiny photo back inside the locket. If she looked at her family now, she'd lose her nerve.

Maeve thanked the pawnbroker and hurried them outside. Teresa tugged her friend's sleeve. "Maeve—that's crazy. What if someone else buys them? How will I pay you back?"

"You'll repay me when you're earning three thousand dollars a week like Eva Tanguay." Maeve's lashes were wet. "Friends are more precious than diamonds." She gave Teresa a quick hug. "No time to waste. We need a fabric store and some notions. We'll be sewing like mad on the train. You can't go west on America's fastest train looking like a schoolgirl."

36.

A few hours later, Teresa stood once again under the domed sky at Grand Central Station. She held the dogs while Maeve bought animal passes. The dogs strained at their leashes, tangling themselves up at Teresa's feet. "Sit," she said. "Stay." They ignored her—except for Edna, who leaned against her leg and stretched out her neck, waiting for a scratch behind the ears.

Teresa looked up. The stars sprinkled across the ceiling shone brighter than the real stars outside, hidden behind a scrim of clouds. So much had happened in the few days since she had arrived in New York, a green country girl. Now she was part of a troupe of performers headed west. Would she ever see her family again?

Teresa glanced at the ticket line. The pink feather in Maeve's hat bobbed closer to the ticket booth. A familiar voice sang out, "*Meet me in St. Louis, Louis.*"

Edna and Dixie let out some happy barks as Pietro and his father hurried toward Teresa, satchels slung over their shoulders. They wore heavy overcoats, in spite of the warm weather, and Pietro carried a rolled newspaper under his arm. "Hello!" she cried. "You keep turning up."

"I could say the same to you," Pietro said. "You made the cut?"

"Yes. I'm one-third of the Singing Toronto Triplets—for six weeks, anyway."

Pietro shook his head. "Mmm, mm. You got your work cut out for you. That tall girl thinks she's the cat's meow. Guess you won't need me on backup." Before Teresa could think of what to say, Pietro held up two tickets. "Ready to go?"

"We have our tickets. Maeve's just finding out about the dogs."

"See you on Track Twelve." As Pietro turned away, his rolled newspaper fell to the floor. It was tied with twine. "Pietro—you dropped something!" she called, but a big family hustled between them and Pietro disappeared into the crowd. "Dixie, fetch!" Teresa dropped Dixie's leash. The terrier ran for the paper, picked it up, and trotted back. The ends of the paper swept the floor. "Good dog." Teresa tucked it into her valise. Maybe she'd done something Pietro would appreciate, for once.

Teresa clucked to the dogs. "Come on, boys and girls. Let's get you untangled. We need to catch the train." She moved among them, sorting out their leashes, glanced at the big clock that stood watch over the station—

And froze.

The policeman who had come to the boardinghouse last night stood under the clock, scanning the room. Was he looking for her—or for Pietro and his father? Was Papa still here? Teresa ducked her head and dragged the dogs toward the ticket booth, where Maeve was waiting. Teresa grabbed Maeve's hat and plunked it down on her own head, pushing her curls up underneath.

"Teresa—what are you doing?"

"Hurry," Teresa said.

"Take it easy, Miss," said the man behind the grate. "She needs to get her papers for the dogs. Plenty of time to catch the train."

"What's going on?" Maeve whispered.

The ticket seller handed over the dogs' papers and Teresa yanked Maeve away from the booth. "The policeman's here, from last night. Run!"

They took off in a tangled mess of dogs and baggage. Maeve's prop bag slammed against Teresa's leg, nearly knocking her down. She caught herself and kept going, dodging passengers, steamer trunks, and porters pushing carts laden with bags. Was that a man's voice, calling her name? She didn't dare stop.

They hurtled down a set of marble stairs and ran out onto the platform. A conductor put out his hand. "Hold on, ladies—do you have permission for these dogs?"

Maeve waved her papers. "Yes—but my elderly aunt needs me. *Please* let me by!"

The conductor protested, but Fido growled and he drew back. They dashed through the gate and onto a bright red carpet that ran alongside the train. Maeve peered over her shoulder as they reached the first car. "The policeman's through the gate," she said, gasping for breath. "I'll take the dogs. Get on the second or third car. Hide in the lavatory . . . until we leave the station. I'll handle him."

Teresa pushed through the door. "Do you think he's after the Joneses?"

"Warn them if you see them. Go."

Teresa ducked into the first car, pushed through the heavy doors, and dashed into the next car, where she found Pietro and Mr. Jones stowing their luggage. "Mr. Jones! Pietro!"

"Why, Miss LeClair—what you all het up about?" Mr. Jones asked.

"The policeman is here. The one who came last night—" How could she explain?

Mr. Jones looked puzzled. "What'd we do wrong?"

"He thinks you kidnapped me in Vermont," she said. "Please hide."

"But you went of your own free will—"

"Hush, Daddy." Pietro grabbed his father's sleeve and yanked him up to standing. "He gave us the evil eye at the Lafayette. Remember how I dragged you from the lobby? Come on. Leave our things. Lavatory's at the far end of the car."

In moments, Teresa had locked herself into one dank, smelly toilet while the Joneses had somehow squeezed into another. She lowered the lid on the commode, sat with her bag on her lap, and waited. Passengers called out to each other on the platform, baggage scraped and bumped against the door, and railroad cars clanged against each other as trains came into the station. Would their train never leave? Someone knocked on the door. "Anyone in there?" a woman called out. Teresa didn't answer. When the knock came again, Teresa made a retching noise, as if she were vomiting. "Disgusting," the woman muttered. Then silence.

Another knock, and a man's brusque voice: "Police. Open up. I'm looking for a red-headed girl. A runaway." When Teresa didn't answer, the door handle waggled up and down. Teresa swallowed hard. This time, she might be sick for real. Surely the cop could hear her heart beating right through the door? A low growl sounded. "Hey—get this dog away from me!" the man shouted.

More growling. Teresa grinned. Good dog, Edna!

"Whose mutt is this? Hey—leave me alone!" Edna's growling became a snarl. "All right, all right—good dog—I'm going—good doggeee . . ."

The policeman's voice went from bass to tenor and disappeared. Teresa clapped a hand over her mouth to smother her laughter.

"Board!" the conductor's voice echoed along the platform. "All aboaarrd the 20th Century Limited, the most famous train in the world! Boooaard!!"

Teresa shivered. Should she open the door?

"Board!" The conductor bellowed one last time. The train lurched and the wheels screeched along the tracks.

Teresa heard snuffling outside the lavatory door, then whimpering. The train was moving now, faster and faster. A quick rap sounded on the door. "Teresa? You can come out now."

Maeve. Teresa let out a long breath and unlocked the door. Edna jumped up, nearly knocking her down. Teresa squatted and wrapped her arms around the dog's neck. "Good dog. You saved me." Edna lapped at her face and wrists. "You're not a 'mutt,' are you?" Teresa said.

Maeve laughed. "She got away from me on the platform and chased after you. Sure scared that cop. He jumped off the train as it started to move."

"What about the Joneses?" Teresa asked.

The small door to the other lavatory opened and Mr. Jones stumbled out, followed by Pietro. "Whew!" Pietro said. "That smelly hole's barely big enough for one, much less two. We safe?"

"You are," Maeve said. The train leaned into a curve. Teresa grabbed for the back of a seat as Pietro nearly fell into her. Mr.

Jones spoke softly. "Conductor's coming." They took off toward their bags.

Edna led the way, head and tail held high, as Teresa and Maeve staggered through the aisles of each car, grabbing on to the backs of seats to keep their balance. Maeve had saved two seats facing each other. They cleared a space between bags and dogs and Teresa collapsed, leaning her head against the window. She pulled Edna close and scratched her between her shoulders in the spot that made her back leg thump. "Brave dog," she said. "You're our hero."

"That policeman was *mad*," Maeve said. "He didn't believe me when I said you had disappeared. And you were right—he was after the Joneses, too." She settled into the seat across from Teresa. "Any sign of your so-called 'triplets'?"

Teresa shook her head. "I forgot all about them. I hope they made the train."

She pulled her cloak around her. They were out of the tunnel now, slipping past apartment buildings, brick warehouses, lumberyards, streets, and bridges. They crossed a river, where scrubby trees along the banks were just leafing out, their spring green a feathery contrast to the cold jumble of steel, brick, and stone. Teresa leaned against the glass.

Edna jumped up onto the seat and rested her head on Teresa's lap. Dixie did the same with Maeve. The wheels sang an iron lullaby: *Pockety pockety pocketa*. Teresa's eyes felt heavy. "Rocky Mountains, here we come," Maeve said.

37.

The train stopped on a siding west of Buffalo, where Maeve and Teresa climbed out to walk the dogs. "Keep them on their leashes," Maeve said. "Look—the Joneses are here." She waved. As Pietro and his father came to join them, Maeve gave Teresa a nudge. "Handsome, isn't he?" she said.

"Who?" As if she didn't know.

Maeve laughed. "Your face matches the feather in my hat."

"Stop it," Teresa whispered.

Mr. Jones touched his cap and glanced around. "Your police going to follow us all the way to Denver?"

"I hope not," Maeve said.

Pietro pointed to the front of the train. "Quite the engine. They switched to steam outside the city."

The engine was massive, with six wheels on each side, some as tall as the conductor. Steam hissed from the smokestack. Teresa couldn't speak. Maeve's teasing had suddenly made her tongue-tied and she was relieved when the engineer signaled to the conductor, who waved his flag. "Board!" he called. The whistle responded with a quick toot.

Maeve beckoned to Mr. Jones. "Come sit with us."

Mr. Jones hung back. "Well . . ."

"Come on, Daddy," Pietro said. "We're not down south."

"Praise be," Mr. Jones said.

"Oh!" Teresa said. "I forgot—I have your newspaper at my seat. Dixie picked it up in the station."

"I wondered where that went," Pietro said.

Maeve waved to the dogs. "Line up!" The dogs scrambled onto the train and pranced down the aisle as if they were making a stage entrance.

"Mama, look at the doggies!" a little girl cried.

"What is this?" a woman asked. "A circus act?"

"Almost," Teresa said. "We're part of a vaudeville troupe." *We.* Teresa couldn't help grinning.

Maeve shooed the dogs onto the floor when they reached their seats and beckoned to the Joneses. "Sit down, won't you? Plenty of room."

Mr. Jones glanced around the car. "I guess the coast is clear." He opened his coat but kept it on as he settled into the seat next to Maeve. Pietro perched on the arm of the other seat as if he were about to bolt.

"New York State goes on forever," Maeve said. "I remember that from when I first came east. Let's have some stories. How did you get started?"

"Harlem was still country when I came up," Mr. Jones said. "Lots of white folks. Italians raising goats where the fancy houses are now. No subway. I worked in hotels by day; at night, my wife and I danced wherever we could." His eyes narrowed. "Back when we got along."

Pietro frowned and nudged his father with his foot. "Come on, Daddy. That's our private business." He glanced at Teresa. "You got that newspaper?"

She handed it to him. Pietro took the paper without unrolling it. "Which one is it?" Teresa asked.

"*Amsterdam News*, out of Harlem. I pick it up whenever I can."

Mr. Jones glanced at them. "My boy tries to convince me he's interested in the local news. Truth is, he's looking to read Du Bois's column. All right with me." He smiled. "Any sign of your singer girls on the train?"

"Not yet." Teresa frowned. "I hope it works out. Julie sings sharp."

"That girl is sharp in more ways than one," Pietro said.

Maeve laughed, and Teresa felt the tension slip away.

"How'd you get started singing, Miss LeClair?" Mr. Jones asked.

"I traveled with my parents from the time I was born. They called me a 'trunk baby.'"

Mr. Jones nodded. "A trunk was Pietro's first cradle, too."

Pietro rolled his eyes and looked out the window, as if fascinated by the fields passing by.

"When did you first go onstage, Resa?" Maeve asked. "Do you remember?"

"I was six. I performed with my parents a few times. Then my grandmother died, my great-grandma was home alone, and Pascal was born. So we stopped touring." Now it was Teresa's turn to study the newly plowed fields, the blush of spring green on the trees that sped past. Thinking about her family—especially Mama and Nonnie—was like picking a scab that wouldn't heal.

The train swung from side to side, throwing Mr. Jones against Maeve. Suddenly a fat man with a contorted face leaned over the seat behind them. "What's going on here?"

Maeve looked up and gave him her sweetest smile. "Why, nothing much. Just having a nice conversation. Is something wrong?"

"I'll say there is. These *boys* bothering you ladies?"

Pietro and his father froze. A bad taste, like castor oil, swirled in Teresa's mouth. She glared at the man. "No, sir. These *men* aren't bothering us. Mind your own business. Please."

The man's face turned nearly purple. "Why—"

Maeve snapped her fingers and whispered a command. Fido growled; the other dogs jumped to their feet, whining and yipping. Maeve didn't stop them.

"Seymour." A woman standing behind the fat man clutched his arm. "Please don't make a fuss. We'll sit somewhere else."

"Fine with me. I don't need this menagerie." The man lurched sideways as he hoisted his bag. "You ladies better watch yourself, if you know what's good for you." As he pushed through the door, his wife gave them a look of regret that said, clear as day, *I'm sorry.*

"Whew. Who could be married to a man like that?" Maeve asked as the door closed, taking them away.

"So much for being comfortable up north." Pietro reached into his coat pocket and pulled out the book he always carried around. For the first time, Teresa was able to read the whole title: *The Souls of Black Folk: Essays and Sketches.* Pietro opened the book, skimmed through a few pages, and pointed to a passage he had underlined. "Du Bois says it in the Forethought, Daddy: 'The problem of the Twentieth Century is the problem of the color-line.'"

"All too true," Mr. Jones said.

"True in Illinois, where I'm from," Maeve said. "Things weren't so good in Springfield."

Pietro stared at her. "That's where you're from?"

"It was," Maeve said. "My family farms outside town. Not my home anymore, thank goodness."

"Chicago's all right. Wouldn't boast on Springfield if I were you." Pietro tucked his book back into his coat pocket and left without saying goodbye.

How rude! Teresa's neck felt hot. Could Maeve help where she was born?

Mr. Jones stood and gripped the seat to steady himself. "Pietro thinks I don't care about all this. Of course I've read Du Bois's work. He's brilliant. Right now, I got to make sure we keep up our routines, give the audience a good time, make sure the boy has three squares a day—and that he's safe. I won't hold on to him long." He touched his cap. "See y'all in Chicago."

Maeve's eyes filled with tears as Mr. Jones took off down the aisle. "It's my fault. I should never have asked them to sit with us. That man was awful—but why shouldn't we sit with our friends?"

"*Mr. Jones* is a friend, but I don't know about Pietro," Teresa said. "Who's the writer he talks about?"

"W.E.B. Du Bois," Maeve said. "My father pounded the kitchen table whenever the Chicago paper printed his articles. All I've heard is that Du Bois is trying to help his people. He sounds very smart."

Teresa ran her fingers through her hair and scrubbed her scalp, as if that might help to clear her head. "I feel stupid, not smart," she said. "Papa was right. I should have learned my history."

"Maybe," Maeve said. "But there's a lot they never taught us in history class."

38.

"I'll walk the train and look for the Toronto girls," Teresa said later. "We need to choose our songs."

"Good idea. Take Edna, in case you run into that angry man," Maeve said. "She won't let anyone bother you—will you, girl?"

Edna leapt to her feet, her tail wagging as Teresa leashed her and pushed the heavy door open against the wind. The couplings moved and slid beneath Teresa's feet when she passed from one car to the next. She staggered from side to side like a tipsy woman, grabbing for handholds, but Edna trotted along without missing a step.

They walked the length of the train, passing hundreds of seated passengers. The waiter in the dining car scowled when she came through. "No dogs in here," he said. Teresa nodded and hurried on. She finally spotted two identical gray hats, set on blonde curls, near the front of the train. Like Maeve and Teresa, Cat and Julie had set themselves up in two seats facing each other. Teresa reached them just as the train swept around a steep curve. Fighting to keep her balance, she grabbed ahold of Julie's armrest and fell into a small space next to a hatbox.

"Nice entrance," Julie said, in a dry voice.

"Hullo, Teresa!" Cat smiled and scratched Edna behind the ears. "Where are the other dogs?"

"With Maeve, near the end of the train."

"Back where the colored folks sit?" Julie's blue eyes were cold. "I saw you talking to those two men when we stopped on that siding."

"So what if I was? Pietro and Mr. Jones are our friends."

"You're greener than swamp grass. Just like Pantages said." Julie leaned toward Teresa, keeping her voice low. "It's fine to have ideals. But you have to be smart—unless you want to lose your job."

Julie made Teresa feel tired, and they hadn't even tried to sing. "Let's talk about something else. We need to pick some songs and practice."

"She's right, Jules," Cat said. "We have a long train ride ahead." She pulled a small book out of a satchel. "I have a list of songs we've performed. Want to see?"

∽∾∽

The train sped west as Teresa and Cat wrote up a list of songs they all knew. Julie participated, but only when Cat asked, "What about that one, Jules?" For the most part, Julie gazed out the window, even though the train hurtled through darkness, with only an occasional glow of light in a distant farmhouse.

"Let's figure out who sings lead on which songs," Teresa said, guessing—correctly—that Julie would respond.

"You can't just barge into our group and expect to be the star," Julie said.

Teresa took a long, slow breath. "I didn't 'barge in.' Mr. Pantages chose me. And who said anything about being a star?" Teresa handed Julie the piece of paper.

Julie scanned the list and frowned. "I say we should only sing songs that we *all* know by heart."

"Jules, that's silly," Cat said. "Our act was getting tired—Lydia said so—and Mr. Pantages told us to come up with new material."

She glanced at Teresa. "Anyway, it's two against one, so I say we learn some of Teresa's songs—"

"And I'll learn yours," Teresa added quickly.

"Sing something now," Cat said.

"All right. 'Hard Times' has nice harmony." Teresa closed her eyes, listened for the first note, and began to sing. Cat hummed softly on the second verse and Teresa realized, with relief, that Cat had a good ear. By the third chorus, Cat was singing the words along with her. *"Tis the song, the sigh of the weary . . ."* Julie frowned and stayed quiet, but a few passengers turned around in the seats ahead of them; one woman stood up to listen and her little boy leaned toward them, his thumb in his mouth. The door to the next car opened, but Teresa didn't pay attention—until she started the fourth verse and heard a voice behind her.

"Someone's a little sharp."

Pietro? Teresa turned around, but he was already gone.

Julie glared at Teresa. "Who does he think he is?" she asked.

"Who?" Teresa bit her lip, trying not to smile. Pietro was right, of course: Julie *did* sing off-key.

"You can't fool me. He has no right to insult us." Julie picked up her coat. "I'm going to complain to the conductor."

Teresa leaned over to block her way. "Wait. I'll speak to Pietro. He and his father have a fine dance routine. They're too busy to bother us. And we need to practice."

"She's right, Jules." Cat tugged Julie's hand. "Let's get going. How about 'Let Me Call You Sweetheart'? You could take the lead on that one."

"Good idea," Teresa said, though it was a schmaltzy song.

Julie perched on the edge of her seat and crossed her ankles as if someone were about to take her picture. "All right." She cleared her throat. "Damned Lydia—she could have left us the pitch pipe, at least."

"Try this note," Teresa said, humming.

Julie sang a few bars and shook her head. "Too low."

Teresa pitched it higher. Julie swayed along with the train and tipped her head in a fetching way, but she still sang sharp, with movements as stiff as her voice. However, Cat's voice was sweet and Teresa found a line of harmony just above her alto line. Would their voices ever blend? If Julie always sang off-key, they'd be "all wet"—as Papa would say—after their first performance in Denver. How had Julie been hired in the first place?

That was obvious: Julie was pretty, and her eyes had what Nonnie called a "come-hither look." Yet her voice sounded like Papa's fiddle when his bow slipped on the strings, causing it to shriek.

They needed a miracle.

39.

Teresa, Cat, and Julie sang together for an hour—or rather, Teresa and Cat sang while Julie pouted, criticized, and occasionally chimed in. Her voice even annoyed Edna, who huddled on the floor under the seats. When Teresa suggested they sing "The Sidewalks of New York," Julie stood up. "Who's going to care about that song in Denver?" She left for the lavatory without waiting for an answer.

"She hates that song because of her fiancé," Cat said. "He didn't want her to try out in New York, so he ended their engagement. He thinks vaudeville is improper."

"That's what my papa thinks, too—even though he used to perform himself."

Cat bit her lip. "If Jules changes her mind, I don't know what I'll do."

"She can't go anywhere as long as we're on this train. Let's try the song anyway." Teresa whistled the first four notes. They sang the first verse and the train's swaying rhythm mimicked the song's waltz tempo. A few passengers turned around and joined in. Then the conductor, passing through with a wad of tickets in his hand, added a bass line on the final refrain.

"Time for a lullaby," the conductor said when the scattered applause died down. "The porter will make up the sleeping compartments soon." He nodded to Teresa. "Nice voice you have there, Miss. You part of a troupe?"

"We are," Teresa said, and nodded at Cat. "My friend's harmony makes me sound better."

The conductor passed into the next car. "You didn't have to say that," Cat said.

"I meant it," Teresa said.

"Julie says I'll always be a backup—not a star."

"What does she know?" Still, Julie could be right. Cat might be too shy, her voice too soft, to make it on her own.

"Julie's not always like this," Cat said.

When she didn't explain, Teresa asked, "Where are you from?"

"A farm in Ontario. It's lambing season now." She winked back tears. "I'm homesick."

"Why did you leave?" Teresa asked.

"Pa said he had too many mouths to feed." Cat wiped her eyes with her sleeve. "I thought it would help him if I left. When Julie's fiancé jilted her—" Cat took a deep breath. "Here she comes," she said quietly.

"It's late. I'll see you in Chicago." Teresa nodded at Julie—although the girl ignored her—and slipped away. Jilted? No wonder Julie was upset.

Teresa pushed through one heavy door after another and finally collapsed into the seat next to Maeve. Even Edna seemed exhausted; she jumped into Teresa's lap and closed her eyes. "This will never work," Teresa said.

Maeve stretched and yawned. "What's wrong?"

"The so-called 'Singing Triplets' are doomed. Julie hates me, and she sounds like a fiddle out of tune."

"Ouch," Maeve said. "I'm worried, too. My act was so much better with Pascal. He covered my mistakes, distracted the audience. Who will take his place?"

"Not me, that's for sure—I'd fall flat on my face." Teresa huddled into her cloak and pulled Edna closer. Her stomach growled. They'd finished their snacks long ago and had little money left for food. Better to sleep off her hunger.

The train was an hour late reaching Chicago. Maeve led their troupe through the cars to the front of the train as it crawled into the station. They waited at the door, the dogs lined up and ready. "Ready to dash? We can't miss our connection," Maeve said.

They jumped the gap between the train and the platform and raced toward the station. The dogs barked and yipped; Teresa's bag slammed against her shins. She passed a young man and a woman caught in a passionate embrace, the woman arched back with the man leaning over her. He held his hat in front of her face to hide their kiss, but Teresa recognized the yellow curls and the powder-blue coat. She scooped up the gray hat lying on the platform.

"Julie? You dropped your hat."

"Resa, hurry! We're out of time," Maeve called.

Julie grabbed the hat and the man drew her into the shadows beneath the stairway—but Teresa saw the flush on Julie's cheeks, her triumphant smile.

"Dogs! Come!" Maeve's shrill whistle sounded from along the platform. The three dogs in Teresa's care leapt forward, yanking Teresa with them. She ran.

They reached the gate just as the conductor called out, "ALL ABOOAARD!"

Teresa stepped onto the bottom step of the nearest car, shooed the dogs into the train, and clung to the railing as the other passengers wrestled their bags inside. "Teresa!" a high voice called.

"Cat!" Teresa leaned out as Cat ran for the train. "Grab my hand. You'll make it." The conductor blew his whistle and waved a red flag. "Hurry!" Teresa cried.

"I can't." The train began to move. Cat trotted alongside, gasping for breath. "Julie's fiancé changed his mind . . . he came early on the Philadelphia train . . . they're getting married . . . after all. I'm sorry! I want to go—ho . . ."

The clattering of the wheels drowned her last word, but Teresa understood: Cat was headed home to Ontario. She waved until the girl's tiny figure disappeared. She liked Cat. Now she'd never see her again. But that was the least of her problems.

Maeve poked her head out, struggling to hold the door open while the train picked up speed. "Resa—what's wrong? I thought you were right behind me."

"I was. I'll explain later." Teresa untangled Edna's leash and tried to find the train's rhythm as she followed Maeve through one car, then another and another, grasping for the seats as she lurched from side to side. The wheels sang a new song this time: *What now? What now? What now?*

40.

Maeve and Teresa finally found two open seats near the front of the train. Maeve hoisted her prop bag onto the shelf overhead and fell into the backward-facing seat. "Phew! We made it. Denver, here we come." She winked at Teresa. "You certainly attracted attention as we went through the cars."

"Me? Why?" Teresa sank into the opposite seat. "They were looking at the dogs. Weren't they, Edna?" She pulled *her* dog—for that's how she thought of Edna now—into her lap.

Maeve rolled her eyes. "Resa, dear Resa—your flaming curls and copper eyes turn heads—and now you've learned to walk like the Queen of England, with Edna strutting beside you. You're the best advertisement for both our acts. I'm just glad we have the dogs to protect us."

Teresa's face felt warm. "People notice me, even in this wrinkled shirtwaist?"

"Even so. Once I finish your new frock, you'll have every audience at your feet."

"*If* I can go onstage." Teresa explained what had happened with Cat and Julie.

"Oh, dear. What a pickle."

"I know. Not that I liked the group—well, Cat was all right. But what will Pantages do to me? I'm supposed to be part of the 'Singing Toronto Triplets.' Now I'm all by myself and I'm not even from Canada. Although my papa was born in Québec."

"There you go. One problem solved." Maeve sat forward in her seat. "It just so happens that you're the only one of the triplets who can sing."

"The Denver stage manager doesn't know that. He could still toss me out."

"Not right away. He'll have his lineup all figured out, and he won't be able to fill that spot with someone else. If you slay them at the first house, the stage manager will think he can't *live* without you." Maeve placed her palm over her heart and batted her eyes.

Teresa couldn't help laughing. "You're dreaming. How will I slay them?"

"The same way you did in New York, only better. Practice, practice, practice. You'll go onstage in your wonderful new costume, open your mouth—and they'll throw you jewels, instead of pennies. But first, we need to finish the skirt and blouse." She dug into her valise, took out the silky yellow fabric they had bought in New York, and held it up to Teresa's face. "This will bring out the color of your hair—"

Teresa laughed. "It's not obvious enough already?"

"Trust me. You like *my* costumes, don't you?"

Teresa nodded, although she was glad that Papa hadn't seen Maeve onstage in her short pants, tights, and plunging neckline. Never mind. Papa wasn't on this train—and Teresa couldn't perform in schoolgirl clothes.

Maeve had cut out and pinned the fabric on the first leg of their trip. Now she spread it across her lap and rummaged in her prop bag for a needle and thread.

"What songs were you working on with the triplets?"

"A real mix—oh! Lucky me. I made the list." Teresa pulled a crumpled piece of paper from her skirt pocket. "Cat and I each wrote down the songs we both knew." She studied her scrawled notes. "There are ten numbers. A few were for Julie to sing lead— and I didn't like those."

"So scratch them. You'll pick four or five songs you love and sing your heart out. We'll listen and decide which ones sound best."

"*We?*"

"Mr. Jones and Pietro, of course." Maeve sat back. "I haven't seen them since Union Station—have you?"

Teresa shook her head. "Maybe they missed the train."

"Not likely. I'll bet they needed a rest from all the commotion yesterday." Maeve pressed her face to the window, as if looking for someone in the passing scenery. Dixie leaned against her while Fido and Bronwyn sat at her feet, their ears pricked as if to protect her. They seemed to sense Maeve's moods. The farmland rolled and tucked into itself, the lush green pastures alternating with dark, newly plowed fields.

Maeve turned to Teresa, her eyes glassy with tears. "I thought this wouldn't bother me."

"Are we near your farm?"

"So close. When I was a little girl, playing outside, I used to hear the train's lonesome whistle as it neared the crossing." She took Teresa's hand. "I had eight brothers. I always wished for a younger sister. Now I found one—so you *have* to do well on this tour. We'll figure it out."

Teresa moved closer to Maeve, shifting Dixie gently out of the way. What should she do to comfort her friend?

She thought of Mama, who liked to say, "Singing scares our troubles away." So Teresa hummed the tune to "Hard Times" and sang a soft round of the chorus. Maeve tapped her fingers, though she didn't open her eyes. They leaned against one another and the train rocked them to sleep.

Hours later, they crossed the Mississippi River and pulled over at a siding. "We're waiting on an eastbound freight," the conductor called from the back of the car. "Twenty minutes, if you want to stretch your legs."

They tumbled out into a brisk, cold wind. Teresa pulled her cloak around her and squinted. "Look!" She waved at two familiar figures near the rear of the train. "There they are."

She and Maeve hurried to meet the Joneses. "Where have you been?" Teresa asked.

Pietro and his father shared a look. "Here and there," Pietro said at last.

"Seems like a long ride," Mr. Jones said. "At least we're not down south where they make coloreds sit in the last car, then use that car for target practice."

Teresa felt sick. "Is that true?"

"Afraid so. Listen to this." Pietro pulled a scrap of paper from his pocket and read. "'*The morning breaks over blood-stained hills. We must not falter, we may not shrink. Above are the everlasting stars.*'" When no one spoke, Pietro said, "That's the end of the speech Du Bois gave at Harpers Ferry, to start the Niagara Movement. So many states are 'blood-stained.'"

Harpers Ferry? Was that where John Brown was killed? Something else she might have learned in history class—if only she'd paid attention.

Mr. Jones glanced over his shoulder. "Pietro, be careful. You quote that man in the wrong company, you'll get us all in trouble." He coughed, drew out a handkerchief, and wiped his face. The dogs tugged at their leashes as they waited for him to finish. Finally he nodded at Pietro. "Still, I'm glad we're out of Illinois. I was thinking President Lincoln would be rolling in his grave if he knew what had happened in Springfield, his hometown."

"That was a few years back, Daddy. Don't fret." Pietro put an arm over his father's shoulders and Teresa hung back. Had she ever tried to comfort Papa? No: He was bristly, like a wire brush. She touched her locket, thinking of the tiny photograph inside, how Papa had once looked so proud of his little family. Did Papa miss her now? Was he worried about her? She walked slowly along the verge of the tracks, fighting tears, and almost bumped into Pietro. "Sorry," she said.

"No problem." He glanced up at the train. "Where's the rest of your troupe?"

"Gone." Teresa explained what had happened in Chicago.

Pietro shook his head. "Hope her fiancé knows what he's got himself into, poor devil. What you going to do now?"

"Sing," Teresa said. "What else?"

When Pietro shrugged, she asked, "Are you and your father doing the same routines?"

"I guess. Daddy tells me they expect blackface—that right?"

Mr. Jones nodded. His face looked tight from coughing.

"Wish I'd joined that all-black troupe," Pietro said.

"You did fine against those white boys in the contest," Mr. Jones said.

"Oh!" Maeve cried, catching up to them. "We forgot to ask you. What happened?"

Pietro's smile flickered like heat lightning. "Twenty-dollar gold piece is what happened. Bought me a new suit, new scarf, new gloves and taps. Wait until you see." He jumped in the air and clicked his heels.

Two short, high-pitched blasts sounded from the engine. "B-flat," Teresa said. Edna howled in response and everyone laughed, which sent Mr. Jones into another fit of coughing.

"Come sit with us," Maeve said. "This ride goes on forever."

"Well . . ." Mr. Jones hesitated.

"Resa needs an audience for her songs." Maeve gave him her most dazzling smile. "Don't worry. If anyone bothers you, I'll sic these dogs on them."

Mr. Jones shook his head. "Dogs that smile and wag their tails won't scare anybody." But he followed them onto the train.

41.

Mr. Jones carried two small harmonicas. When Teresa showed him her list of songs, he pointed to a few he could play. "What about 'Shine On, Harvest Moon'—that's an easy one to warm up with." He blew a reedy note on one harmonica, then the other. "Either one of these work?"

Teresa picked the lower key and breathed deep. She was shy at first, singing in the crowded car, but the harmonica gave her voice some depth and Pietro added his harmony. Then a few passengers joined in. One burly white man scowled and left the car, but a small crowd gathered in the aisle. People made requests, sang along, and laughed when the train threw them sideways around a curve. If someone suggested a song that wasn't on her list, Teresa jotted it down. If this crowd liked them, maybe a Denver audience would, too.

Two performers came on board in Des Moines and found their way to Maeve and Teresa's car. Both men had curly black hair and were tall and skinny as beanpoles. "I said to Sammy, if there's music, that's our car," one man said, pointing to his friend. "We're acrobats. I'm the Italian Sammy; he's the Spanish Sam."

Teresa laughed. "How confusing!"

The man called Sam shrugged. "What can I tell you? They gave us the same names when we were kids, just off the boat at Ellis Island. What's the next song?"

Mr. Jones pointed to the list. "How about 'Listen to the Mockingbird'—you know that one?"

"It's sad," Teresa said.

"Not completely—it has a bit of jive, if you sing it right," Mr. Jones said. "You could use a little variety, and the audience needs a tearjerker now and then. Besides, it was composed by Richard Milburn, a colored man, though he never gets the credit."

Teresa glanced at Pietro. Would he approve? For once, Pietro nodded.

"Let's hear it!" Sammy said.

Mr. Jones played a chord and she started in, but her voice caught in her throat like a fishbone. She remembered Mama singing that song to Pascal, walking him up and down the front hall of the boardinghouse when he was a baby, to stop his crying.

Mr. Jones pulled out the bigger harmonica. "We pitched that too high. Let's try the other key." Teresa found the melody and tried again. "*I'm dreaming now of Hallie*," Teresa sang, "*My sweet Hallie . . .*"

The passengers hushed and the train slowed, as if it listened along with them. Teresa had never paid attention to the words before. The thought of a bird singing over a girl's grave made her sing more sweetly. "*Listen to the mockingbird*," she sang, and Pietro joined in, his tenor right on pitch. The second acrobat whistled a warbling tune and a few passengers whistled back.

Mr. Jones picked up the tempo and Teresa sang the next verse in a more rollicking way, in spite of the lyrics. Pietro swayed as he sang harmony, and by the third chorus, the whole car was either singing or whistling.

"*For the thought of her is one that never dies.*" Teresa bowed low when the applause started and waved her hand toward Pietro, to include him. To her surprise, he smiled and tipped his hat. "Thank you, thank you!" she called, and bent to Mr. Jones. "My voice is tired. But thank you for playing."

"My pleasure." Mr. Jones looked up at Pietro. "You do make a pretty sound together. Too bad you can't sing that number onstage."

"Are you sure?" Maeve asked.

Mr. Jones lowered his voice. "Positive. In vaude, we travel together, get to know each other, treat each other right. It's almost like family."

"That's what my mama always said." Teresa felt a pang of homesickness.

"Things are different out in the world," Mr. Jones said. "So don't push it. Folks aren't ready for that." He beckoned to Pietro. "Come on, son. Let's get some sleep."

They were gone before Teresa could say goodbye. She glanced at Maeve. "Did we say something wrong?"

"No, hon." Maeve sighed. "He's right: You have to be careful. Both of you."

Teresa sighed and smoothed the song list out on her lap. Somehow, she'd have to persuade the stage manager that she could sing on her own, without Pietro. If not—

Then she was headed back to Brattleboro. And Estey. And the mockingbird would sing over *her* grave.

42.

Denver's Union Station was ice cold, even inside. Teresa shivered and Alix, with her short hair, trembled all over. Teresa picked the dog up and held her under her thin cloak. The dog was stinky. How long since anyone in their troupe had had a bath? Teresa's hair was so tangled she couldn't comb it, her shirtwaist was wrinkled and stained, and her joints were stiff from sitting so long.

But she couldn't complain. Not while Mr. Jones, sitting on a slatted bench nearby, coughed and hacked into his gloved hands. As they had crossed the rolling plains of Kansas and climbed slowly onto Colorado's dry prairie, Mr. Jones's cough had grown worse. Pietro had hovered over his father, bringing him hot drinks and wrapping a wool scarf around his neck, but nothing helped.

"Can I get you anything, Mr. Jones?" Teresa asked now.

He shook his head. "Not unless you got a nice warm bed nearby." His eyes had lost their sparkle. "It's the altitude. The thin air makes hammers ring in my head. Feel it?"

"Some." Her ears buzzed and her head felt too light for her body.

Mr. Jones reached into the pocket of his overcoat and brought out a small, tattered book. "Look up Denver; see what they say about this Princess Theater."

The book was a guide to vaudeville theaters in cities and towns west of Kansas City. Teresa flipped through the worn pages. "Wow," she said. "It tells you what trains to take, where to eat, and where to stay . . . it even gives the names of stagehands and conductors." She found the section on Denver and glanced at Mr. Jones. "It says, 'take care of your voice in Denver's thin air.' Sounds like it's hard to sing here."

"And to dance. The acrobats will have a tough time, too."

Teresa searched the list of theaters. "The Orpheum, the Tabor Opera House, the Empress . . . Here it is: Princess Theater, Curtis Street."

"Got your start at a Princess, didn't you?" Mr. Jones said.

"Maybe that's good luck." She returned the book and he tucked it into his jacket.

"Just hope I can go on," Mr. Jones said. "I wasn't this weak last time I was here. Good thing we don't perform until tomorrow."

Teresa was relieved when Pietro and Maeve showed up with a baggage handler and a cart, but the man gave them a nasty look. "Don't tell me you're going to the *same* hotel?"

"No, sir," Mr. Jones said. "A nice Negro man runs a place close by. You take us there first, then help the ladies to their hotel." He took Pietro's arm.

"No need to call *him* 'sir,'" Pietro said.

"Don't make trouble," Mr. Jones murmured.

They made a scraggly line following the cart out of the station. The dogs strained at their leashes and refused to obey, no matter how much Maeve cajoled and threatened.

"They've been cooped up too long," she said. "We should walk them, once we get settled in."

Teresa leaned close to Maeve. "Mr. Jones is really sick."

"I know. Let's hope it's only the altitude. They say we'll get used to it in a few days. But you notice that smell?"

Teresa nodded. The bitter scent of burning coal made her eyes smart. "I thought the air would be clean."

"Me too. Poor Mr. Jones."

And poor me. Would her own voice hold up?

They passed through an enormous iron arch with "WELCOME" spelled out in big letters on top. A wide boulevard stretched out beyond it. Everything seemed open and new, compared to New York, but the city had cars, buses, and streetcars, too. "Don't miss the view," Mr. Jones said.

When Teresa turned around, her jaw dropped. A double wall of mountains loomed in the distance, the closer ones low and brooding, the craggy peaks in the distance snow-covered. Even though it was hard to make them out through the smoky haze, these mountains made Rattlesnake Hill look like a wart on her little toe.

They parted with Mr. Jones and Pietro outside their rooming house. "See you tomorrow," Teresa called. Mr. Jones was coughing again, and Pietro had to help him up the short flight of steps to the front door. Neither man answered.

The baggage man pocketed Pietro's coins and set off again. "I'm surprised at you ladies," he said. "They say the West is free and easy—but watch out for the company you keep."

"Don't insult our friends," Maeve said. Fido picked up on Maeve's warning, growling until the man picked up the pace. When they reached their rooming house he took his pay and hurried away without a word.

"Good riddance," Maeve said. "I'm winded and we didn't even walk far." She gazed at the rooming house, a simple wood building with a red door. "A bath, a walk with the dogs, maybe some food, then bed—how does that sound?"

"Perfect." Teresa's eyes were heavy. She couldn't tell Maeve what else she was thinking: They were in Denver at last—but what if she didn't have a job?

43.

After a long sleep, followed by a bath in a tiny, claw-footed tub, Teresa tried on the skirt and blouse that Maeve had stitched for her on the train. "Don't look until I've buttoned you up," Maeve said. "All right—now."

Teresa turned to face the mirror and gasped. She had watched Maeve work the pleats into puffy sleeves on the blouse, and had even hemmed the skirt herself—but it was different, seeing it on. The neckline plunged, the skirt barely covered her knees, and the short sleeves left her arms bare. "I can't wear this," she whispered. "I'm almost as naked as Eva Tanguay."

"Nonsense," Maeve said. "If I can perform in short pants and tights, you can wear this skirt and blouse. Besides, I didn't go to all that trouble for nothing." She touched Teresa's hair, still wet from her shampoo. "The dry climate will tame your curls, and the yellow fabric highlights the color, just as I thought. You look wonderful!"

"Not like a carrot?"

Maeve hugged her. "Stop worrying. You need to walk into that theater like you own the place."

"Should I wear this to first band call?"

"Definitely. Pull out the stops; convince the stage manager you're ready to go. Where's your necklace?"

Teresa settled her locket around her neck. Though the photograph was hidden, she felt as if she carried her family with her. The warm gold gleamed against her freckled skin.

Sam and Sammy, the acrobats from the train, were already rehearsing on the slack wire when Teresa and Maeve walked down the aisle of the Princess Theater. Sam balanced on the metal line, four feet above the stage, while Sammy did flips and tumbles nearby. The metal slack wire rose and fell like breathing, but Sam's feet never faltered. Halfway through their act, Sammy tossed Sam a ball, then another one, then a third, and Sam began to juggle on the wire. A rolling drumbeat escalated from the orchestra pit as their tricks grew bolder.

"Pascal would love this," Teresa said.

Dixie whined and wagged her tail as the balls sailed through the air. Maeve's face lit up. "That's it!" she whispered. "Maybe one of the acrobats could help me do Pascal's trick." She headed down the aisle with the dogs at her heels.

Teresa followed, only half listening. Where was the stage manager? Sam and Sammy cartwheeled into the wings, leaving an empty stage. Maeve nudged Teresa from behind. "Take off your cloak and find the stage manager, before things get too busy."

Pietro's voice rose from the wings. "It's the altitude! He'll be fine this afternoon; I promise. Let me run through our numbers for the band. He'll dance later."

Teresa and Maeve crept closer to the stage. The stage manager paced up and down in the wings, running his hands through his bushy white hair. "And if he's *not* ready?" the manager demanded. "What then? Better to scratch you now. Our patrons won't think much of one measly colored boy dancing alone."

"But you'll be missing an act. And how do you know what I can do until you see me? Give me a chance."

Pietro, pleading? The stage manager shook his head. Teresa tossed her cloak over a seat and hurried up the steps to the stage. "Excuse me. Sir?"

Pietro tried to warn her off as the manager whirled around. He gave her the once over, and waved her away. "Later, Miss. Can't you see I'm busy?"

Teresa stood her ground. "Pietro's a good dancer," she said. "We saw him perform many times in New York. He and I sang together there. Maybe we could do a number here, after Pietro dances on his own."

The stage manager folded his arms across his chest. "And who—if I may ask—are you?"

"Teresa LeClair. I'm part of Pantages's troupe."

The manager pulled a crumpled program from his pocket and ran his finger down a list of names. "No LeClair here."

"I'm one of the Toronto Triplets."

"Fine. You girls can run through your songs later. Now, if you'll please let me finish—"

The stage manager turned away, but Teresa blocked his path. "That's the trouble, sir. The other two girls ditched the act in Chicago. I'm here alone—and if Pietro is alone, too—well, I thought you might not want two solo acts—"

"I don't care *what* you think," the manager said, "or how they do things in *New—York—City*," he said slowly. "You may be friends offstage, but races don't mix on this stage. I can't help it: Those are the owner's rules."

Pietro shook his head at Teresa from behind the manager's back, but she ignored him. "What if we both wore blackface?" she said. "Then our skin wouldn't show."

The stage manager gave a harsh laugh. "Are you serious?" He pointed to her hair. "Who's going to believe that, with your orange mop?"

Mop? Teresa bit her lip and stood up as straight as she could. She wouldn't cry in front of this wretched man. "If the audience thinks we're both white underneath, my frizzy hair wouldn't matter—would it?"

The manager rolled his eyes, as if asking heaven for help. Teresa glanced at the pit. The band members were listening intently, leaning forward in their chairs. Pietro didn't move, though a muscle twitched on the right side of his jaw. Was he angry with her for barging in?

Maeve's cheery voice rose from below the stage. "Sir! Excuse me for interrupting. I'm Maeve Cullen, with the dog act. I've seen these two perform, and they're good, alone *and* together. Why don't you let them rehearse, see what you think? Otherwise, you'll have two empty spots in your program."

"The day is wasting," the bandleader called from the pit.

The manager groaned. "This is absurd—but you're right; I've got too many solo acts now." He loosened his collar and his small brown eyes darted from Teresa to Pietro and back. "First we'll see how you do on your own. Then we'll decide if you go onstage together."

Teresa's mouth was dry, but at least he was giving her a chance. She had opened her bag and was searching for her sheet music when a high voice sounded from the back of the theater. "Just a minute! Stage manager, Sir—wait just a cotton-picking minute!"

Teresa froze. Where had she heard that voice before? She glanced at Pietro, who rolled his eyes. "Sounds like the so-called 'Rose of Abilene.'"

Sure enough, Miss Stanton herself tripped down the aisle in high-heeled shoes. Her hair was a brassy red now, rather than blonde, and her dress was even shorter than last time. She clicked up the stairs onto the stage apron and planted herself in front of the manager. "This is outrageous!" Miss Stanton sputtered. "I'm the Rose of Abilene and I *know* this girl. She's nothing but a song plugger. And she's a runaway! I saw what happened, with my own eyes! Left her family weeping and wailing. Besides, she's too young. The Gerry Society will shut you down if you let her perform."

The manager tried to speak, but Miss Stanton leaned in close. "What kind of theater lets a white girl perform with a colored boy?" She was nearly spitting.

The manager's face turned a mottled red. "Mind your manners. I don't care if you're a rose or a prickly pear, this is *my* theater. We're trying to put a show together here." Miss Stanton hissed, but the stage manager ignored her. "Now, could we please carry on? I've had enough interference for one day." He glanced at Teresa's low neckline. "How old *are* you?"

"Sixteen," she said promptly, then gritted her teeth to keep them from chattering. Was it true, what Miss Stanton had said about her family?

"She's lying!" Miss Stanton cried. But the manager strode past her and beckoned to Maeve. "Come with me, Miss Cullen. I'll show you where you can park your dogs." He waved at Teresa and Pietro. "Get ready. I'll be back in a few minutes to watch your acts."

Miss Stanton's high heels clipped across the stage, her breast heaving in a fake way. "I know the truth about you," she whispered to Teresa. "You had to be fifteen to enter that contest. And what sort of girl steals her baby brother away from home?"

"Pascal is safe, with my parents." Teresa struggled to keep her voice steady.

"So you say. Don't think you can get away with this." Miss Stanton disappeared into the wings.

"Phew," Pietro said. "Prickly pear indeed." His hands trembled.

"I just hope she won't turn the manager against us," Teresa said.

"Who's first?" the bandleader called.

"Be right with you," Pietro said. "Let me get my shoes." He lowered his voice as he crossed the stage to fetch his bag. "You crazy, or what? You'll hate being corked up. And you'll wreck your pretty dress."

Was that a compliment? You never could tell, with Pietro.

44.

Pietro ran through his dance routine with the bandleader. His feet looked weighted, especially during the number where he danced up and down a small fight of stairs. He tripped once, and dropped his walking stick when he twirled it above his head. "Play it again, please," he said. The musicians grumbled, but they repeated his last tune. Pietro's face was stony until Maeve hissed, from the wings, "Smile!"

He pasted a smile on his face, danced offstage, and bent over in the wings, gasping for breath. "Break . . . a leg," he managed to whisper to Teresa.

"Play to the stage manager. He's in the third row," Maeve told her.

"Will we do 'Mockingbird?'" Teresa asked Pietro.

"Sure . . . can you waltz?" He mopped his brow.

"I used to waltz with my mama a long time ago. Why?"

"Tell him we'll do 'The Sidewalks of New York,' if he has the music."

"You want to *dance* together?" she whispered.

"Not exactly," Pietro said, as the stage manager clapped his hands.

"Come along!" he cried. "We haven't got all day."

Teresa wiped her damp palms on her dress and lowered her music to the bandleader. "I'll do 'Cousin of Mine,' 'You Are My Sunshine,' and 'Hard Times.' Do you know them?"

"Of course." The bandleader's smile was warm, and Teresa felt welcomed for the first time all morning. "Good choices," he said. "Let's have a sense of your tempos."

She hummed a few bars of each song and snapped her fingers to give him the beat. The band played the first four measures of "Cousin" as an introduction and she pitched the song to the stage manager. She felt like a phony, singing to a white-haired man in an empty theater about a girl flirting with a cousin, when she'd never even walked out with a boy. Her voice felt as thin as the mountain air. The stage manager nodded when she finished, but his expression told her nothing. "Go on," he called.

Teresa drank a glass of water. Her voice felt stronger on "Sunshine." She sashayed a few steps right, then left, snapping her fingers. On the last line of the chorus, she stretched her arms out, pleading with the invisible audience not to "take my sunshine away."

Someone in the pit clapped. Teresa bowed, and finally hit her stride with 'Hard Times,' sending the song up to the balcony. It was so quiet when she finished that she heard floorboards creak backstage. Finally, the manager grunted and waved his hand. "Not bad." He beckoned to a stagehand. "Get her stage name and take the Triplets off the sign outside."

Stage name? Teresa's mind went blank. Never mind; she'd invent one. She had a job.

Teresa and Pietro sang "Mockingbird" straight through, but they were out of sync. Teresa's voice cracked twice in the chorus, Pietro's tenor barely covered her mistake, and the high ceiling swallowed their voices. Could the stage manager even hear them? He was chatting with an older woman halfway up the aisle, his back turned to the stage. Maybe he'd already scratched their duet.

"We'd like to do 'The Sidewalks of New York,'" Pietro told the bandleader, "but we don't have the music."

"No trouble." The bandleader played a chord on the piano. "This all right with you?"

Teresa hummed a few bars. Pietro shrugged. "Sounds fine."

They practiced the first few verses. Teresa swayed from side to side while Pietro added a lazy waltz rhythm behind her with his tap shoes, mimicking the sound of brushes on a snare drum.

The bandleader held up his baton and checked his watch. "We're way behind. Practice offstage somewhere. Don't worry; a full house gives this place better acoustics." He peered up at Teresa from the pit. "Such a pretty girl—you really want to hide behind blackface?"

"No." She glanced at Pietro, but he was studying something at the back of the theater.

The bandleader beckoned to Pietro and spoke to them both. "Bert Williams wore blackface even though his partner didn't. Audiences accepted that. Black and white together isn't common. But if the boy's in blackface and you're not—who's to know what color he is beneath the cork?"

"*I* know," Pietro said. "Neither one of us is Williams or Walker. And I'm not anyone's 'boy,'" he muttered.

"Think about it," the bandleader said. "Nothing worse than being sent home without pay."

They gathered their coats and bags and headed for the wings. The stage manager was nowhere in sight. "Where can we practice?" Teresa asked.

"Our rooming house. You remember—just beyond the station." Pietro stowed his tap shoes in his bag. "I'll go along first. Follow me in ten minutes or so." He squinted at her. "How do you do that thing—where you pluck the note out of thin air?"

"Luck. I was born with perfect pitch. That's why my papa wanted to lock me up in the tuning rooms." Teresa didn't want to think about Papa, or Estey Organ Works, right now. "Go ahead." She understood why they had to walk to the rooming house separately. She didn't like it—but what else could she do?

45.

Teresa stood in the stage doorway, feeling lonesome. Maeve's music was playing as she whistled to the dogs, calling them onstage. Teresa drew her cloak around her, stepped out of the wind—and caught her heel on something lying on the floor. She stooped to pick it up. Even in the dim light, she recognized the book that Pietro carried with him everywhere: *The Souls of Black Folk: Essays and Sketches*, by W.E. Burghardt Du Bois. Pietro must be really rattled to leave his precious book behind.

She traced a finger over the author's name. Papa would say it the French way, "Do Bwah"—"of the wood"—but Pietro pronounced it differently, like "boyss." She looked through the book, turning the pages carefully. Pietro had underlined sentences all the way through, including the one, at the beginning of Chapter II, that he'd read to Mr. Jones on the train: *The problem of the Twentieth Century is the problem of the color-line.*

Teresa turned the pages and a slip of paper fell out. In neat handwriting, Pietro had written: "*The morning breaks over blood-stained hills. We must not falter, we may not shrink. Above are the everlasting stars.*" *Spoken at Harpers Ferry.*

She tried to put the paper back in the right place. One page was bookmarked with a newspaper column written by Du Bois. Pietro had also turned down the corner of a page where Du Bois had written a poem—or was it a song? In the margin, Pietro had written: *What's the tune?*

She looked behind her to make sure no one was coming. She felt as if she were reading someone's personal diary without permission. Pietro's notes in the margins were questions for the author—as if they were having a conversation. The writing in the early pages was so complicated it made her head spin. She was about to shut the book when a chapter called "Of the Meaning of

Progress" caught her eye. It began like a story: *Once upon a time I taught school in the hills of Tennessee, where the broad dark vale of the Mississippi begins to roll and crumple . . .*

Pietro had written in the margin: *Was Du Bois teaching where Daddy grew up?*

Teresa leaned against the wall, caught up in Du Bois's descriptions of the valley where he taught, the children he grew to love, the little school with its "rough benches" and few books, the families struggling to survive. She was so lost in his words that she yelped when a man's voice called, from below, "Miss LeClair? You still here?"

"Yes, sir!" Teresa shut the book, stowed it carefully in her bag, and ran downstairs to the dressing rooms. The stage manager waited in the hall with the gray-haired woman he'd been talking to earlier. "This is Mrs. Handley, our costume designer," the manager said. "We need to show you something."

Teresa followed them to a tiny dressing room that smelled of cigar smoke, stale greasepaint, and sweat. Mrs. Handley held up a wooden sun, attached to a stake. The sun's rays radiated out from a smiling face with big green eyes. Mrs. Handley balanced the sun up behind Teresa. "Perfect, ain't it?" she asked. "Her hair is like the flames themselves."

The stage manager nodded. He and Mrs. Handley turned Teresa sideways in front of the mirror, as if she were a store mannequin. "What is this for?" Teresa asked.

"No cork," the stage manager said. "Mrs. Handley and I agree: You shouldn't cover that comely face. And what would we do with your hair? Besides, it makes no sense for you to perform in cork when you're onstage alone. You'll sing 'Sunshine' first, with this behind you—thus—" He gave her the stake and helped Teresa position it behind her shoulder, so that the flames fanned out around her face. "We'll call you 'Little Miss Sunshine.' That's your stage name, for now."

"*Little* she's not," Mrs. Handley said, in a dry voice.

"Just 'Miss Sunshine,' then," he said. "Do the 'Cousin' song next, and the sad number last."

"But—I don't understand," Teresa said. "Will Pietro and I sing together?"

"We'll try it at the matinee. The bandleader's right: If the boy's in blackface and wears gloves, no one will know his true color beneath the cork. Whites did that in minstrel shows—so why not try it here? If there are no complaints, we'll go ahead with the other three shows." He took a deep breath. "You must understand—I don't own this theater. If my boss finds out I've mixed races on our stage—" He ran a finger across his throat.

Suddenly, a familiar voice screeched from the end of the hall. "Disgusting!"

The stage manager rolled his eyes at Mrs. Handley. "She's a hard case. Doesn't want to perform after a colored boy."

"Henry, you could lose your shirt over this," Mrs. Handley said.

To Teresa's surprise, the stage manager laughed. "It wouldn't be the first time. I survived the California Gold Rush, so I hope I can deal with a prickly cactus."

Miss Stanton cried out again. "There's a roach in my dressing room!"

Mrs. Handley rolled her eyes, which only made Teresa laugh. The manager sighed. "Mrs. Handley, see if you can calm her down. Tell her she'll have a good spot in the lineup." Mrs. Handley hurried away and the manager turned to Teresa. "Miss Stanton is right about one thing. Pantages won't want two women singing solo *and* a solo dancer on this tour. So do your best. We'll let the audience decide who stays on the program."

He turned on his heel, leaving Teresa with that ultimatum. Her shoulders sagged, but she caught sight of herself in the mirror. She heard Maeve's voice in her head—*Queen of England*—and then Nonnie: *Reach for the stars.*

Teresa stood tall. She hadn't come all the way to Denver to be beaten by a poisonous rose—or a prickly pear.

46.

Pietro yanked the door open when Teresa finally reached the boardinghouse. He must have been watching for her. "Where the heck have you been?" he demanded.

She explained what the stage manager had planned. "That figures." Pietro stomped down the hall, slicing at the air with his walking stick. "Bad enough that Daddy and I have to pretend to be someone else. Now I have to black up to sing with a white girl?"

"So don't." Teresa put her hands on her hips. "You do your act, I'll do mine—but the manager told me he can't use three solo acts. One of us will get the hook if the audience likes Miss Stanton best."

"And it's my job to keep you in business?" Pietro's eyes blazed and Teresa bit her cheeks to keep from crying.

"Take it easy, you two."

Teresa whirled around. Mr. Jones lay on the couch behind them, propped up by pillows. "I'm sorry, Mr. Jones," she said. "I didn't see you. Are you all right?"

"Barely. Still breathing." He turned to Pietro. "You knew you'd be in blackface here."

"Doesn't mean I have to like it."

Mr. Jones swung his legs to the floor and sat up. "We're all lucky to have any job at all—and you're wasting time . . ." He began to cough and his eyes bulged. Teresa rushed over and patted his back.

"I'll get some water." Pietro sent Teresa an accusing look as he left the room. As if this were *her* fault!

Pietro returned with a full glass and watched his father drink it down. Mr. Jones settled back against the pillows. "I wish I could play my reeds for you," he whispered, "but I'd better save my wind."

"That's all right." Teresa opened her bag to get her sheet music and found Pietro's book. "I found this on the floor of the theater."

Pietro snatched it as if she'd stolen it and caressed the cover with his fingertips.

Teresa turned away. Did anything she owned matter that much? Her voice. That was her most prized possession—yet no one could see it. The locket—and Nonnie's photograph: that was all she owned. She took out her sheet music and cleared her throat. "Shall we sing?"

They practiced "Mockingbird" twice, singing in the key of G, without looking at each other. "Stiff as boards, the both of you," Mr. Jones said. "Add some bounce to it. And you gotta at least *pretend* you're friendly."

Teresa blushed, but she still didn't dare meet Pietro's eyes. "Show her some steps," Mr. Jones said. "Go on, Son."

"Like this." Pietro sidestepped in front of Teresa and whistled the tune.

Teresa tried to imitate him, but she felt big and clumsy.

Pietro stepped behind her, put his hands on her waist, and swayed her from side to side. "Relax," he said.

Impossible. The feeling of his hands on her hips sent fire into her face.

"Don't worry," Mr. Jones said. "He won't touch you onstage. Close your eyes and imagine you're all alone, learning a new dance, with no one watching but the four walls." He slapped the beat on the arm of the sofa. "'*Listen to the mockingbird*'—clap clap. Snap those fingers and let Pietro do the dancing."

Teresa shut her eyes and pretended she was in her attic room with no one home, and it helped: The music flowed into her body. Pietro dropped his hands, Teresa opened her eyes, and they followed the beat. "*Now* you've got it!" Mr. Jones said.

They practiced for an hour. When they switched to "The Sidewalks of New York," Pietro showed her how to waltz in place while he danced around her, twirling his cane and easing into a smooth routine. They dropped into the empty chairs, out of breath. Teresa still felt lightheaded, but not as dizzy as when she'd arrived. She pulled out a handkerchief and wiped her face, hoping sweat hadn't stained her new dress.

Applause broke out in the hall. A tall colored man with a wide smile stood in the doorway. "Mr. Bertram here," he said. "You've got a powerful voice, young lady. I was humming along in the kitchen. And nice harmony," he told Pietro. "You'll slay them." He rubbed his chin. "I don't mind you singing together in my parlor. But how will folks act when you show up on stage together?"

"I'll be wearing cork," Pietro said.

"And she won't?"

"That's the plan," Pietro told him. "Sound crazy?"

"You'll find out soon enough," Mr. Bertram said in a dry voice. "Best of luck to you."

"We need it." Pietro raised one eyebrow at Teresa. That was as close as she would get to a smile.

47.

Mr. Bertram fed them sandwiches before they returned to the Princess. Mr. Jones leaned heavily on Pietro; he waved Teresa on ahead. "You go on," he said. "I'm a slowpoke."

Teresa lifted her skirt to keep it off the dusty sidewalk and hurried through town. Now and then she glanced behind to be sure they were all right. Pietro was dressed in the new suit he'd bought in New York, with a handsome striped cutaway jacket and a red bowtie. He looked taller, more dignified. Teresa felt awkward, wearing clothes that were too old for her. Papa wouldn't approve—though maybe Nonnie would. Thank goodness her cloak covered her knees.

Mr. Jones claimed he was feeling better, but he used his dancing stick as a cane and his cough wouldn't quit. If the Joneses could dance together tomorrow—would Teresa have to sing on her own? Would the stage manager like that? She knew what Nonnie would say: *One day at a time, child. One day at a time.*

Nonnie. If only she had some way to reach her, to let her know she was all right. But she needed every penny she might make today—and she couldn't let Papa know where she'd gone. Teresa nearly bumped into a streetlight. She caught herself, pulled her cloak tight, and pushed thoughts of her family away. She had a job to do.

When they arrived at the theater, Teresa, Mr. Jones, and Pietro went downstairs to the dressing rooms. Two signs were tacked up on the wall, over chipped paint: *Such words as Liar, Slob, Son-of-a-gun, Devil, Sucker, and Damn are unfit for Ladies and Children.* A second sign read: *Don't send out your laundry until after the first show.*

"What does that mean?" Teresa asked Mr. Jones.

He managed a weak smile. "If you're all wet at the matinee, they throw you out. You don't want to leave town with your laundry wet, too."

Teresa's heart hammered in her throat. "What if we get the hook after the matinee?"

"Don't worry. You'll be fine," Mr. Jones said.

Maybe. A stagehand showed Mr. Jones and Pietro to a dressing room under the stairs that was as small as a closet—maybe it *was* a closet—and pointed Teresa to a room at the end of the hall. She hesitated. Wasn't Miss Stanton down that way? Just then, Maeve poked her head out of another door. "Teresa—where have you been? Pietro, Mr. Jones—you can't do your makeup in that cave! Come in here. I'm presentable."

Pietro and his father glanced at each other before they followed Teresa into Maeve's room. The dogs went wild, yipping and jumping. "Lie down, dogs! All of you." Maeve waved the dogs into a line under the vanity tables and made space for Pietro and Mr. Jones on two spindly chairs. Her eyes sparkled as she looked at Pietro. "You're quite natty today."

Pietro actually looked embarrassed. "You're not too shabby yourself."

He was right. Maeve's emerald pants and blouse, along with her eye shadow, brought out the green in her eyes. Silver barrettes, shaped like butterflies, glittered in her dark hair. Her cheeks shone and her lips, painted a deep maroon, lit up her smile.

"You look wonderful," Teresa said, then explained the manager's plan. "No cork for me."

Maeve turned to Pietro. "But you'll be in blackface?"

"Afraid so," Pietro said. A muscle twitched in his cheek.

"I'm sorry," Maeve said.

Pietro shrugged. "Come on, Daddy. Let's get it over with." They moved into a corner, where Pietro perched on an old crate at one end of the vanity table. Teresa sat on a chair at the other end. The row of lights made her squint. Scribbled notes from previous performers were tacked on the wall next to the mirror. One note warned about rooming houses with bedbugs; another begged friends to come find him. Someone named Shirley scrawled the names of restaurants with "decent, cheap grub." Another post, from "Lazy Mary," boasted that she would give someone "a nice roll in the hay." Teresa blushed and turned away. Was this what Papa meant, when he said vaude wasn't proper for young girls?

Greasepaint and lipstick stained the vanity table, and a torn dress, limp with age and sweat, hung from a hook behind the door. It wasn't the Palace, but it was better than an amateur night, for sure. Teresa held still while Maeve tried to make sense of her hair.

"Your curls don't want to be combed," Maeve said. "I'm just going to pin your hair up." She twisted Teresa's curls into a small knot at the back of her head and held it with a comb and heavy clips.

Mr. Jones draped an old sheet over Pietro's collar and shoulders and spread thick, black paste on his face. Pietro's cheeks, once a ruddy mahogany, became pitch black, as if he worked in a coal mine. Mr. Jones painted a wide, false grin on Pietro's lips and Teresa stared at the floor. Even though she'd seen them wear blackface in Brattleboro, it was worse, now that she knew them both so well. "It must feel awful," Teresa said.

"You said it," Pietro said. "Like wearing a mask. I'm the worst kind of fake." He stood up and pulled on his gloves. "Admit you hate it, Daddy."

"I do." Mr. Jones slumped into a chair and coughed into his handkerchief. "Believe me—I wish we had a choice."

"We do, Daddy."

Mr. Jones waved him away. "Can't fight that battle now. You taking a big enough risk as it is."

His cough seemed louder in the small room. Even the dogs were quiet. Teresa felt as if the walls were closing in on them. She closed her eyes as Maeve rubbed rouge onto her cheeks. A sudden knock made them all jump. "Come in!" Maeve cried.

Mrs. Handley pushed open the door, holding Teresa's wooden sun on its stake. "Well!" She took in the room, glancing at the dogs—all dressed up in their pompoms and satin coats—then at Pietro and Mr. Jones. "Excuse *me*," she said. "I didn't mean to intrude on this cozy little group. Don't forget your sun—'Miss

Sunshine.'" She shook her head. "Every time a new group comes to town, I think I've seen everything—but this takes the cake." She shut the door firmly behind her.

Teresa's stomach lurched. "Mrs. Handley told the manager he could lose his shirt if we all perform together."

"With his paunch, that's a sight I'd rather not see," Maeve said.

Mr. Jones laughed; even Pietro smiled. He pointed at Teresa's prop. "Don't tell me you have to perform with that thing."

"I'm afraid so. I'm 'Miss Sunshine' now."

Pietro whistled and Mr. Jones grabbed his arm. "Bad luck to whistle in the dressing room," he said.

Whistling was bad luck? So was a feather on the windowsill, according to Maeve, not to mention wishing someone *good* luck. Nonnie was the one who might help Teresa sing "like an angel," but her picture was buried at the bottom of her valise, back at their hotel. Teresa tried to hear her great-grandmother's encouraging voice inside her head, but the footsteps shuffling above their heads, and the scraping of furniture and props across the floorboards, drowned her out. An oboe played an A, and a chorus of instruments chimed in.

"They're tuning up," Mr. Jones said. "Time to go." He fiddled with Pietro's bow tie. "*Merde*," he said in a low voice. Teresa giggled and Mr. Jones gave her a quick look. "You know French?"

"*Mais oui*. My papa is from Québec." And a good thing Papa wasn't here.

"Then excuse my French, as they say. You'll do fine." Mr. Jones squeezed her hand. His palm felt hot to the touch. Did he have a fever?

Teresa glanced at her reflection. She was a stranger to herself, with her flaming cheeks, her hair pulled up high, and her chest exposed by the plunging neckline. Only the gold locket remained from her past life.

48.

The matinee crowd was sparse and restless. Children ran up and down the aisles, tossing peanut shells, and the audience talked through the acrobats' act, even though they performed some wonderful tricks on the slack wire. "Sitting on their hands," Sammy complained as they dashed into the wings.

"You were great," Teresa told him, but he blew her a raspberry. The next act—two comedians—was stupid; no wonder the audience booed. Their best slapstick move was slapping each other with rolled-up newspapers. "Puerto Rico would have shot them dead at the Lafayette," Teresa whispered. "Where's Miss Stanton?"

"Waiting in the best dressing room," Maeve said softly. "She's too 'important' to stand in the wings. Don't think about her. She's next to last, where she wanted to be. She'll be sorry, having to go onstage after you two."

If only.

The band launched into a ragtime number. Pietro pushed past Teresa as if she didn't exist and danced onstage, his feet flashing in his new black-and-white spats. Teresa's stomach roiled and her palms were sweaty.

"Breathe," Maeve whispered.

But breathing deep only made her more lightheaded. Pietro kept dancing. The band's music rushed in her ears like water, and the applause that followed his ragtime sounded like distant drumbeats. She was so far away, so lost in terror, that when Pietro came offstage, Maeve had to jostle her elbow. "You're next," she whispered, and placed the wooden stake, with its sunshine medallion, into her hand.

Teresa stood on tiptoe, waiting for her music to start, when the stage manager strode out from the wings, his belly protruding under his ill-fitting jacket. "We have a little change in the program." The audience rustled and he put up his hand. "Two of the Toronto sisters decided to go back home. But they left the best member of their group behind. Please welcome . . ." (he paused for the drumroll) "Miss Sunshine!"

Scattered applause broke out and the band played her opening bars. Teresa couldn't move. Maeve shoved her from one side and Pietro whispered, "Go!"

Somehow, she found the nerve to sashay out from the wings as the band played the first verse of "You Are My Sunshine." A few people laughed and hooted as she hoisted the wooden sun above her head. It was too heavy and made her feet feel rooted to the stage floor. Teresa glanced at the bandleader. He nodded, brought the band around to the opening chords again, and she began to sing.

The bandleader was right: Even this small audience gave the theater better acoustics. Teresa found a way to brace the sun, as if it were a tree in the woods, and let her voice go. By the third chorus, she heard people humming. She dared to try something she'd never done before: After the final verse, she beckoned to the audience and cried, "Sing it with me!"

They did—badly, but with enthusiasm. By the end of the song, most of the chatter had stopped. Setting her prop aside, she began singing "Cousin of Mine." That song brought a few laughs, so she was more relaxed for "Hard Times." It wasn't her best performance, but the small crowd gave her a decent round of applause.

As she bowed low, the bandleader played the first few bars of "Mockingbird," and Pietro strutted onstage in his tap shoes, whistling. Teresa whirled around, pretending surprise, then shrugged at the audience as if to say: *What can I do?*

The crowd was suddenly still. Teresa began to sing, and when she sang *"listen to the mockingbird!"* the flute answered with a birdlike trill. Pietro tapped out a lazy rhythm, adding some steps that took him back and forth across the stage. The audience gave them polite applause. The band picked up the pace on "The Sidewalks of New York," playing it almost too fast for Teresa to keep up. Pietro danced around and behind her, until she was afraid she'd bump into him. She was relieved to dash offstage when the song was over.

"Did we die?" she gasped, trying to catch her breath.

"*You* didn't," he said. "I'm not sure about us together."

Three actors went onstage for a comedy act and the stage manager beckoned to Teresa and Pietro. They followed him downstairs. "Good job," he said to Teresa. "Don't be afraid to ham it up a bit, put a little more oomph into it." He turned to Pietro. "You're dancing well, but you need a partner. It's too one-sided."

"My father will be better tomorrow," Pietro said. The fake smile, painted on over the cork, didn't match the worry in his eyes.

"I hope so," the manager said. "They don't know what to make of the two of you. Only one duet next show—maybe "Mockingbird." They all know the tune, and the band does a good job, answering with the flute. We'll see how it goes."

Teresa went limp with relief. "Thank you, sir." She rushed into the wings to help Maeve get ready.

The next two shows went smoothly and Teresa settled into the rhythm: She watched Pietro dance, sat quietly as she waited to go onstage herself, hammed it up a bit when he joined her onstage for her final number, then joined Maeve in the wings to help with the dogs.

Maeve's act was a big hit. In fact, Teresa decided, she and her dogs were the stars of the show. Maeve had worked out a routine with Sammy the acrobat, who performed a version of Pascal's trick with Dixie and the ball. The audience loved it, and the crowds grew as the day wore on. They remained lukewarm when Pietro and Teresa sang together, but each audience gave Teresa a warm hand; by the third show, they called her back for a second bow before Pietro came on.

Miss Stanton was another story. She received hoots and whistles for her low-cut gown and her daring skirt and tights, but when she started to sing, her small, breathy voice made the crowd restless. People began to talk; a few even walked out. In spite of this, the stage manager didn't give her the hook.

"Thank goodness her act follows mine," Maeve said.

"Do you think he'll keep her and fire me?" Teresa asked.

"That would be idiotic," Maeve said.

Scattered boos broke after Miss Stanton's third performance. She stalked offstage and drew up in front of Teresa, her face the color of her scarlet dress. "You'll pay for this." She clicked away in her high heels before Teresa could respond.

The theater was packed for the final house of the night. Teresa was so tired she could barely stand, but the crowd's energy carried her through her three solo numbers, and they called her back for three bows before Pietro came on. Teresa sang directly to Pietro this time, even though she couldn't read his expression under the cork. "*Listen to the mockingbird*," she implored. "*The mockingbird is singing o'er her grave . . .*"

Tappita tappita tap, Pietro's shoes answered. When they finished, Pietro motioned her toward the edge of the stage, where they took their bows side by side. "Smile and stand close," he told her, under his breath. "They expect it." They bowed low, Teresa curtsied, the audience kept clapping—

And a shrill voice rang out, from someplace above the crowd—from a box, perhaps?—"Disgusting! She sings and dances with a colored boy!"

Teresa froze. "One more bow," Pietro said.

Teresa's smile felt as phony as Pietro's. A raw egg splattered at their feet. Teresa jumped out of the way and dashed offstage with Pietro right behind her. A chorus of boos and a low buzz, like a swarm of bees, rose from the audience. The stage manager waited in the wings, wringing his hands. He jerked his thumb toward the stairs and they followed him to the narrow hallway outside the dressing rooms. Teresa's heartbeat whooshed in her ears.

"The truth is out now," the stage manager said. "It was madness, putting you onstage together." He tugged at his thinning hair. "Tomorrow you do your acts separately, on different parts of the program. And you," he said to Pietro. "Either you're with your father—both of you in cork—or you're washed up."

"That's not fair," Teresa said. "It's Miss Stanton's fault."

"What do you mean?" the stage manager asked.

"She's the one who screamed. I recognized her voice."

"Why would she do that?"

"Because she's jealous," Pietro said. "Miss LeClair here sings better."

A compliment from Pietro? Teresa couldn't believe it.

"*Boy*," the stage manager said through gritted teeth. "Don't get uppity with me. Miss Stanton is a trained professional. I'm sure she's in her dressing room."

"Really?" Teresa turned on her heel and knocked on the first door on the right. Sammy the acrobat poked his head out, a half-eaten sandwich in his hand, his shirt unbuttoned.

"Sorry," Teresa said. "I'm looking for Miss Stanton."

"Next door," Sammy said, his mouth full.

"You're trying my patience," the stage manager called.

Teresa ignored him, rapped on the next door, and opened it. Dresses littered the backs of chairs, makeup was strewn across the vanity table, and a feather boa lay coiled on the floor—but the room was empty. Teresa left the door open and faced the stage manager, who had followed her down the hall. "*Now* do you believe me?"

He glanced inside. White spots appeared on his cheeks. "Don't test your luck, young lady. I'm giving you one more day here—but only because I don't have replacements. Thank the Lord you go to Leadville on Sunday. Now get out of my sight, before I send Pantages a telegram."

He stomped down the hall. Pietro gave a low whistle. "Watch your temper. You nearly got us both fired."

"Me! *You're* the one who—"

Before she could finish her sentence, Pietro ducked into the dressing room under the stairs and shut the door firmly in her face.

49.

Mr. Jones was better the next day, and he did manage to dance with Pietro—though without his usual style. Teresa couldn't pay attention. She was too worried about her own performances. Perhaps because it was Friday, even the matinee brought in a full house. Teresa tried to put her heart into her songs, but she felt deflated without Pietro's dance steps and harmony.

Worse, the Joneses weren't speaking to her—or to anyone else. They used their own closet-sized dressing room to apply their blackface, and Mr. Jones huddled there between performances. When Pietro wasn't running back and forth to a café for hot drinks and soup, he sat on a folding chair at the end of the hall, reading a newspaper. Teresa caught a glimpse of the paper's title—the *Chicago Defender*—but she didn't dare ask why he hauled that old paper around. Plus, she hated to look at his blackened face. Even Maeve seemed quiet and distracted.

After the third show, Teresa slumped onto a chair in their dressing room and faced herself in the mirror. Her hair was falling out of its pins, her makeup was smudged, and her dress was stained under the arms. "I look terrible," she said.

"Join the crowd," Maeve said. "Could you fix Edna's pompom? It's falling off."

Teresa cut some ribbon from a roll on the table and retied the pompom to Edna's harness. "Why is everyone mad at me?" she asked.

"We're just nervous," Maeve said. "You and Pietro could have spoiled it for all of us."

"But I was helping *him* out! He needed someone to dance with. Besides, the audience loves you and the dogs. You're the headliners, even though you're not listed that way."

"Not today. They're sitting on their hands for everyone. They're just waiting to catch us in a mistake, so we're all tripping up. Dixie missed the ball in the third show, Sam nearly fell off the slack wire, and Mr. Jones dropped his cane. Meanwhile, Miss Stanton got some applause, even though her voice broke."

"And that's my fault?" Teresa blinked back tears.

"Remember what I said: You and Pietro *must* be careful."

It wasn't fair! Pietro didn't even like her. Teresa buried her face in Edna's tangled fur. "You're my only friend," she whispered.

Thank goodness the jump to Leadville was on the night train, so Teresa didn't have to talk to anyone. She managed to sleep, using Edna as a pillow on a hard seat, and woke to bright sunlight glinting on slick rock. The train rattled across a long trestle, suspended in space above an abyss. She tapped Maeve's shoulder. "Look."

Maeve murmured, "The Rockies?" but didn't open her eyes.

They passed under a long shed laden with snow and came out on a hillside dotted with emerald pines, their branches weighted with fresh powder. Deer with jackrabbit ears ran from the train, their tails waving like small flags. Dixie and Bronwyn set their paws on the windowsill and whimpered. Passengers stretched and twisted in their seats as the train climbed onto a wide, bleak plateau. They passed freight cars loaded with chunks of stone. Caves and tunnels were dug into the sides of a mountain, and rickety wooden structures sprouted everywhere. "What is all this?" Teresa asked.

Maeve slept on.

Teresa walked through their car to the toilet and then headed to the rear of the train, where she found Mr. Jones standing against a window, looking out. Pietro was curled up awkwardly on the seat behind him, legs dangling, his book tucked under his cheek for a pillow. Mr. Jones tipped his cap to her. "Morning, Miss LeClair. Quite the view, isn't it?"

"It's beautiful." She pointed to a group of men digging into the side of the hill. "What are they doing?"

"Mining. Let's hope they want some entertainment at the end of the day." The men waved as they passed.

The train leaned into a curve and Teresa grabbed the back of the seat. "I'm sorry about what happened in Denver," she said.

"So am I," Mr. Jones said. "The world's not ready for y'all—not yet." He glanced behind him, keeping his voice low. "Tell you what, though—we walked the whole train last night before we found these seats. No sign of Miss Stanton anywhere."

"Is this the only train?"

"No. There's also the narrow gauge. But we can always hope, can't we?"

Teresa crossed her fingers and held up her hands. "Definitely."

Teresa, Maeve, and the dogs straggled down Leadville's wide main street. Their bags knocked against their legs as they searched for a rooming house. "What a strange place," Teresa said. Women in long gowns, hoisting their skirts to avoid grimy snow, walked beside miners carrying shovels and pickaxes. Mules strained to pull heavy freight wagons through the wide, muddy streets, while glossy black automobiles stood in front of stores with decorated, fake storefronts. Rundown shacks leaned up against elegant brick buildings. Within a few blocks the dogs had muddy paws, and Teresa was glad she had worn her oldest dress for traveling.

She glanced behind her. Pietro and his father followed them at a slow pace, Mr. Jones using his dancing stick for balance. Teresa felt lightheaded again. "I hope Mr. Jones can dance," she said.

"I know," Maeve said. "I feel woozy myself. We're that much higher than Denver here—look!" She pulled up the dogs. "There's our theater. Isn't it grand?"

A three-story brick building rose above the sidewalk on the far side of the street. The raised words "Tabor Opera House" stood out above arched second-story windows, and the building stretched back into the next block. An elegant hotel flanked the theater on one side. "Too bad we can't stay there." Teresa patted her skirt, where she had pocketed her earnings from Denver. At least she wouldn't have to borrow money again.

"It's not worth asking." Maeve clucked to the dogs. They walked the main street and tried four or five rooming houses, but they were all full. "There's a run on molybdenum up here," one owner told them. "Try the Miner's Refuge—they might have room."

The "Refuge" turned out to be three small cabins leaning up against one another like tired old ladies. "Glorified shacks," Maeve said, but she knocked on the closest door. The owner, a jowly man in suspenders and a red flannel shirt, scowled at the dogs but offered a choice of two rooms: one not much bigger than a closet, but with a door; the other a larger room separated from the hallway by a thin curtain. They took the smaller room and Maeve settled onto the bed, which sank under her weight. "Prickly horsehair," she said, rubbing the mattress. "Never mind. I could sleep on a board, if I had to." She yawned and made space beside her. "Need a nap?"

"Not now. I'll take the dogs for a walk. Maybe I can get inside the Opera House."

"Good idea. Find out when band call is, and wake me in time—will you?" Maeve closed her eyes.

At least Maeve was herself again. Maybe this town would be all right.

On her way out, Teresa asked the owner if he could save the last room for their friends. "I think they'll be along soon," she said. "They're part of our troupe."

"First come, first served," he said.

Teresa swallowed a laugh. As if he had something decent to offer!

50.

Teresa stopped outside the theater to catch her breath. A poster announcing their show leaned up against the brick wall. The "Singing Toronto Triplets" were still on the list, as were Maeve and the Joneses—but at the bottom of the bill, someone had drawn a thick line through "The Rose of Abilene" and scrawled above it:

"FAVORITE SHAKESPEAREAN SKIT RETURNS!"

"She's gone!" Teresa crowed. Cleo, usually the quietest dog, made a low crooning noise. Teresa gave her a pat. "Yes, it's lovely.

Good dog." Had Pantages fired Miss Stanton—or had she quit in disgust? Either way, it was good news.

The theater door stood open. Teresa tugged the dogs up a wide staircase and went into the hall, pulling the door closed behind her. The space was dimly lit. She waited a moment, with the dogs at her feet, until her eyes adjusted to the light. She was standing at the back of the parquet, with the dress circle above her. Rows of plush maroon seats, each one topped with a wrought-iron decoration, lined red-carpeted aisles. She looked up. Cherubs, flowers, and ribbons seemed to dance on the frescoed ceiling. "Dear Mama, dear Nonnie," she whispered. "If you could see me now."

She pulled the dogs together. They seemed to understand that they were in a special place, and trotted down the aisle in an orderly row. Teresa reached down to touch a seat. It was soft as velvet. Gauzy lace curtains lined the special boxes on either side of the stage, and a wide orchestra pit, with at least a dozen chairs, ran in front of the stage apron. She looked up—and sucked in her breath. A painted scene formed the stage backdrop. It showed lines of craggy peaks marching in rows to fainter, white-covered mountains in the distance. A waterfall cascaded over a stony bank in the foreground, surrounded by pines. Would she sing in front of this beautiful painting?

"Stay!" she told the dogs, and climbed onto the stage. She touched her locket, cleared her throat, and hummed an E-flat to warm her voice, then sang a few scales. When she began to sing, she closed her eyes to get a sense of the theater's acoustics. Even without an audience, the placed sounded warm.

She begged the hard times to disappear, pleaded with them to quit lingering "around my cabin door"—yet, even as she sang of troubles, and the "sigh of the weary," she also knew that this was what she was meant to do: send her voice up to the frescoed ceiling, to the last row of seats in the dress circle, and out to the busy street.

The final note drifted away and she was startled by the sound of clapping. The dogs leapt to their feet, barking and snarling, and raced up the aisle, the fur bristling on their backs. A tall, silver-haired man stood up in the last row and raised his hands over his head. "Call them off!" he yelled.

"Dogs—sit!" Teresa jumped off the stage and hurried up the aisle. "Calm down." The dogs obeyed, except for Fido, who went down on all fours, a low growl rumbling in his throat, as the man started down the aisle.

"Easy, boy." The man glared at Fido. "Is this mutt part of today's show?"

"They're all with Madame Maeve and her Marvelous Marching Dogs. Fido, leave it." Teresa picked up Fido's leash and wrapped it around the arm of an aisle seat. "They're usually friendly." No need to tell him that Fido protected them both against men with "bad ideas," as Maeve put it.

The man stepped out of the shadows and put out his hand. "Rupert Harrison," he said. "Stage manager."

If only her palms weren't damp with fear. "I'm Teresa LeClair."

"So I guessed." He cleared his throat. "You have a lovely voice. But I heard about your—uh—little fiasco in Denver. I trust we won't see any of that here."

"No, sir." Teresa studied the plush red carpet under her dirty boots.

"Look at me, young lady."

She did. His eyes were a cold gray-blue. "I'm sorry," she whispered. "We thought—"

"Never mind what you thought. I also heard that you could sing, and you just proved that to me here. But no more shenanigans—understand?"

"Yes, sir." Teresa hated sounding like a servant, but what choice did she have?

"If you know what's good for you, you'll keep to your own kind." His words stung, but Teresa said nothing. "What songs are you planning to sing?"

She pulled her list out of her pocket. He looked it over and nodded. "Check these out with the bandleader at first band call. 'Sunshine' might sound sappy to these men—I'd give them 'The Sidewalks of New York.' 'Hard Times' could be too close to home—but you sing it well, so leave it in." He waved at the painted backdrop. "'Mockingbird' would match the setting, with those trees and mountains." He handed her the paper. "I also heard that you sang better than that so-called 'Rose of Abilene.' She was already washed up when she performed here last year, so we scratched her. Hope you can prove we made the right choice. Band call at noon."

He turned on his heel and strode back up the aisle, leaving Teresa with her mouth open. His welcome was as cold as this town—but at least the "Rose" was gone.

51.

After a stingy breakfast, Teresa and Maeve discovered that the Miner's Refuge offered little more than a sponge and a basin of hot water for a bath. "We'll clean up at the theater," Maeve said. "And let's bring our luggage with us. I don't trust this place."

The theater's lavatory was tiny but clean. Teresa washed at the basin and winced when she pulled her yellow skirt and blouse from her bag. "Look how wrinkled it is," she said. "I can't go on in this."

"We'll find an iron," Maeve said. "That's the least of our worries. From what you told me about the stage manager, we all have to prove ourselves today."

Someone rapped on the dressing-room door. "Who's there?" Teresa pulled on her cloak to cover her underwear.

"Wardrobe mistress." A plump white woman stepped inside and stared at Teresa. "You're that singer girl, aren't you?"

"Yes."

"I was listening upstairs, when you was practicing." The woman's face reddened. "Sorry for eavesdropping, Miss, but Mr. Harrison had no business talking to you that way; you such a young thing. Thought I'd look in on you, see what you might need."

Teresa blinked back grateful tears. "How kind." She scooped up her yellow costume. "I was going to wear this—but it's so wrinkled."

"Hmm. I've got something better suited to your coloring." She bustled away and returned a few minutes later carrying a royal-blue gown. "Let's see if it fits you." The woman's speech was slurred from the straight pins sticking from her mouth. She slipped the dress over Teresa's head and buttoned it up the back.

Teresa looked at herself in the mirror. Like the dress Maeve had stitched for her, this one had a low neckline, though not as revealing. The skirt swung just below her knees. And the woman was right: The royal blue set off her hair and didn't highlight her freckles as the yellow outfit did. "It's beautiful," Teresa whispered. "Thank you."

"You'll need some decent tights, maybe some black shoes," the wardrobe mistress said. "I'll check my storeroom." She glanced at Maeve, then at the dogs. "Anything you need, Miss? And what about these furry critters?"

"A whole new canine wardrobe?" Maeve smiled. "Just teasing." She held up a pair of green tights. "I was mending these, but they're in terrible shape. Maybe a pair to match my shorts?" She showed the woman her emerald satin outfit, then picked up a shredded pompom and pointed to Fido, who was curled up under the vanity table. "He chewed this up on the train last night. If you had some fresh ribbon—"

"Naughty boy," the wardrobe mistress said, but she gave Fido a pat. "These dogs are better behaved than the monkey we had last week. Not to mention what the visiting zebra left onstage."

They all laughed. "You're very kind," Maeve said. "What's your name?"

"Miss Feingold—but folks just call me Goldie. I'll be back shortly." She paused at the door, looking at Teresa. "Sing like you did this morning, and you won't have nothing to worry about."

She was gone before Teresa could thank her.

"You see?" Maeve gave Teresa a quick hug. "As long as you do your job and sing like an angel, the audience will love you."

"I hope so." Teresa plopped down onto a hard chair. "Do you have to prove yourself every time you start in a new town?"

"Every single town, every single theater, every show," Maeve said. "It keeps us on our toes, trying new things. Right, dogs?"

The dogs jumped to their feet, tails wagging, ears pricked. Dixie did a little jig on her hind legs—and Teresa imitated her, twirling around the tiny room until her head spun.

An hour later, as Maeve and Teresa were putting the finishing touches on their makeup and costumes, they heard familiar voices in the hall. Dixie and Edna leapt up, tails wagging, but Teresa froze.

"Daddy, if I'm dancing alone, I'll do it my own way," Pietro was saying.

Teresa opened the door and peered out. Pietro was hauling their luggage down the narrow hallway while Mr. Jones limped behind, leaning on Pietro's shoulder. "Is everything all right?" she asked.

"Afraid not." Pietro set down their bags and wiped his brow on his sleeve.

Mr. Jones gave Teresa a sad wave. "I'm slow as a tortoise at this altitude." He touched the brim of his cap. "Don't you ladies look nice."

Pietro didn't even glance in their direction. He squinted at the label on the dressing room across the hall. "Looks like this is our spot. And it's not your fault we're late, Daddy. It's this town, and you know it. *No room at the inn.*" His voice was like cold iron. "That's what they all say."

Maeve emerged from their dressing room. "Our place—the Miner's Refuge—was supposed to save you a room."

"Some 'refuge.' We showed up just after you, but they said someone had taken the last bed."

"Then they lied. Where will you go?"

Pietro shrugged and shoved their bags into their dressing room. "Maybe a boxcar, but that won't help Daddy's cough. Right now we need to get ready for band call. Come on, Daddy."

Mr. Jones didn't budge. "Let's see what our friends think about our question."

"Our *question*—if that's what you want to call it—is none of their business—begging your pardon," he added.

Mr. Jones ignored him. "Pietro here says he's dancing without cork."

Pietro leaned close to him. "I am, Daddy. That's none of their worry—or yours. If Walker could perform without cork, then so can I."

"Son, we've been through all this. George Walker was one of the most popular entertainers ever known, until his collapse—God rest his soul. Williams still *is* one of the funniest men alive.

But you're just a young man, hardly more than a boy, starting out." He bent over coughing.

Pietro patted his father's back. "Williams and Walker were boys once, too. Personally, I'm sick to death of being a 'boy' to all these stage managers."

"Then maybe it's time for you to pack it in," Mr. Jones said, when he caught his breath.

Teresa bit her lip. Did Mr. Jones mean that? She backed away. It was too awkward to hear them fight. Maeve touched her elbow. "We'd better finish dressing," she said, and ducked inside their dressing room.

Pietro held up his hand. "Resa, wait. Let me get Daddy settled." He took his father's arm and ushered him into their dressing room.

Resa. Had he ever called her that before? Pietro's voice was low and reassuring behind the closed door. When he emerged from their dressing room, he glanced at Teresa. "Daddy's right. You sure do look nice." He glanced along the hall. "Coast is clear. We need to talk."

Teresa followed him past the dressing rooms to a bench in a corner. They perched at either end, careful to keep their distance. "How *is* your father?" she asked.

"He's still got a fever. We could be all washed up after tonight."

"But you're fine, dancing on your own."

"I need to be more than *fine*. If the stage manager won't accept me without cork, that's the end. It might not be the worst thing."

When he didn't explain, Teresa said, "I read some of your book." She stole a look at him, expecting him to be angry, but he smiled.

"I know."

"How?"

"You put my notes back in the wrong place. What did you think?"

"I'm not the best reader. It's—it's complicated writing. I can see why you'd have to study it a lot. I liked the part where he wrote about being a teacher. But what—I feel dumb that I don't remember—what happened to John Brown at Harpers Ferry?"

She expected scorn, but Pietro's tone was patient. "Brown and his sons and followers tried to take over a federal arsenal. There was a massacre, people killed on both sides. Some folks say the Civil War began at Harpers Ferry. That's why Du Bois gave his speech there—"

"I read it," Teresa said. "He—makes me think about things." She felt stupid and tongue-tied. Pietro didn't seem to notice.

"The man's a genius. He's a poet and teacher, he writes essays, he went to *Harvard*, amazing for a colored man—and he understands how the world *works*." Pietro's toes tapped a nervous rhythm on the floorboards. "And I want—" He glanced down the empty hall. "Don't say anything about this."

"Of course."

"I want to be near this man, learn from him, work for what he believes in. So that someday—" He glanced up and down the hall, then leaned close, pulled up his shirtsleeve, and held his arm against hers. Teresa shivered when their skin touched. "See that?" Pietro asked. "Black against white? No different than day touching night. White folks can't handle that now. Someday, maybe they will."

Footsteps clattered on the stairs. Pietro jumped to his feet as a stagehand ran past. "Band call in a half hour," the stagehand said, and kept running.

Pietro's brown eyes met her own. "I haven't said a word to Daddy. Du Bois has this organization, the National Association for the Advancement of Colored People; NAACP, they call it. That Harpers Ferry speech was the start of it. In the NAACP, whites and blacks work together to stop the lynchings; help us get schooling, jobs, and houses like white people have now. I've been reading about it in the newspapers. Might see if I can work with them, get better educated, try to change things."

Teresa's mouth went dry. "You'd leave the stage?" Her voice sounded as small as she felt. "You're such a good dancer."

"Good, sure. But fabulous? Not yet; maybe never. Dancing is Daddy's calling, not mine. I do it because he's my daddy. If they toss me offstage tonight, maybe that's a sign." In spite of what he said, Pietro tap-danced in a lazy beat as he talked.

"What would happen to your father?"

"He'll be all right when he gets down from the mountains. I'll take him back to New York. He could find another partner— maybe a woman. Or teach people to dance. You see how he was, helping you: so patient. Not like me," Pietro added, with a rare smile.

"Twenty minutes!" The same young stagehand pulled up in front of them. "Everything all right, Miss?" he asked.

"Just *fine*." Teresa stood to face him. "I'm completely fine, thank you very much." When the stagehand disappeared, she plucked Pietro's sleeve. "Could I borrow your book for a few minutes? I promise I'll be careful. I want to copy something."

He gave her a rare smile. "I didn't take you for a reader."

"I'm not," she admitted. "Except for song lyrics. But could I?"

He shook his head in disbelief. "You're one confusing girl, know that? Sure; borrow it until band call." He drew circles on the floor with the toe of one shoe. "Better go to Daddy now." He didn't move. He was so close, Teresa felt his breath. She lifted her hand, longing to touch his face—but he turned away. "I'll get the book," he said. And was gone.

52.

The bandleader skimmed Teresa's sheet music and checked a card on his music stand. "Looks like you're on after the acrobats, so come back in a few minutes."

"Second, before Maeve?" Teresa's heart skipped. "Could I see?" He handed her the list and she scanned it quickly. The scrawled handwriting was hard to read, but she found her name: *#2: Singer LeClair*—followed by Pietro and his father. She skipped over the other names to the end. Maeve and the dogs were in the plum spot, next to last, followed by a movie short. "Thank you," she said.

Teresa stopped at the end of the downstairs hall and hugged herself with delight. The narrow passageway buzzed with activity. Sammy the acrobat was upside down in a handstand, his shirt fallen over his face. The comedian from the Denver performance dashed past, his coat open, fake mustache dangling, calling "Goldie! Where are you?" Edna, Bronwyn, and Cleo were loose; Bronwyn nipped at the pointy shoes of three men dressed in tights and blousy short trousers—were they the Shakespearean actors? Stagehands bustled past, handing out props, while Goldie appeared at the end of the hall, a fur coat over her arm, her mouth bristling with straight pins again.

Teresa wound her way through the chaos. How could Pietro give this up? She rapped on their door to return the book. Pietro slipped into the hall. "Daddy's too sick to dance."

"Should we call the doctor?"

"He says no. He's stubborn."

Like you, Teresa thought. "Listen—I'm on second and you're third. If I don't see you—then *merde*."

"Break a leg yourself," he said.

﹏∽◠◡◠∽﹏

Teresa's new high heels put her off balance and the thin air made her lightheaded again. The bandleader asked her to run through her last number twice and he didn't even nod when she finished. Teresa flopped in front of the mirror in their dressing room. "I'm all wet," she said.

"Nonsense." Maeve looked up from mending Dixie's pompom. "You just need to relax and forget about Pietro."

"Who says I'm thinking about Pietro?"

"It's obvious." Maeve squeezed her knee. "You look like a star in that dress. You'll be wonderful—you always are. Belt your heart out. Now help me with the dogs."

The matinee audience was tepid and didn't call her back for a second bow. Maeve met her in the wings. "You were fine. First house always sits on its hands."

Like Pietro, Teresa wanted to be more than "fine." She was walking her own slack wire to stay with the troupe. She watched Pietro from the wings. The stage manager gave him a nice plug while the stagehands slid Pietro's stairs onstage. "Mr. Jones is ill," Mr. Harrison told the crowd. "Luckily, his son dances well enough for two. Please give a big hand to . . . Pietro Jones!"

The crowd applauded politely, the music began, and Pietro danced out of the shadows—wearing his fancy striped cutaway suit and his own brown skin. Teresa wanted to cheer. Mr. Harrison did a double take as Pietro cakewalked past him. "You're asking for trouble," he said, but Pietro ignored him.

Pietro *did* dance as if he were two people, his feet and arms a blur of motion. He was elegant in his new suit and top hat. The crowd was quiet during the cakewalk, but a low hum started up as he began his tap routine and soon became a buzz. *Tappetta*

tappetta tap tap tap . . . buzz buzz buzz. Finally, someone shouted, "Where's the cork?"

Teresa held her breath. Would he falter? But Pietro never missed a beat, and his smile, when he danced up and down the stairs, brandishing his cane, seemed genuine. The stage manager had disappeared. Pietro launched into his third dance without waiting for any applause. The band played his ragtime number. Pietro's movements seemed loose and free, as if he had no worries in the world. A few people in the front row began to clap in time to the music. The clapping spread, and Pietro beamed, his body swaying and bending with the beat, his feet moving faster and faster.

"Not in my theater." The stage manager reappeared beside Teresa, holding a hook. He started forward, but Teresa grabbed his arm and held on with all her might.

"Wait," she said. "The audience likes him. Listen."

Mr. Harrison twisted out of her grip and stalked toward the stage, but the crowd clapped and stomped in unison until the theater seemed to vibrate. Pietro finished with a flourish of his cane, swept off his top hat, and bowed deeply. The audience roared. He danced offstage, tipped his hat to Mr. Harrison in the wings, and danced back out for another bow.

"What cheek," the stage manager said. But the hook was gone.

Teresa slipped away and waited for Pietro downstairs. "You were wonderful!" If only she could give him a hug. He tipped his top hat to her, breathing hard. "Thank you, Resa LeClair."

Pietro and Teresa each found their rhythm by the third performance, although every house was cool until Pietro proved himself. Maeve had suggested that Teresa play to someone in the audience.

On "The Sidewalks of New York," she focused on a woman with sparkling eyes who mouthed the words along with her. The band picked up the tempo and Teresa waltzed in place as Mr. Jones had taught her.

As she belted out the chorus, she even imagined Papa in the audience, listening as she praised New York's street life. "*Boys and girls together,*" she sang. "*Me and Mamie O'Rourke. We'll trip the life fantastic on . . . the sidewalks of New York.*" She knew she'd botched the words—the song was about dancing the "light" fantastic on Broadway—but it was the *life* she longed for. Someday she'd perform on a real stage in New York. The crowd hushed when she sang "Hard Times," and called her back twice.

Sam and Sammy stood in the wings, applauding, as she ran offstage. "Good job," Sam said. Teresa bent over, gasping for breath. Sam pointed to the stairs. "Maeve needs you in the dressing room," he said.

Teresa ran downstairs, though she had wanted to stay and see the Shakespeare scene. She pushed the door open. "Two curtain calls!" she sang, and skidded to a halt. Maeve sat at the vanity table, her face ashen. Teresa drew back. "What is it?"

"You have a telegram," Maeve whispered. "You were onstage so I signed for it."

The Western Union envelope rattled in Teresa's hands. "Who knows I'm here?"

"Pantages."

"Has he fired me? Maybe I should read it later." But Teresa tore it open in spite of herself.

The telegram was in French, with the stops in English:

MA CHÈRIE STOP NONNIE EST MORTE
STOP VIENS ICI STOP PAPA.

Teresa's knees buckled and she sank to the floor, wailing like a tiny child. "Not Nonnie! She can't be dead! I never wrote her a letter. Now she'll never know . . ." Teresa drew up her knees and buried her face in her skirt.

"Who's Nonnie?" Maeve knelt beside her, stroking Teresa's hair. "Here, use my hankie."

"My great-grandmother. She was very old. I love her so much." Teresa gave way to deep, heaving sobs. Maeve held her tight. The dogs whimpered, and Edna licked Teresa's hand. "Everything's ruined," Teresa wailed. "I have to go home."

"Is that what she'd want?"

Teresa held her head in her hands, as if someone had boxed her ears. "I don't know. Papa says, *Viens ici*: Come here. Did that policeman in New York tell Papa I was on that train?" Teresa sat up, very still. Only a few hours ago, she'd remembered Nonnie telling her to follow her dreams. Had Nonnie sent her a message? Teresa pulled her valise out from under the vanity table and rummaged in the bottom for Nonnie's photograph. "Here she is."

Maeve held the picture gently. "You have her bright smile."

"She was nearly blind—but she taught me all the songs I know. She was—" Her voice broke. "She was everything to me."

Applause rang out upstairs and someone tapped on their door. "Ten minutes, Miss Cullen," a stagehand called.

Maeve let go of Teresa. "Will you be all right?"

"Maybe," Teresa said, though she felt stripped and broken inside. She struggled to her feet, swept the jars of makeup to the side, and set Nonnie's picture on the vanity. "I'll feel better if I help you." She snapped her fingers at Edna and Alix. "Come on, girls," she said, her voice shaking. "Pompom time."

She bent to her work. But when Maeve and the dogs were set to go upstairs, Teresa grabbed hold of the dressing table. "I still have one more show. How will I sing again? Look at my eyes!"

Maeve kissed the top of her head. "You'll be fine. Put a cold compress on your face; that will help the swelling. And you *will* perform once more today. Sing to your great-grandma in heaven."

Maeve must have told everyone what had happened, because when Teresa climbed the stairs for her evening performance, she found Maeve, the dogs, the acrobats, and Pietro waiting for her in the wings at stage right. "Sorry about your loss," Pietro whispered. His dark eyes were sad. Even Mr. Jones was there, perched on the prompter's stool. He beckoned to her and whispered in her ear. "Sing your heart out, Resa. It will ease your pain."

"Thank you," she whispered, and went out onstage. Her smile felt pasted on at first, but then she imagined telling Nonnie about "tripping the *life* fantastic"—instead of the "light"—on the sidewalks of New York. It was harder to sing "Listen to the Mockingbird" without weeping, especially when she pictured the birds that Nonnie loved, singing over her grave—but her voice only broke once.

After the flute's final trill, she walked slowly to the edge of the stage apron and held up her hand. The audience settled, with a few curious murmurs. She looked out over the gas footlights. "I'd like to dedicate this last song to my great-grandmother, Aurelia Baxter, who just passed away."

Murmurs rippled through the crowd. Teresa glanced at the wings. Pietro stood there, listening intently. The stage manager shook his head violently, but Teresa ignored him and pulled a folded paper from her pocket. "The famous American writer W.E.B. Du Bois said these words." She smoothed out the paper and read, "*The morning breaks over blood-stained hills. We must not falter, we may not shrink. Above are the everlasting stars.*"

"I believe my great-grandmother is in the stars, so I'm sending this song to her." Teresa turned to the bandleader. "I'll sing my last song a cappella."

She returned to center stage. The lights went down and left her standing in a single spotlight. Teresa closed her eyes for a long moment. She saw Nonnie's cloudy blue eyes and twinkling smile, smelled her lilac scent. She remembered sitting beside her on the piano bench, as a little girl, learning her notes. An E-flat sounded from the wings. Was that Mr. Jones, on his harmonica?

"*Let us pause in life's pleasures, and count its many tears,*" she began. The full house gave warmth and depth to her voice. When she reached the first chorus and begged the hard times, with all her might, to "come again no more," a pure tenor joined by a sweet harmonica sounded from the wings at stage right, while a bass added rich tones from stage left. And an alto voice chimed in—was that Maeve? Teresa smiled through her tears. *Do you hear me, Nonnie? We're all singing to you.*

Her voice cracked when she reached the last verse and its lines about "the lonely grave," but she was steady on the final chorus, and the voices of her friends, in the wings, felt like an embrace. "*Oh!*" she sang, with all the power in her lungs, "*hard times, come again no more!*"

A hush, as warm and thick as fur, fell over the theater. Teresa pictured her last note drifting up into the last row of the dress circle, through the ceiling with its painted frescoes, and up into the dark sky to heaven. When the applause began, she was startled; she'd forgotten where she was. She ran offstage and bumped into Pietro, who squeezed her hand. He didn't speak, but his eyes shone.

"You sounded beautiful, all of you!" Teresa leaned over, gasping for breath. "Thank you, Mr. Jones. Who sang bass?"

"Sammy." Mr. Jones gave her a little shove. "Go on—the crowd wants you."

Teresa ran back onstage. She curtsied low and then stood tall, kissed her hands and blew the kisses up to heaven. The crowd roared, and pennies rained onstage. She bowed deep once more, then hurried off for the last time and collapsed in Maeve's arms.

53.

Goldie was waiting for Teresa when she stumbled into the dressing room. The wardrobe mistress pulled her close and dabbed at her cheeks with a hankie. "You sang like an angel," she said. "Your grannie must have heard you."

"Thank you," Teresa said. "You've been so kind." She pulled away gently. "I need to change."

"Turn around. I'll unbutton your dress. It fits you like a dream." Goldie's fingers flew over the cloth buttons.

"I hate to give it up." Teresa pulled the dress over her head.

"It's yours," Goldie said. "Another actress left it behind. Quite frankly, she didn't have the bosom to fill it the way you do." She chucked Teresa under the chin. "Don't go blushing on me. You're lucky for your pretty figure. It matches your voice."

Teresa hugged her again. "How can I thank you?"

"You already did. Tonight you sang for all of us that ever lost someone. Send me a card once in a while; let me know how you're doing. And don't forgot me."

"How could I? You've been good to me." Teresa remembered Mama, in that long-ago chat in the kitchen, saying she "missed the feeling of family" on tour. This was what Mama meant. "I'll write to you, Goldie," Teresa said. "You're wonderful."

Teresa embraced her, shut the door, and leaned against it, her heart thumping. She couldn't bear to tell Goldie that Papa had ordered her home. *Viens ici*, Papa had said. Mama would want her home for Nonnie's funeral—

Or would she? Teresa picked up the telegram and read it again. Papa had called her *ma chérie*—my sweet. Was that a trick, to bring her home? Or did Papa mean it? Teresa felt stretched and tugged in every direction, like saltwater taffy.

❧

It was after eleven by the time Teresa, Maeve, and Mr. Jones stood outside under the gaslight, waiting for Pietro. Snowflakes angled through the lights onto the street. "Snow in June," Mr. Jones said. "That's a first."

The door slammed and Pietro strode toward them, lugging their bags. "Well, Daddy. Say goodbye to this no-count town."

"What happened?" Maeve asked.

"Stage manager had a telegram from Pantages. He says if Daddy can't dance with me, we're through. I have to say, I agree." Maeve gasped, but Pietro held up his hand. "It's all right. Resa can explain it to you—and I think Daddy understands."

"I'm working on it," Mr. Jones said, but his dark eyes were sad.

"We're headed east tomorrow," Pietro said.

Me, too, Teresa almost said, but held her tongue. She rubbed her ribs to ease the ache that was lodged there. A broken heart actually hurt.

"Good thing we didn't leave our bags at the so-called 'Refuge.'" Maeve's eyes shone with tears in the gaslight, but she managed to sound cheerful. "I've always wanted to sleep in a boxcar. How about you, Resa?"

"Of course." Teresa hoisted her bag. "Let's find one before we freeze our toes off."

"Don't you have a bed?" Mr. Jones asked.

"A horsehair plank with fleas is *not* a bed," Maeve said. "Besides, the dogs will keep us warm."

Mr. Jones shook his head. "You're wearing me down. Never mind. Even fools won't come looking for us out here." His dry laugh turned into a cough. Maeve steadied him.

"I'll go on ahead, find us an empty car." Pietro took off. The dogs ran free beside Maeve, snuffling the frozen snow lining the streets. Thick, wet flakes caught on their fur. They sneezed and rolled in the snow. Mr. Jones stopped coughing. "I'll be right as rain, soon's I get back to sea level," he said.

Maeve matched her steps to Mr. Jones's slow pace and Teresa lagged behind. A few days before, they didn't dare walk down the street with Pietro and his father. Here in the dark, no one seemed to care.

A light bobbled up ahead and she heard Pietro's whistle. He hurried toward them holding a lantern high overhead. "Found one." He tucked one arm through his father's. "A few bales of straw, along with the dogs, and we'll be warm as toast."

They climbed over steel rails, skirted an engine and its coal car, and followed Pietro to a boxcar that stood alone on a siding. Pietro pulled a wooden crate to the open door to use as a step. Teresa waited, handing the baggage up to Pietro, before she clambered onto the overturned crate herself. "All aboard," Mr. Jones said softly.

A shout rang out. Teresa listened, holding her breath. "Someone's calling me. I'll be right back."

"Wait!" Maeve poked her head out. "Take Edna. She'll protect you."

Teresa ran back along the rails with Edna loping beside her. A tall, skinny figure jogged toward her. "Teresa LeClair! Is that you?"

"Sammy? Over here!" Teresa cried. Edna barked and raced to greet him, her tail wagging in circles.

The acrobat strode through the dark, a long cape swirling at his knees. "What are you doing in this godforsaken place?" he asked. "Goldie told me you had headed out this way."

Teresa looked up at him. Her teeth were chattering. "What's wrong?"

He reached under his cloak. "Another telegram," he said. "Goldie found this on the floor of your dressing room." He squeezed her shoulder. "Hope it's good news this time."

"I hope so, too. Thank you, Sammy. And thank you for singing with me. Your voice is beautiful."

"My pleasure," he said. "See you on the first train out."

Would she? Sammy touched his cap and hurried away before Teresa could say goodbye.

Her feet were as heavy as the lead that had named this town. She followed the glow of the lantern back to the boxcar and climbed inside. "Who was it?" Maeve asked. She was curled up in the corner, her voice already thick with sleep.

"Sammy, with another telegram. Pietro, could I borrow the lantern?"

Pietro stepped over his father and held the lantern above her head. Her hands shook as she tore open the telegram.

DEAR RESA STOP NONNIE SINGS WITH THE
ANGELS STOP ALWAYS REMEMBER THE CANARY
ONLY SINGS WHEN FREE STOP LOVE MAMA.

Teresa laughed, even as the words swam across the yellowed paper.

Pietro squinted at the message. "What's that supposed to mean?" He cleared his throat. "Excuse me for being nosy."

Teresa glanced at Mr. Jones, curled up with Fido, Bronwyn, and Dixie, and at Maeve, wrapped in her cloak next to Cleo, her head pillowed on Alix. "Come outside," she whispered.

They jumped down into the snow. Pietro cocked his head. "Well?"

"It means," she said, "that I'm not going home."

"I knew *that*. But what's this about a bird in a cage?"

"It's complicated." Teresa explained about Lebo the canary, who only sang when he was flying free. "Mama wants me to keep singing," she said. "Even though Papa says I should come home."

"Your mama sounds smart."

"She is." For a moment, Teresa longed to feel Mama's arms around her, ached to hear her mother's laugh, to feel her hands—rough from so many years of dishes and washing—smooth the hair from her forehead. "She's brave, too." Teresa rubbed her hands to warm them. "Would *your* mother tell you to keep dancing?"

Pietro stared off across the rail yards. "I don't see her much, with all this traveling. But if I did, I'm guessing she'd say: 'Do what's right.'" He stepped close. "Resa, you've got the hunger. I don't."

"What do you mean?"

"You know. You're hungry for all of it. You love to strut onstage. You feel the spark when the crowd's with you. When you finish a song, and the last note floats and the crowd goes still—you want to hold on to that moment forever. Don't you?"

Teresa nodded, her throat too thick for speech. So he felt it, too.

Pietro glanced around the empty rail yards and took her hand, his touch firm and steady. "Look at me, Resa." She met his gaze, though it made her shy. "I'm hungry for other things," Pietro said. "The end of lynchings. Schools where my people can learn. A time when I can hold the hand of whomever I please." His voice was like iron. "That's *my* hunger. And I won't find it onstage."

"Where *will* you find it?"

"I don't know yet. I got to work for it. The way you'll work for your success. Someday, I'll see Teresa LeClair's name in lights on some big New York theater—like the Palace. If they let me in, I'll be there, cheering you on."

"And I'll read about *you* in those newspapers of yours."

"Maybe." A rare smile flickered in his eyes. Then Pietro's lips brushed her own; a kiss as delicate as the touch of a butterfly's wing. "Good night, Resa. We'll be gone before first light. But I'll see you in my dreams."

He climbed into the boxcar, leaving Teresa alone in the dark.

"In *my* dreams, too." Teresa looked up. The snow had stopped, and clouds scudded across the brightest stars she had ever seen; as bright as the lights on the Great White Way. *Above are the everlasting stars.* She picked a song that Mama loved—and Papa, too.

"*Irene, good night,*" she sang. "*Irene, good night. Good night, Irene, good night, Irene, I'll see you in my dreams.*"

Pietro's warm tenor echoed from inside the boxcar. "*In my dreams,*" he sang. "*I'll see you in my dreams.*" Their harmony wheeled up to the velvet star-studded sky.

FINAL CURTAIN.

HARD TIMES

by Stephen Foster
(1854)

Let us pause in life's pleasures and count its many tears
While we all sup sorrow with the poor
There's a song that will linger forever in our ears
Oh hard times come again no more.

Tis the song, the sigh of the weary,
Hard times, hard times, come again no more
Many days you have lingered around my cabin door
Oh hard times come again no more.

While we seek mirth and beauty and music bright and gay
There are frail forms fainting at the door
Though their voices are silent, their pleading looks will say
Oh hard times come again no more.

Tis the song, the sigh of the weary,
Hard times, hard times, come again no more
Many days you have lingered around my cabin door
Oh hard times come again no more.

Tis a sigh that is wafted across the troubled wave,
Tis a wail that is heard upon the shore
Tis a dirge that is murmured around the lowly grave
Oh hard times come again no more.

Tis the song, the sigh of the weary,
Hard times, hard times, come again no more
Many days you have lingered around my cabin door
Oh hard times come again no more.
Oh hard times come again no more.

The Songs

(in order of appearance):
Hard Times
Shoo Fly
Gypsy Davey
(I Dream of) Jeanie with the Light Brown Hair
Cousin of Mine
Heaven Will Protect the Working Girl
Down by the Old Mill Stream
The Sidewalks of New York
When Irish Eyes Are Smiling
By the Light of the Silvery Moon
A Bird in a Gilded Cage
After the Ball
Meet Me in St. Louis, Louis
Let Me Call You Sweetheart
Shine On, Harvest Moon
Listen to the Mockingbird
You Are My Sunshine
Irene, Goodnight
Everybody Works But Father

AUTHOR'S NOTE

Vaudeville has fascinated me since I was a small child. That's when my father told me the romantic story about my great-grandmother, Carrie Lebo. She stole away from home in the night to elope with a vaudeville musician, leaving her pet canary behind. The family found the bird dead in its cage the next morning and declared it a bad omen.

William Patton, Carrie's sweetheart, was a charming red-headed violinist. Carrie had a lovely voice and played the piano. The couple sang and played with a vaudeville troupe that moved from town to town, performing in small theaters. They had two children: a son, and my paternal grandmother, Thelma June.

The couple's elopement created a scandal in the small town of Shreve, Ohio, as did their divorce a few years later. Growing up, I often asked my grandmother about her parents. She told me that Carrie loved to sing, and that she was a skilled seamstress and music teacher. Although my grandmother had inherited her parents' love of music (she also played piano), she refused to speak about her father, except to mention his red hair, and the fact that he seldom visited. Sadly, she was ashamed of her parents' history.

For my grandfather George Ketchum, who started working when he was eleven, vaudeville was the only entertainment he could afford on his meager earnings. From the time I was four or five, Grandpa and I sang vaudeville songs together. He taught me silly, off-color tunes such as "*Everybody works but Father, he sits around all day,*" and "*There lay Brown, upside down, lapping up the whiskey off the floor.*" Grandpa described what it was like to sit in the cheapest gallery seats, high above the stage, enjoying the shows with a rowdy audience.

I have always loved theater; I enjoyed acting in high school and I went to theater school before college—so I wondered: What was life like for vaudeville performers of all ages and backgrounds? One summer, while driving across the country, I stopped in the town of Leadville, high in Colorado's Rocky Mountains, and visited the Tabor Opera House, which had been restored to its former grandeur. As my footsteps echoed in the quiet aisles, I looked up at the empty stage, with its beautiful forest backdrop, and tried to imagine the theater packed with miners and other residents who were grateful for entertainment in their remote mining town. Since my grandmother couldn't—or wouldn't—tell her parents' story, I decided to invent one myself.

In 1913, the year this novel takes place, vaudeville was still the country's most popular and affordable form of entertainment. Thousands of theaters, in small towns as well as big cities across the country, hosted vaudeville troupes. Performers appeared in lodge halls, riverboats, and small opera houses, as well as in ornate, grand theaters such as Hammerstein's Victoria in New York. People who loved vaudeville tunes bought sheet music of the most popular songs, so that they could sing and play them at home.

Imagine a world without movies or television. There were no computers, no video games or smartphones. Though inventors had discovered radio waves, and Thomas Edison had figured out how to record sound, movies were still silent, black and white, and grainy looking. Private telephones were rare and many parts of the country (especially in rural areas) didn't have electricity, so people were thrilled when a lively vaudeville troupe came through town.

The life of a traveling vaudevillian wasn't easy. Performers lived out of their trunks and duffels. They slept in fleabag hotels or on trains between "jumps" (the moves from one town to the next). They often performed as many as six shows a day in theaters with unheated, basement dressing rooms where the only running water came from an outdoor pump. The pay was low and audiences could be ruthless, pelting performers with rotten eggs or tomatoes when they didn't like a performance. Yet many vaudevillians from that time spoke fondly of the camaraderie that grew among the musicians, jugglers, comedians, actors, singers, and animal trainers as they crisscrossed the country together.

The vaudeville experience was far more challenging for African-American entertainers. While prejudice wasn't as common onstage, it was rampant throughout the country in 1913. "Separate but Equal" was the law of the land. Lynchings were common in many parts of the country and strong laws had been enacted—especially in southern states—to prevent blacks from voting. Public schools, swimming pools, restaurants, churches, prisons, theaters, hospitals, buses, funeral homes, sporting events, orphanages—and even the military, where blacks fought as valiantly as whites—were segregated. The Ku Klux Klan terrorized blacks throughout the country.

When black performers went on tour, they often had to ride in separate railway cars. They were turned away from hotels and restaurants that served white vaudevillians. Black women were sometimes forced to stay in whorehouses. And onstage, African-American performers had to hide their true identities behind blackface (burnt cork). Usually, they couldn't appear as themselves.

Blackface had its origins in minstrel shows, where whites blackened their faces to impersonate blacks, usually to ridicule them and to perpetuate cruel stereotypes. White members of an audience didn't want to sit *below* a black person—but if they knew that a white actor hid behind the black mask, they didn't mind. This carried over into vaudeville. African Americans were expected to cover their skin with black cork or greasepaint so that audiences could imagine the actors were actually white. Black performers—such as Pietro in this novel—found the practice demeaning. The famous comedian Bert Williams complained that whites "made me a fool and now I got to go out here and make money laughing at me." Williams's stage partner, George Walker, was one of the few blacks who dared to perform without blackface.

In 1905, the great African-American leader W.E.B. Du Bois co-founded the Niagara Movement to address racial inequality in the United States. In 1909—soon after white rioters in Illinois burned a black neighborhood and lynched black women, men, and children—Du Bois and other concerned citizens, black and white, met in New York. As the country honored Abraham Lincoln's 100th birthday, the people assembled with Du Bois formed the National Association for the Advancement of Colored People (NAACP), which is still active today. Young people around the country—such as Pietro in this story—were drawn to the goals and ideals of the NAACP, fighting for equal rights. Sadly, our country still struggles with issues of inequality and racism that African Americans faced more than a century ago.

As sound was added to film, vaudeville slowly disappeared and movies became more popular. But talented vaudeville performers from all backgrounds made a successful transition from vaudeville to become superstars on Broadway, on the silver screen, or in recorded music. Many gained international fame. That list includes Fred Astaire and Ginger Rogers, Julie Andrews, Louis Armstrong, Jack Benny, Charlie Chaplin, Cab Calloway, Duke Ellington, W.C. Handy, Buster Keaton, Bert Lahr, Jelly Roll Morton, Bill "Bojangles" Robinson, Ma Rainey, Mickey Rooney, Bessie Smith, Ethel Waters, Mae West, and many others.

GLOSSARY

A cappella:
Singing without musical accompaniment.

All washed up; All wet; A fish:
A few ways of saying that the act is a flop.

Big time:
Theater that played vaudeville, without movies, and usually had only two shows a day.

Blue:
Material that was off-color, in bad taste, or obscene. Supposedly, the term arose because theater managers left blue envelopes in performers' dressing rooms, fining them for use of bad language.

Cakewalk:
A strutting dance that originated in a nineteenth-century African American contest. Walkers with the most amusing or skillful steps won a cake as a prize.

Curtain call:
The appearance of performers, at the end of a show, in response to applause from the audience.

Death Trail:
Small-time vaudeville tours, in the Midwest or Canada, with long "jumps" between towns, performing in theaters that required five or six performances a day.

Fine pair of pipes:
A singer's beautiful voice.

Flies:
The area above the stage; used to store lights, curtains, and equipment for raising and lowering the sets.

Gerry Society:
The Society for the Prevention of Cruelty to Children, which in some states kept young children from performing on stage. It gets its name from Elbridge Gerry, its cofounder.

Handcuffed:
An audience that refuses to applaud. Also described as "sitting on their hands."

Jump:
The distance between one town or city and the next.

Next to closing:
The next-to-last act, usually saved for the biggest star on the program.

Perfect pitch:
The ability to name or sing a musical note without help.

Pitch pipe:
A small reed pipe that produces a specific pitch or tone when blown. Also: a tuning fork, a two-pronged metal fork that vibrates when struck. Both produce exact tones for tuning an instrument or to give singers the correct starting note for a song.

Scrim:
A rough gauze cloth, used as a stage backdrop.

Song plugger:
A singer hired by a music publisher to sing new songs and encourage sales of sheet music.

Stage left:
The part of the stage to the actor's left, when facing the audience.

Stage right:
The part of the stage to the actor's right, when facing the audience.

Vaudeville (Also "Vaude" or "Variety")
Stage entertainment offering many different acts. A typical show bill might run as follows: a "dumb act" (acrobats, jugglers, animals, or bicyclists, who were silent onstage); a female singer or minor comedian (not a choice spot); an act to "wake up the audience" such as a comedian, a dramatic sketch, a magician, or even a swimming act; a big name, top singing act, or comedy team; a skit or another big name; a solid dance team to get the audience excited before the biggest star on the program (this star would get top billing in ads); and finally, a chaser—another dumb act or a silent film, shown as the audience leaves.

Wings:
The unseen area, on either side of the stage, where performers wait to come onstage, or exit at the end of their acts.

RESOURCES/ BIBLIOGRAPHY

Books

Atkinson, Brooks. *Broadway*. New York: Macmillan, 1970.

Barry, Harold A., Michelman, Richard E., Mitchell, Richard M., Wellman, Richard H. *Before Our Time: A Pictorial Memoir of Brattleboro, Vermont from 1830 to 1930*. Brattleboro, VT: Stephen Greene Press, 1974.

Du Bois, W.E. Burghardt. *The Souls of Black Folk*. Chicago: A.C. McClurg & Co., 1903.

Finney, Jack. *From Time to Time*. New York: Scribner Paperback Fiction, 1995.

Furman, Evelyn E. Livingston. *The Tabor Opera House: A Captivating History*. Aurora, CO: National Writer's Press, 1984.

Gerstle, Gary. *American Crucible: Race and Nation in the Twentieth Century*. Princeton, NJ: Princeton University Press, 2001.

Hill, Errol G., and Hatch, James V. *A History of African American Theatre*. Cambridge, England: Cambridge University Press, 2003.

Hine, Darlene Clark, and Thompson, Kathleen. *A Shining Thread of Hope: The History of Black Women in America*. New York: Broadway Books, 1998.

Kisseloff, Jeff. *You Must Remember This: An Oral History of Manhattan from the 1890s to World War II*. San Diego: Harcourt Brace Jovanovich, 1989.

Marks, Edward B. *They All Sang*. New York: Viking, 1934.

McDaniel, Melissa. *W.E.B. Du Bois: Scholar and Civil Rights Activist*. Danbury, CT: Franklin Watts, 1999.

McNamara, Brooks, Ed. *American Popular Entertainments*. New York: Performing Arts Journal Publications, 1983.

Meltzer, Milton, Ed. *In Their Own Words: A History of the American Negro 1865–1916*. New York: Thomas Y. Crowell, 1965.

Rasenberger, Jim. *America, 1908: The Dawn of Flight, the Race to the Pole, the Invention of the Model T, and the Making of a Modern Nation*. New York: Scribner, 2007.

Short, Ernest. *Fifty Years of Vaudeville*. London: Eyre and Spottiswoode, 1946.

Smith, Bill. *The Vaudevillians*. New York: Macmillan Publishing Co., 1976.

Snyder, Robert W. *The Voice of the City: Vaudeville and Popular Culture in New York*. New York and Oxford: Oxford University Press, 1989.

Stein, Charles W., Ed. *American Vaudeville As Seen by Its Contemporaries*. New York: Alfred A. Knopf, 1984.

Tate, Eleanora E. *The Minstrel's Melody*. Middletown, WI: Pleasant Company Publications, 2001.

Waring: Dennis G. *Manufacturing the Muse: Estey Organs and Consumer Culture in Victorian America*. Middletown, CT: Wesleyan University Press, 2002.

Articles

Sullivan, John Jeremiah. "'Shuffle Along' and the Lost History of Black Performance in America." *New York Times Magazine*, March 24, 2016.